D1498454

PRAISE

"Duran is back and Ward has drawn the beguiling contradictions in his character in bright and bold relief to drive the second book in this series. Struggling with British Intelligence's new yolk around his neck, Duran takes on the challenge of his career and it takes him beyond the walls of Granada for the first time. Stuck in a web of deceit and playing cat and mouse with murderous foes, Duran's loyalty and humanity are tested, and Ward's epic depictions of the world and people around him give the book a unique richness and drama. I'm ready for book three already!"
SAM HIERSTEINER, CONTRIBUTOR, *BOSTON GLOBE*

"*The Sovereign* is taut, intense, and disquieting as it is rewarding. Ward is the type of thriller writer who grabs you by the collar and won't let go." BILL NEWMAN, CIVIL RIGHTS ATTORNEY AND AUTHOR OF *WHEN THE WAR CAME HOME*

"With this smart, seductive thriller, Ward takes us even deeper into Special Agent Duran's immersive world. At every propulsive turn, you'll feel the sun's heat at your neck, smell food simmering on a stove, and taste the burn of a stiff drink in your throat. It's an eerily prescient adventure that raises worthy questions about contemporary geopolitics."
MEG LITTLE REILLY, AUTHOR OF *EVERYTHING THAT FOLLOWS*

"Reading *The Sovereign* is like watching a Hollywood spy flick while micro-dosing acid. Stark, pacy and strangely intoxicating, Ward's prose makes every high calibre gun shot and Machiavellian double cross pop off the page in post-apocalyptic high definition." KADE CROCKFORD, BLOGGER, CONTRIBUTOR, *THE GUARDIAN*

ABOUT THE AUTHOR

John Ward is communications director for the ACLU of Massachusetts. He has written and lectured extensively on politics, urban public policy and criminal justice reform. In a prior, weirder life, he was a hip-hop artist and producer. Seriously.

He lives in Boston with his patient wife, three wildling sons and an old, smelly dog.

Visit John Ward online: *johnward.ink*

THE
SOVEREIGN

JOHN WARD

Vine Leaves Press
Melbourne, Vic, Australia

The Sovereign
Copyright © 2018 John Ward
All rights reserved.

Print Edition
ISBN: 978-1-925417-75-3
Published by Vine Leaves Press 2018
Melbourne, Victoria, Australia

This is a work of fiction. Any similarity between the characters and situations within its pages and places or persons, living or dead, is unintentional and coincidental.

Cover design by Jessica Bell
Interior design by Amie McCracken

 A catalogue record for this book is available from the National Library of Australia

Who's your hero?

Mine's a stalky Irish guy from Boston named Jerry.

This book is for him.

PART ONE

MOJA

The AC was broken. Open windows offered little but a view of the hot night. An old brass deck clock hung above the doorway, but overlapping shadows masked its weathered face. Every few minutes, Abasi Lotto craned for a look at the clock, as if the floor lamp's halo had magically swelled to expose it. But time remained cloaked in darkness. The air, burning and gluey. Abasi's wife, Kesi, slouched on the sofa like an opium fiend, lids at half-mast and the kids—save Darweshi—snoozed in a sweaty tangle on the floor.

Babu, however, remained animated as an imam before a throng of rapt worshippers. "Life is about choices. It's about taking charge. Otherwise, you know, you're subject to other people's whims … Malia, for example."

Darweshi's eyes widened.

Abasi extended a palm toward his father. "Babu—*please*."

"It's true," the old man said with a shrug. He arched forward, liver-spotted hands clasping the sloped handle of his cane. "She lost control."

Abasi shook his head in disgust, twisted to check the clock again.

"I'm sorry—do you have somewhere to be?"

"It's a hundred degrees in here."

"So open a window."

"The windows *are* open."

"My god," Babu huffed. "Show some resilience."

Abasi tilted his face toward the ceiling and pinched his eyes shut. "We've been sitting for hours listening to you."

"Yet," Babu said, gravelly Swahili blooming with affected gravitas, "you remain deaf to my concerns."

"Oh, you are *relentless*."

"And you're naïve."

"Because I don't agree with you?"

"No," Babu said. "Because you would place your faith in these people."

"*Which* people?" Abasi growled.

There was an abrupt jitter of limbs below; a loud yawn from Kesi. The silent had been roused from their heat-induced comas. But this only encouraged the old man.

With a restored audience, he gradually rose from the couch and cleared his throat. "*Which* people? The doctors? The nurses? The laboratory technicians? Take your pick." He paused, raising the butt of his nubby cane and wobbling it at Darweshi. "If I've learnt one thing in this life—and you'd do well to remember this, young man—discretion is a thing often promised, but *rarely* honoured."

Abasi dismissed the comment with a flick of his fingers. "What does that even mean?" Receiving no response from the old man, he shifted his attention to the boy. "Don't listen to your Babu, Darweshi—he's far too senile to be offering you advice."

"Don't talk to your father like that," Kesi said. She was upright now, brown lips pursed with consternation. "Especially in front of the kids."

"The kids aren't listening," Abasi said. "And for the record, I'll speak to my father however I please."

Babu's face tightened, a hundred hidden wrinkles unveiled by the insult. "Quit being obstinate, and just listen, Abasi—for once in your life."

Abasi lifted his hands in mock surrender.

Babu bent to retrieve his tea cup from the coffee table and winced. Kesi edged forward to help. "No, no. Thank you, love. I've got it." His palm trembled but reached its mark. Then, in between slow sips, Babu issued his declaration. "It's very clear to me at this point that we need to hide him."

Abasi squinted. "What?"

"You heard me."

"Are you insane?"

"I'm thinking somewhere inland … perhaps your cousins' house."

"You want us to hide in the bush?" Abasi said. "I'm sorry … I can't sit through this anymore. Truly, I'm done." He sprung up, marched to the door and whipped it open. Halfway over the threshold, though, he pivoted. "Darweshi."

"Yes, *mjomba*?"

"Don't let this old fool scare you."

Outside, darkness washed over Abasi like a slow river. He waded in gradually, pupils adjusting with each measured step. Above him, the sky was heavy and starless, emissary cumulus announcing the return of the truant rains. Below him, the bone-dry earth exhaled plumes of dust. When Abasi reached the road, a sudden wind came tumbling forward and the drooping foliage flanking the road whistled with satisfaction.

With the feverish talk behind him, Abasi's posture finally relaxed. Hands pocketed, he ambled the winding back streets, ears tuned to the sounds of night. Crickets and nocturnal songbirds. A distant racket echoing up from the cafés along the waterfront. Bursts of laughter. The clank of dishes. The wail of a toddler in gastronomic revolt.

Stone Town had changed since Abasi's youth. But tonight, it sounded vaguely the same. Not so different from those many evenings he'd spent with friends on the big terrace of the Africa House.

The Africa House. Onetime temple to the virtues of secularity. During high season, its deck heaved with sunburnt tourists; fair-haired bohemians who drank with abandon and fancied things like snorkelling and rail travel. Then there was Abasi, and the other local boys. They'd show up in droves every weekend to trade sanctity for indulgence, regaling female travellers with tall tales of the exotic. These days, the Africa House hosted a more subdued variety of patron. All Zanzibari, most enjoying only what the Quran permitted.

Yes, things certainly were different now. No more foreign women. No raucous debates. No American cigarettes and Italian beer. After the Great Tilling, the island became an island in every sense of the word.

But at least the Africa House survived.

***

John Ward

Perhaps it was the weather, but tonight the terrace was a particularly faint shadow of its former self. Almost silent, save a few lonely diners scattered among the empty tables. Abasi found a seat facing the harbour, and with a nod to old ghosts, sent the waiter off in search of scotch. When the drink arrived, he immediately slugged down two numbing gulps. Then two more, this time slower, savouring the heat and mustiness. He took the fifth draw with his eyes closed, letting the world around him fade.

"Care to join me?"

Abasi twisted in his seat, and found a plump figure in pinstripes seated at the table just behind him. "Yes, you," the man said, flicking the filter of his cigarette and taking a draw. "Would you like to join me for a drink?"

"I'm just finishing up," Abasi said.

"One more, for the road, then. Please, be my guest." Abasi scanned the deck. The man smiled. "Mr Lotto, correct?"

"Yes," Abasi said, eyes contracted. "Have we …"

"One of my companies does business with you."

Abasi stood, extended his hand. "Sorry—and you are?"

"Mm," the man said, tipping his glass back and swallowing a gulp. "Ebrahimi. Sattar Ebrahimi. Please, sit down." After a brisk shake, Ebrahimi flagged the waiter. "What are you drinking, Mr Lotto?"

Abasi studied his empty glass for several seconds. One could never tell who the pious ones were these days. "Whiskey," he finally said.

"Good. Two whiskeys then."

The waiter shuffled off behind them. Abasi pulled up a chair and sat. Ebrahimi drained the remainder of what he'd been drinking and looked around. "Beautiful night, isn't it?"

"Might rain," Abasi said.

"A possibility."

"We desperately need it."

"I suppose it depends on the business you're in," Ebrahimi said, casually.

Abasi eyed the man's tailored lapels. "I apologize, but what business did you say you were in?"

"I didn't," Ebrahimi said, wearing a coy smile. "Few things, though. Your fleet—it gets its fuel through us. Biggest petrol brokerage on the island, if I'm not mistaken."

"Again—I don't mean to be rude," Abasi said. "But your accent."

"Ah, quite perceptive. *Persian.*"

"You're Persian."

"Indeed." Ebrahimi chuckled. "One of the few foreigners to make it on the island twenty years ago. I'll tell you, certainly worse places to start your life over."

The waiter returned with fresh whiskeys. As he placed them down, Ebrahimi's tongue traced the bulbous contours of his lower lip.

Abasi averted his eyes. "It's a nice place."

To that, Ebrahimi raised his glass. "To new beginnings." After the toast, he added, "Interesting times though, no?"

"In what sense?"

"Let me count the ways," Ebrahimi said, grinning again. "This little haven of ours—it provides many things the world is quite admiring of. It's really a bit of a miracle, if you ask me."

"Miracle?"

"Oh, yes. I consider myself very lucky to be here." Ebrahimi raised his index finger toward the sea. "Insulated from the big mess out there. While the rest of the planet limps on, we're sitting pretty, as the British say. Plenty of food … relative peace … beautiful beaches."

"It certainly could be worse," Abasi said. "I do wonder, though …"

"What's that?"

"I don't know … the big mess, as you say."

"Go on."

Abasi shrugged. "You ever wonder if we'll be drawn into it?"

"Yes, I suppose I do. But, then, what would the world want from us besides our business?" Ebrahimi suddenly grew thoughtful. "Although these recent rumours are really something." Abasi remained silent. "You think there's anything to them?"

"Rumours?"

"You know—all that stuff about the kid?"

"The kid?"

"Who's immune."

"Oh, yes—*that*."

Ebrahimi smiled. "You sound sceptical."

Abasi took a long swig, wiped his lips with the back of hand. He then nodded toward Ebrahimi's cigarettes. "Would you mind?"

Ebrahimi pushed the pack across the table and levelled his gaze at Abasi. "How amazing if it were true, though. I'm no scientist but, my goodness, what a breakthrough that would be."

Abasi lit up, cocked his head, and exhaled from the corner of his mouth. The smoke spiralled up and rapidly dissipated in the breeze. On the periphery of the balcony, the palms dipped and swayed in the wind. "Yes," Abasi said. "Incredible."

"You like the whiskey, don't you?"

"Yes, it's quite good."

"It better be … cost me a fortune to import."

"Cost *you*?"

"Oh, yes. I pay handsomely to keep it on the menu. We don't sell much of it, these days. But I make sure the top shelf is stocked with at least one bottle at all times." The Persian's palm made a broad, slow circle in the air. "If for nothing other than show."

"You *own* the Africa House?"

"That, I do," Ebrahimi said. He tilted his glass toward Abasi. "Another?"

"No, no. Thank you very much, though … the drink was really, very good. But I do need to get home."

"Understand, fully," Ebrahimi said, rising from his seat. "Domesticity beckons."

Abasi extinguished the smoke, shook the man's hand, and strode carefully toward the balcony doors, steps a touch wobbly. But when he reached the exit, he abruptly reversed course.

The Persian chuckled. "*Ah*—you reconsidered."

"If only," Abasi said as he reached into his pocket. "I forgot to pay."

"Oh, don't be foolish—you're my *guest* tonight."

"No, no. I couldn't. A stranger paying my tab?"

"But we're not strangers, now, are we?" Ebrahimi said with grin. "Tell you what—next time, it's on you."

Abasi nodded so deeply it was almost a bow. And with another flurry of thanks, he left through the broad French doors at the rear of the terrace.

***

The waiter approached Ebrahimi's table, placed a small, unmarked envelope at its centre and scuttled off without a word. Ebrahimi withdrew a narrow, ivory-handled pocket knife from his jacket, pried it open with his manicured fingernails, and slipped the blade gently beneath the sealed fold of the envelope.

The note came out with a single word scrawled at its centre in black ink.

Upstairs.

Ebrahimi rose with a sigh. On his way to the stairwell, he tossed the note in a small barrel behind the interior bar, then mixed himself another drink. At the top of the stairs, he removed a key from his trousers and made for a door several metres beyond the carpeted landing. As he inserted the key, the door clicked slightly ajar, unimpeded by its deadbolt. He pressed a palm to the door and swung it wide. "Hello? Kamkin?"

When he received no immediate answer, Ebrahimi stepped inside and turned to close the door. With his back to the room, he instantly froze, something cold and hard pressed to the base of his skull.

"Walk into a room like that, you never walk out," the woman behind him said in coarse but serviceable Farsi. She lowered the gun from Ebrahimi's neck and transitioned to her native tongue. "Wake up!"

Ebrahimi spun in a fury. "What the fuck are you doing?" he said in low growl, his Russian far better than her Persian. "You scared me half to death."

"I'm fucking with you," she said. "Relax." Then she turned from him and marched to the open window of the suite. "What's the deal?"

John Ward

Ebrahimi withheld a response, too busy studying Kamkin's arse. The curve of it hung high and flexed athletically in the tight seat of her black slacks. With the gun returned to its holster, she faced him, took a pack of smokes from the sill, and said, "So?"

"It was my first conversation with him."

"You spoke about the boy?"

"I tried … got very little, though."

"You need to try harder, clearly."

"Listen," he said, lighting his own smoke. A wet draft of air flowed in and Ebrahimi twisted his torso to protect the flame. "I know your lot is short on patience, but there is such a thing as subtlety. Twenty minutes ago, the man was a complete stranger."

"Well, we've got only a few days—so get to it. Otherwise, I will be forced to intervene."

With the smoke lit, Ebrahimi pivoted to fully face her. "Don't jeopardize my reputation here, Kamkin. It's a small island. Things get around."

"Spare me," she said, tone razor sharp. "Most of these people don't even know you exist. And let me be clear—because I know things move slowly in this little fiefdom. Moscow will not be left waiting around. Either you get it done your way—and soon—or I'm dropping the hammer."

Ebrahimi took a big swig of brown liquor and chased it back with a long drag. As he exhaled, he squeezed out his parting words: "Whatever suits you, dear."

DOS

In a modest flat above a winding road at the foot of the Albaicin, Amir Duran stood naked in the bathroom mirror examining his reflection.

"So vain, *mi amor*," Cristina said, slipping out of her thong.

"I'm getting fat."

With an impish grin, she slapped his backside and opened the shower curtain. "Maybe you're just getting old."

"*Misma maldita cosa.*" As he turned around to get in, he was arrested by the sight of her nude figure. He'd seen it a thousand times, sure. But tonight, it looked particularly supple and sun-browned. In a better state of mind, he'd have sprung into action immediately. But the day's sedentary chore of case file maintenance had eroded his sense of vigour. "Fucking job … making me soft."

"*Pobrecito.*"

"You know how much time I spent at my desk today?"

"Tell me," she said with a tilt of the head as if talking to a child.

"Don't condescend me." To that, Cristina puckered her lips and beckoned him with an upturned palm. "All day," he said. "I was in the office all fucking day. Didn't get out once."

"Amir," Cristina said, impatience wiping the smile from her lips. "I'm getting cold. James will be home in a half hour—*vamos.*"

He stepped over the lip of the shower basin, closed the curtain behind him and watched her bend toward the faucet. As the water came down and the steam rose, Cristina turned around, extended her arms above his shoulders, and drew him in under the warmth of the shower head. "*Mi amor*," she whispered, "*me gusta tu nuevo trabajo*. So does James. You're home at a normal hour. And frankly, I don't have to worry as much."

"You won't like it if it turns me into a paper-pushing slob."

"*Si, carino*," she said quickly. "*Verdad.* I'm going to run off with one of those big, blond soldiers." She gave Amir a sensuous smile and pressed her breasts fully against him. "*Amor*, you are perfect to me."

As she kissed his neck, she slowly slid her right hand down his ribs and along his upper thigh. Truth was, he was still in very good shape. And with Cristina intent on stroking things other than his ego, even Amir was bored with this indulgent conversation.

***

Amir sat at the kitchen table, pecking at his laptop, drinking a beer. James sat beside him and scribbled out long division on a worksheet. Cristina was cooking a simple but masterful rendition of paella over the rangetop behind them.

"Papi," James said, without looking up.

"*Sí?*"

"*Necessito ayudame.*"

Amir glanced over the edge of the computer, then stood from his seat and leaned over James's shoulder. "*Mira,*" he said, then took the boy's pencil and made a minor correction. "See?"

"*Sí.*"

"How was practice?"

"Good, but our goalkeeper is moving," James said.

"Where?"

Cristina turned from her work at the stove. "Sector 3. I talked with his mom on Saturday during the game."

"Why?" Amir asked. A scent of chicken and saffron rose from the iron skillet on the rangetop and Amir drifted closer for a damp waft of it.

Cristina backed him off with a nudge. Work in progress successfully defended, she took a celebratory sip of white wine, and said, "Rent was getting crazy."

Amir looked down at Paco and thought about it. The dog yawned widely, tail spread like a furry dust brush on the cool tile of the kitchen floor. "I hope they know what they're doing," Amir said. "Three's more of a mess than ever."

"Sounds like they don't have much of an option."

"Jesus," Amir said. "I thought Marcos's father did well."

"He was a supervisor at F," she said. "Guess he lost his job when they restructured last summer. Now he's working as a truck driver or something."

Amir thought about last year's labour negotiation. The fucking debacle it was. Though the whole episode arguably changed his *own* life for the better. If one considered more paper work better, that is. Shit. Hadn't even used the gun once this year. And that's a good thing, he reminded himself. Plus, the paychecks signed by the British Foreign Secretary were substantially fatter than the ones made out by the Municipal Police Department.

Nevertheless, he itched for more action.

"Amir," Cristina said. "*Hola*—I'm talking to you."

"Yes, I know, it's hard," he said, somewhat absently. "Things needed to change, though. The Africans needed the wage concessions."

"At what cost?"

"*Mi amor*, have you ever been to the camps?"

"Of course not."

"Eye-opening experience," he said and sat back down. "Talk to Kwame about it sometime. Place is a fucking hell hole."

"Papi," James said. "Language!"

"Sorry," Amir said with a chuckle. "But it's true. You know—if I was in charge of the school system—"

"And here we go," Cristina said.

But Amir heard her. "Seriously—I'd make it standard for every twelve-year-old to do community service there. *Todos*," he said with a wave of his hand.

"I'm sure that'd sit well with parents," Cristina said.

"I want to go," James said.

Cristina scowled. "*Absolutamente no.*"

Amir looked at James and they both smiled. Amir said, "I could arrange it."

"Are you out of your mind, Amir?" Cristina obviously didn't appreciate the direction things were heading. Neither did Paco. He stretched out his front legs, sniffed around at his bowl and then scampered off to the living room. Cristina smiled. "*Mira*, James—even the dog thinks it's a bad idea."

James giggled. Amir also found it hard to contain a laugh.

"Okay, *caballeros*," Cristina said. "Dinner is served. James, clear your stuff. Amir, set the table, *por favor*."

The two boys went to it with great efficiency, the paella's aroma a piquant motivator. And as they sat and ate, Amir's heart was filled too full to hold onto whatever vanity still lingered from his pre-shower pity party. They talked football. They talked politics. They discussed the merits of Cristina's cooking.

Soon, James was in bed and, in direct challenge to Amir's paternal authority, Paco with him. "Tough," Cristina had said with a laugh. "Overruled by a two-thirds majority. Three-fourths if you count the dog." Amir wondered why James had so much agency in the matter. Choose your battles, he told himself. The boy'll be hitting puberty before you know it ... that's when the real fireworks begin.

They were on the couch now, Cristina draped across it lengthwise, her feet on Amir's lap, typical of their arrangement. When his phone buzzed, she was dozing and he, reading a rather entertaining account of Putin's rise and fall.

It was Brit Tillman, with a vague message: *Can u meet me?*
Amir: *Cuando*
After twenty seconds, Brit: *Now*
Amir: *Ahora???*
Brit: *Yes Amir NOW*
Amir: *Ok where*

She was his boss, though he still wasn't used to it. Working for Special Unit was an adjustment in and of itself. Answering to Brit had other distinct complexities.

Brit: *idk pick*
Amir: *what?*
Brit: *you choose where*

Well, at least she was being minutely considerate. Strange though, he thought.

Amir: *El Sevillano*
Brit: *See u in 20*
Amir: *OK. Hardware?*
Brit: *are u joking*
Amir: *haha thought it was going to b more fun ...*

To that, she didn't respond.

He'd bring the piece anyway. Old habits die hard.

≡

When the boat reached the fringe of the harbour, Suzuki pointed at the controls and slashed a thumb across his neck. The man at the wheel cut the engine.

"This is as far as we go," Suzuki said in French, the common language between them.

"Are you sure?" the fisherman said, eyes peering over the bow toward the dim lights of Zanzibar City. "I could get closer."

"Kill it."

The boat gurgled to a glide, low waves lapping at its side. Suzuki disappeared to the stern for a moment and returned with a water-proof duffle bag, black material slick from the drizzle outside.

"What now?"

"This is where we go our separate ways," Suzuki said.

"What is it we agreed on?" the fisherman asked, though they'd confirmed the price several times.

An avarice-sculpted grin appeared on the fisherman's stubbly face as Suzuki bent over and unzipped the duffle. When Suzuki came upright, the fisherman's eyes bulged. There were two flashes, each delivered with a muted snap. The fisherman's head jerked back and his body toppled.

Suzuki stooped to inspect the precise entrance wounds just beneath the fisherman's receding hairline, then parted the man's wind-jacket. The pockets held nothing of value or concern, so he placed the gun back in the bag, and dragged the body out onto the stern. A thin smear of blood trailed in its wake, Suzuki's signature.

After popping the corpse up on the lip of the starboard side, Suzuki wiped the rain from his forehead and lifted a large chain from the deck. With great speed, he wound it in figure eight loops around the fisherman's ankles and lower legs. He finished the process by running the excess chain up to the man's belt, which he then unbuckled, wove through one of the iron links, and refastened to the man's waist. Satisfied, he up-ended the fisherman's legs and allowed weight and momentum to finish the job. With a greedy gulp, the black waters accepted Suzuki's gift.

He checked his watch. It wasn't yet 0200, but an outbound current had the boat drifting. So he wasted no time. First came the wetsuit. Next, he sealed his supplies. Once everything was airtight, he attached the bag to his waist by a thin plastic line and put on his flippers and mask. Finally prepared to jump, Suzuki pulled a cord on his bag and the small inflation balloons at its sides swiftly took in air.

With unceremonious haste, he parted ways with the orphaned trawler and began his swim ashore.

***

It was the quintessential Spanish barroom—narrow and dark, adorned in dense clusters of old photos and artefacts of religious and athletic significance. Several cured boar legs dangled above the service counter. Another lay on a platter at the far end of the bar—hoof intact—half the marbled flesh stripped away. A scent of garlic hung in the air and the affected staccato of an English football announcer blared from a small radio beneath the hard liquor selection. The place was at typical volume for midweek. The front littered with off duty officers sipping lager. A few Spanish old-timers huddled over tapas and sherry toward the back.

Amir and Brit sat at a small wooden table, one edge of it flush to the wall. She'd just delivered the news and he'd almost spit a mouthful of beer everywhere.

"*What?*"

"Un-bloody-believable, no?"

"What," Amir repeated—slowly this time, vowel elongated as if holding a note.

Brit tapped her cigarette against the edge of the ashtray and took another drag. As the smoke drifted from her lips, she nodded and said, "I know."

"You're fucking with me."

"I'm not. I just got off with London two hours ago."

"They're fucking with *you* then."

"It isn't a joke, Duran."

Amir waved his pint glass over the table in a vague circle and shook his head. "It's got to be bad intel."

"It's been confirmed."

"*Confirmed*."

"Multiple channels. Records. Sources on the ground. This is very real."

Amir blinked repeatedly and rubbed the crown of his skull as if suddenly disoriented. After a moment, his voice descended to a near-whisper: "How'd they find out—kid was exposed?"

"No. Blood test picked it up."

"Blood test ..." Amir trailed off, lower lip now pinched between his thumb and forefinger. None of it computed. None of it.

"I'm short on details," Brit said. "But, there was a woman several years ago, apparently. Guess she was exposed but remained uninfected. When they did the analysis—"

"Who?"

"The doctors."

"In Zanzibar?"

"Yes, Zanzibar. They do have doctors down there, Duran." There was no humour in the look she received. "Long story short, they ended up isolating an antibody in her system."

"*Mierda*," he said.

"Shit is right."

"Well, what the fuck happened to her?"

After some hesitation, she said, "Drowned."

"Christ. How the hell did that happen?" Again, Brit balked. "Let me guess," Amir said snidely. "Your lot had something to do with it."

"My lot? Last I checked, you'd an office down the hall from me."

"Tell me I'm wrong."

Brit ground her cigarette into the flat of the ashtray and watched its embers fade. "Isn't important."

"No? Bet her family thinks it is."

"Based on what I've read, it's not clear they ever knew about it."

"How convenient."

"Anyway—the local doctors have been looking for the immunity in the general pop ever since."

Amir dug a smoke from his own pack and shook his head. "Jesus ... the Zanzibari flare for survival ... it's fucking amazing."

"I'll say," Brit said.

As she reached for her water, a faint grin came to Amir's lips. "Still a taste for the strong stuff, eh?"

"Funny bloke," she said. "Genes don't mix well with liquor."

"And you know this from experience."

"Proximity. Bloody close proximity. Returning to the point—"

"Fuck," he said, cutting her off, "I'm still trying to process the fact that people are actually immune to this shit. I can't wrap my fucking head around it."

"Yes, well, life is weird. Nevertheless, we've got to deal with it."

"*Deal with it.* No fucking offence, Tillman—why's London even involving you? They should send an extraction team a-sap."

"Not an option."

"*Porque?*"

"Concerns over provocation."

"Are you kidding? We've got a cure on our hands and they're worried about the Russians?"

"Potential cure. And yes—the Russians ... and the Japanese for that matter. London's convinced they'd both go to the mat on this one."

Amir took a big drag and studied Brit's face. "I'm still not seeing our role in it." Brit averted her eyes and reached for another cigarette. "You're fucking kidding me," he said, prompting several heads to turn in their direction.

"Welcome to the world of espionage, Duran. And quiet down, will you?"

After a quick glance of the bar, Amir's eyes settled back on Brit. "Are you out of your fucking mind? Our guys are so fucking green, I worry every time I put one in the field. And this is Granada ... not some fucking unaligned zone off Africa."

"I don't disagree."

"Well, what the fuck are you—" Amir paused mid-sentence, ran both hands through his hair, then abruptly shot to his feet and marched over to the bar. A minute later, he returned with something strong and slumped down. After a stretch of deafening silence, he edged forward in his seat. "Not in a million fucking years, Tillman. No fucking way."

"I expressed my concerns."

"Good," he said. "London'll have to find someone else."

"It's not *our* choice, Amir."

"Like hell it isn't!"

"Listen," she said, palm raised. "I get your apprehension. This sort of thing demands a very specialized skill set."

"An international exfil? Yeah, I'd say so."

"Honestly, though—the more I thought about it—the more it made sense."

"What? You're giving me the fucking company line?"

"Duran—I can't change what London wants. Would you've been my first choice? No. But can I see why they think you're a good fit? Sure—detective by training, look the part, speak serviceable Arabic."

"They speak Swahili in Zanzibar, Tillman."

"Yeah well, Arabic too, I guess ... to be frank, they also wanted someone who could handle it if shit goes down."

"I'm flattered."

"I'd prefer focused," she said, without humour.

"What if I refuse?"

She tilted her head, almost apologetically. But not quite. "You'd be court-marshalled."

"Cristina will be fucking livid."

"Amir, are you kidding? Cristina can't know about this. That's basic protocol. Besides, you'll be away for no more than a week or two. We'll say you've gone to London for meetings."

"*Two weeks.*"

"She and James will be fine," Brit said. Amir drew rapid, anxious puffs from his cigarette, refusing to look at her. "Oh, come off it, Duran. It's not the end of the bloody world. You're the one who's been complaining about not seeing enough action."

"Wasn't what I had in mind," he said. After a slug of scotch, he re-established eye contact. "How soon?"

"Tomorrow," she said, standing. "We'll go through the plan first thing."

***

After a three-shot inoculation for self-pity, Amir paid his tab, lit a smoke and drifted out into the familiar currents of the Andalusian night. The air was warm and the ancient heart of old Granada was dark and mostly quiet. Somewhere to the west, a squad car's tinny siren screamed its warning to the slums. But the shrillness soon faded, and a whisper of mountain wind rose up in its place.

For several minutes Amir lingered on the cobblestone walk beneath the Sevilliano's gold and black lacquer sign. With every drag his head spun a little faster. Less from the nicotine and liquor. More so, the ground shifting beneath his feet. The immunity. The assignment. The vast universe beyond the wall. The prospect of a different world, and the sudden burden of delivering it.

Then there were those pangs of anticipatory homesickness. Amir's soul had been haunted for years by a host of nasty demons: rage, longing, sadness. But fear of the unknown? This was something new. And he wondered why all that whiskey failed to produce the mollifying effect he'd invested in. And as the vague ache of uncertainty sharpened into a clawing panic, Amir couldn't ignore one basic question: why him? Why had he been put up to this? But the only answer he could think of came in the form of another question: Why fucking not?

Amir tossed his butt and abandoned the curb of Reyes Catolicos for the granite sweep of Plaza Mayor. As he passed the dormant fountain at Mayor's centre, images of Jeddo bubbled up from the silence. There was the old man: perched on the lip of the fountain with a mouthful of guava gelato, crooked feet dipped beneath the gurgling surface. Had his grandfather been there now he'd have scolded Amir for reeking of smoke. Filthy, he'd have called it. Selfish, filthy and dumb.

He drew another smoke from his pack and sparked it. A heavy

gust whipped across the plaza. The pruned oaks along its shoulder shimmied under the blue corona of the half moon, watery shadows dancing beneath. He slowed his pace, took a long drag and smiled. Still lovely, he thought. Despite all that had befallen the world, beauty still survives. Maybe not in the crumbling slums of Sector 3, or out past the wall in the sun-punished feed-lots of 5. But here—in old Granada—some beauty still survives.

On the gentle incline of Calle del Darro, Amir's focus drifted toward Zanzibar. What was it like? How would it measure up to this little world he knew so well? Then he thought of Joseph Coblah—or whoever he really was, the poor bastard. The man had survived that arduous sojourn—braved the Ebola-infested wilds of sub-Saharan Africa—only to end up here, face down in a pool of his own blood. What does it take for a man to abandon his home? What had he been promised?

Strange world it is.

Passing below the floodlit ramparts of the Alhambra, Amir felt a sudden impulse to ascend the winding hill of the Albacin. Maybe he'd wander the grounds of the Grand Mezquita, find a nice spot, pray a little. Come to peace with his assignment.

But then he thought about Cristina, and the pull of devotion soon vanished with the transient haste of a passing cross breeze. Earthlier desires suddenly took root in his sleepy soul. Home. Bed. Her warm body to flop down next to. There were only a few hours left before he'd have to go. And he sure as hell wasn't going to waste them talking to Allah.

There'd be plenty of time for that later.

***

The inflated duffle bobbed like a buoy as Suzuki slashed through the mild cross-current. The moon was draped in rain and every-thing but the agent's chiselled face blended black against the waves. His bag, his wetsuit, his flippers, the .22 strapped to his ribs, the long sheath and ribbed handle of the Hissatsu on his thigh—all of it remained invisible. A less proficient swimmer might've found the gear cumbersome given the task. But Suzuki

John Ward

glided like a seal, surfacing for breath every ten strokes.

The swim only took twenty minutes, and it was low tide when he made ground at the harbour's far side. A stout seawall provided cover as he hoisted his bag onto the seaweed-draped rocks. He spent less than two minutes huddled beneath it, preparing for the next leg. Once changed, he zipped the bag up and threw it over his shoulder. Suzuki then pulled his hood high, scaled the wall and surveyed the landscape.

A rolling mist had replaced the drizzle—perfect conditions for crossing in the open. He set off without hesitation toward the muted orange wash of a single lamp post across the yard. Its ethereal glow gave definition to a paved path along the western side of the property. When he reached the curved edge of the narrow road, Suzuki dug a hand into his pocket. His palm came out clutching a small, wristwatch-like device. He paused to activate it and waited for his directions to arrive. Thirty seconds later, the device beeped twice and emitted a single flash. Suzuki fastened the straps on, and again set off into the shadows.

When he arrived, the hotel's facade was cloaked in darkness. Only a single, yellow light shone dimly from a second-floor window. Suzuki circled round to the rear of the building, and immediately found the garden level entrance by the foot of an emptied swimming pool.

The handler's instructions had been explicit: enter without lingering. So Suzuki withdrew the silenced pistol and unsheathed the Hissatsu without breaking stride. Gun held shoulder level, he pressed the knife butt to the door handle. As arranged, it swung open, unimpeded.

"Come in." The simple command was followed by a second. "Lower your weapons."

Suzuki halted, pupils dilating in the darkness. "Show yourself," he said in French, "or else—" The lights were on before he could finish.

A tall, slender woman stood in profile before a staircase several metres away, her fingers poised over a switch. And, as abruptly, the room went black again.

"Call me Shiv," she said. "Confirmation code: zero, one, nine,

nine, sixteen-forty-two." Her French was impeccable. "Now, please, lower your weapons, and follow me."

She'd appeared to be unarmed, but he kept his distance none-theless. As they ascended the steps, he holstered the Glock, but kept the knife out.

Passing the first floor, Shiv cast her eyes over her shoulder toward the shadowed blade of Suzuki's Hissatsu. "Again, that isn't necessary," she said. Suzuki withheld a reply, still climbing with the knife in hand. "Suit yourself," she said quietly.

At the second floor landing, she turned off the stairs and led him toward a slender, vertical plane of light at the end of the hallway. But instead of opening the door she pivoted around to face him. "This is your room. You'll find what you need inside."

"The coordinates?" he asked, still a safe distance from his guide.

"As I said—it's all there." Again, Suzuki had no reply. "I will be leaving you now," she said, extending a set of keys in Suzuki's direction. "The place is basically yours. But I urge you, don't forget the lights."

"Lights?" he asked, taking the keys from her.

"Only one that should ever be on is in your room. And even then, I'd prefer it shut as much as possible. We don't have visitors these days—and believe me—people in the neighbourhood take notice of the smallest things."

"Who are the neighbours?"

"No one important," she said. "Nonetheless, it's wise to be cautious. Also, call me only in an emergency. Otherwise ..." Shiv brushed by Suzuki, padded down the corridor and paused at the top of the stairwell. "... best if you don't contact me."

Suzuki smiled as Shiv descended into the darkness. Then he turned around, took hold of the doorknob and raised his knife into a defensive position.

***

One palm to the wall, a bleary-eyed Abasi hunched over the toilet bowl, cursing like a sailor. In a haze, he'd left the seat down and every few seconds a sprinkle of piss jumped back at his knees.

The process was too far along to pinch off and go for the lights switch. So when it came time to flush, he grabbed a wad of tissue to mop the mess.

After a few good swipes, Abasi dumped the sopping paper and straightened up. When he turned toward the sink, a square column of yellow light struck his eyes. He immediately squinted, rose to the tips of his toes and craned for a look out the small, high-set window to the right of the sink.

"Oh, who the fuck left the porch light on," Abasi grumbled. He gave his hands a quick rinse and plodded from the bathroom to the kitchen, swearing under his breath. In the foyer, though, Abasi fell silent.

"Hello?" he said, nudging the cracked door open further and peaking outside. Abasi exhaled with relief at the sight of Darweshi. The boy was huddled on the concrete slab of the porch, knees to chest, little head buried in his crossed arms. "It's late," Abasi said, "what are you doing?"

The boy lifted his head for a moment, eyes bloodshot and glassy from weeping. When Abasi crouched and sat next to Darweshi, the boy tucked his brow back into the crook of his elbow.

"Darweshi, what is wrong—why are you not sleeping? A bad dream again?"

"No," Darweshi said, voice muffled under the fold of his forearm.

"Then what is it, son?"

"You're not my father!"

Abasi reflexively drew away, face baring a look of shock. After a few seconds he reached his arm around the boy's back and said, "Darweshi—whether it makes sense to you or not—I think of you as my own son. I always have. Now tell me what is wrong, love." The boy burst into uncontrolled sobs, his thin shoulders heaving under Abasi's embrace. "Shh," Abasi said softly. "Shh," he repeated, pulling the boy closer. "Whatever it is, it will be just fine. I promise you. Calm, now, calm."

"I don't want to be like this," Darweshi said, tears coursing down the tender flesh of his cheeks.

"Like *what*? What are you like?"

"What the doctors said—I don't want to have it."

Abasi patted the boy's neck. "There is nothing wrong with you, Darweshi. In fact, you are healthier than all of us. It's a special thing."

"Then why does Babu say I need to leave?" Another round of loud sobs rolled out, the boy struggling to control his breathing.

"Shh. Don't let Babu frighten you. He doesn't know what he's talking about. You're not going anywhere, Darweshi. Especially not without us. I promise you that."

"I'm not?"

"No," Abasi said, "don't be silly." The boy's body relaxed a bit under his arm. "You're staying right here with us ... at *home*." Darweshi leaned his head on Abasi's shoulder, and the two of them sat in silence, holding each other, peering off into the yard. The faintest blue glimmer of dawn strained through the blackness of the overcast sky.

John Ward

FOUR

For all his carping about the way things worked in Granada, Henry Glass was burning to get back.

London was a drag. Vauxhall Cross, even more so. Christ, it'd become a fucking rudderless institution. Bogged down in bureaucracy. Crumbling under the weight of arrogance and ineptitude. Made his bloody head hurt. And frankly, he wasn't sure how much more he could handle.

The station liaison pow-wow didn't conclude for another week, and he'd had it up to here listening to Tony Mason—the UK's most strategy-deficient case officer—lecture ad infinitum about Russia's rapidly deteriorating coms infrastructure. Glass wanted to stand up and say: *So, Mason—I mean, sir—what do you want to bloody do about it? Oh, I apologize. Providing an answer might require some actual thought on your part now, wouldn't it? Not just a tedious regurgitation of what some low-level analyst already reported ... you fucking duffer.*

But Agent Glass hadn't the bollocks. Hadn't the energy either.

Glass turned away from the gargantuan geometry of Vauxhall's facade, then leaned over the railing, and looked out at the Thames. As he studied its muddy banks, he took a drag from his cigarette and let out a disdainful chuckle. Half at the idiots he'd been surrounded by for the past seven days. Half at himself for being such a careerist pussy.

Unfortunately, the air outside the building was oppressive too. Only 0800, and it was pasty thick, showers having not yet arrived to break the humidity. Glass wiped the sweat from his brow, loosened his tie and wondered how the hell things were going with Brit.

What had SIS reported to her in his absence? Most maddening thing about these goddamn retreats was how much they interfered with actual work. Despite being at the physical centre of the British intelligence apparatus for two whole weeks, he felt entirely out of the loop. Maybe it was by design. Who the hell knew. Glass threw his butt into the river.

Back to the salt mines.

But as he turned toward the building his cell rang. It was Brit.

"Ah, a sound for sore ears," he said into the phone with a laugh. "How are you, dear?"

"Peachy," she said. "How's London treating you?"

"Like shite."

"Well that's good—at least they're consistent about something."

"Very good, General. You're learning to have a sense of humour about these pompous nitwits."

"Glass, listen—has Mason made any of mention of Zanzibar?"

"Not sure what you mean, dear—but then again, coming up here is the operational equivalent of being dumb, deaf, and blind for two weeks, so it doesn't surprise me. They've kept us locked in a conference room reviewing Op Sec protocols for nearly eight hours each day. And when the impulse for variety strikes them, Mason comes in to deliver one of his inane presentations on the FSB. Why?" he said. "What's happening with our friends in Zanzibar?"

"Interesting," Brit said. There was a pause on the line, then, "So nothing about Duran, either?"

"What does Duran have to do with Zanzibar ... other than last year's Coblah fiasco, that is?"

"Henry, where are you right now?"

"I'm standing in front of the Thames, twenty metres from HQ ... Brit, what bush are you beating around, exactly?"

"Well," she said, "this is complicated ... and I'd thought they'd have told you at this juncture."

"Told me what, Tillman. Out with it already—"

"Okay, simmer down. I don't appreciate the hostility."

"Sorry," he said. Then he lit another cigarette and began to pace. "I'm completely in the dark here. It'd be kind of you to relieve me of my suffering."

"We're sending Duran to Zanzibar."

Glass stopped pacing. "Why in hell would we do that?"

It was silent for a beat. Then Brit said, "Because we've—or they've, really—discovered another one."

"Another one? Another what, Zanzibari operative? So? If they know who he is, just let the Russians smuggle him up. We'll snag him at the border, as per usual. And of all people, why would you send Duran down—?"

"Henry, slow down," she said. "That's not it at all … the immunity, it's resurfaced."

Glass stammered. "I'm … I'm sorry dear, what did you say?"

"There's a child," she said, "A boy—found out just recently. He's the son of—"

"The Lotto woman."

"Precisely," Brit said, tone betraying confusion. "Henry, how long have you known about her?"

But Glass was already onto another rant. "You know, I had told Mason to consider extracting the entire family, the damn fool. Or in the very least, test them all. Fucking moron wouldn't do it. Too much noise, as he put it."

"How involved were you?"

"I was involved in the whole bloody thing! Start to fucking debacle of a finish. It was just before you'd come on. They had all of us working on it."

"Too much noise?"

"I don't know," Glass said. "The woman was a handful from the very beginning. Threw a wobbler as soon as our local asset approached her. Told us to stay away. We tried every carrot in the book. 'Course, I was of the opinion we should've taken more decisive action—get in there with a team, snatch them all up, every bloody living genetic relation. You'd think it'd have been worth our while, noise or not. But no—Tony Mason in his infinite fucking wisdom wanted to play nice. Do it the quiet way. Next thing we know, our man on the ground reports in that the fucking miracle woman has taken a long walk off a short pier."

"I saw that in the file."

"Yeah, brilliant. Never even recovered the body."

"Henry, I don't understand something. If the hospitals down there have been testing all this time, why are we only finding out about the boy now?"

"I don't know. That's a question better answered by a geneticist. From what I understand, these sorts of things aren't always apparent. Latency and what have you."

"Right," said Brit, the only response she could muster.

"Hold on," Glass said, pivoting. "You're saying they want to send Duran down there? To get the boy? That's a ludicrous idea!"

"He thinks so too."

"For once, I agree with the man."

"Well, London's briefing him in less than an hour. They've whipped up an entire strategy and it's scheduled for immediate implementation," she said.

"So," Glass said, "the Russians must know. No other reason to move so hastily."

"And the Japanese."

"Jesus Christ." He stood, aghast, shaking his head. "And they've chosen Duran for this? Insane, Tillman. Sheer, unmitigated insanity. He doesn't know the first thing about an op of this sort."

"Don't tell me twice ... I protested, but Mason boxed me into a corner. Said it was a direct order from the Foreign Sec, by way of C, himself."

"What the fuck does the Foreign Secretary know about Duran?"

"Who knows. But there's not much I can do. Thought you needed to know, though."

"Thank you," he said, as sincerely as his current state of agitation permitted. Nothing was right about it. Neither the Duran piece, nor the fact he'd been circumvented.

"Glass."

"Yes?"

"I need to go," Brit said. "Touch base with you later."

"Brit—favour, dear."

"What is it?"

"Don't let Mason know we've spoken yet."

After a few seconds she said, "Fine."

"Good. And don't forget to call."

"Right. Bye, then."

Glass came back over to the railing and drew smoke from his third cigarette with such rapidity and voraciousness, it was as if they'd been discussing the cure for lung cancer—not airborne Ebola.

***

As Tony Mason circled, the studded souls of his suede driving loafers left a trail of dimples in the vacuumed surface of the cream carpet. The agent's choice in footwear screamed Chelsea, but his clipped lilt suggested Cambridge: "I must admit, love—I'm a touch confused. Last we spoke, Mr Matthews was quite satisfied with the terms."

The woman on the line launched into a long-winded rebuttal. Mason ceased pacing and peered through the office's floor-to-ceiling interior window. "Christ," he whispered, eyes fixed on Henry Glass. Glass gave Mason an irreverent wave and disappeared into the conference room at the end of the corridor.

"No bloody order round here." The comment injected a bit of confusion into the phone call and Mason was forced to clarify. "Nothing, it's nothing to do with you. Listen—tell Matthews it's fifteen percent equity stake, or the plug is pulled. Simple as that."

As the caller reiterated her complaint, Mason drew the interior blinds and sauntered over to a putter leaning against the left edge of his desk. Closing his free hand over the club's custom leather grip, Mason grinned. It was a fine club—right weight, perfectly balanced. Two days prior, it delivered a birdie on a rather overgrown eighteenth green. Mason had celebrated by ordering a round of martinis for the three strangers he'd played the round with.

After several short one-handed strokes across the carpet, Mason winced and said, "Delicate? Bloody right ... but that's not my concern, now, is it? Honour the agreement, we'll have no problems." Then he clamped the cell between his shoulder and ear, gripped the putter in both hands, set a stance, and struck the invisible ball at his feet with such precision it made him smile again.

Watching the illusory putt sink, Mason said, "Tell him you've an hour to work it out—no paper." The last bit prompted a lengthy response. Mason shook his head and gesticulated with the putter as if the woman were standing before him. "Love—you seem to be missing the point. The window is closing rapidly on this ... pardon?" After a pause, he said, "Oh, they can't tell their arses from their elbows. And no, I've no qualms with that aspect. Just think of it this way: when it's wrapped up and done with, we'll all be knighted."

With a chuckle, Mason placed the club back against the desk and pivoted toward the broad, outward facing window behind him. Across the wide, sludgy line of the Thames, the low, bleak sprawl of London rolled toward the horizon. A light rain was beginning to sweep in, and the sky was crowded with a dense layer of leaden vapor.

"Good. See to it then," Mason said. "*Ciao*."

He sat in the big, black leather swivel chair behind his desk, flipped through the setting menu on his cell, pressed his selection, and slipped the phone back into the breast pocket of his linen sport coat.

"Always something, now, isn't it?" he said with a grin. "Let's pray this Amir Duran character is up to the task."

***

Henry Glass rose from the table and made for the door. This time, nearly everyone watched him walk out. "Excuse me," he said, "nature calls."

The creak and click of the door brought a faint smile to Glass's lips. It was hard not to relish the blatant fuck-off-ness of his conduct.

Wankers. Have fun in there.

On the elevator up, Glass's grin faded. Whether he'd make through security was anyone's guess. But worth a try, nevertheless. Twenty seconds later, the control panel pinged and the lift's doors whispered open. Glass stepped out into the executive floor's sterile stone and chrome foyer and proceeded directly to the scanner mounted on the wall to the left of the entrance.

With his palm pressed to its reflective black surface, the digital display flashed red. A robotic but rather sexy female voice confirmed his lowly status. "Access denied," she said. "Please refer to security protocol."

John Ward

Within seconds, another voice piped in—female, human, and decidedly less attractive: "Agent Glass, may I help you?"

"Um, yes, I was hoping to see Marissa, if possible."

"Ms White?"

"Yes, Ms White."

There was a pause. "Do you have an appointment?"

"No," Glass said. "I suppose I'm dropping in rather out of the blue. But if it's possible to—"

"I'm sorry, you'll need to speak with her EA."

"But see, that's just it, dear—I'm wondering whether you might inform her I've something critical to discuss." Oh, come on, don't be a fucking cunt, now.

"I'm sorry, sir. You'll need to use the appropriate channels."

Glass glared at the black box on the wall and shook his head at the existential absurdity of the situation. Bloody impersonal technology—can't charm someone without proper eye contact, can you? A bit of blandishment would have to do.

"I'm so sorry," Glass said. "I do realize what a bleeding pain it must be, having to gate keep for these big wigs. An utterly thankless task, I'm sure." Glass coated each word with a thick layer of Oxbridge gentility, his cultivated enunciation projecting a sort of benevolent superiority. "Though, I must say, I've heard from Marissa herself that you've done just a smashing job of it."

"Ms White said that?"

Shocked she'd bitten, Glass smiled. "Oh, *yes*," he said, laying the accent on thicker. "Very enthusiastically, I might add. Said you've become rather legendary with the brass for your unmatched prudence and perspicacity. Tell you what, I'm under a time crunch on this one, dear—how about you simply pick up the phone and tell her I'm right outside her office. If she can't talk, so be it. I'll update her after the op is completed." He paused. "I do hope it goes well, though. Really needed her guidance on one very essential aspect."

"Sir ... just ... please hold for a moment."

It was a long moment. Truth was, he hadn't spoken to Marissa for years. And the way they'd left it—it was anyone's guess how she'd react, him swooping in unannounced. Caution to the wind, old boy.

There was a crackle and the box on the wall said, "Agent Glass? Someone will be with you shortly."

"Um, thank you, dear." *What in the bloody hell is that supposed to mean?*

Glass took a small step backward. The towering door slid open with a hiss. A rather prim, young man in a slim grey suit stood on the threshold, hand out. "You must be Agent Glass," the kid said, tone dripping with condescension.

"And you are?"

"McManus, Ms White's executive assistant."

"Irishman," Glass said, taking the boy's hand.

"Only in name," McManus said. "This way."

He led Glass down a long corridor bifurcating dense rows of predominantly empty cubicles. An occasional computer jockey gazed up as they passed. Glass nearly inquired about the abundance of unused work stations but decided not to afford the prissy little bugger another opportunity to patronize him. At the end of the corridor, they arrived at a row of tall, polished wooden doors. McManus passed the first two, stopped in front of the third, knocked rapidly, and opened it without pause for reply.

"Agent Glass for you, ma'am." McManus looked Glass in the eye, affected a rather dramatic, bowing gesture, and strode away.

For several seconds, Glass and Marissa stood in complete silence, eyes locked. She, behind her desk, fingers of both hands pressed to its paper strewn surface. He, in the frame of the open door, rigid as a palace sentry, past rushing back with the speed and acuteness of an airborne arrow.

Finally, Marissa smiled. "You always were good at talking your way out of tricky situations."

"Or into them," he said. "May I?"

"Oh, yes—please come in." Marissa watched intently as Glass took several hesitant steps forward. "So," she said, "what exactly did it take to get Lucinda to let you in?"

"You know—a bit of this, a bit of that."

"Right. The old this and that," Marissa said. She straightened her suit coat, sat down, and crossed her arms. "Please—sit."

Glass settled into the stiff leather sofa adjacent to Marissa's desk and motioned toward the window with his left index finger. "Great view."

"Perks of leadership. I hear you've a nice set-up, yourself."

"Granada? Yes. Rather wild place, but undeniably pretty. Food is half-decent too." He looked down at his lap and again fell silent.

"So, how are you, Henry? I wasn't sure I'd ever see you again. Not in person, that is ... Mason tells me you're doing a fair job of it down there."

"Does he, now?" Glass asked, tone less diminutive than before.

"That surprises you?"

"Well, that's what brings me here, actually."

"Ah—the special operation you spoke so urgently of."

He had to smile. "What do you know about this whole Zanzibar thing?"

She glanced up at the ceiling. After some time, her wide eyes returned to him. "Better question, Henry, is what do you know about it? Last I checked, they're supposed to keep the liaisons sequestered in a conference room all day."

"They certainly try."

"For good reason. It's a chance for Mason and his lot to test operational efficiency without a mediating party involved."

"Right. But a real op? A full-scale exfil in an unaligned zone? One in which the primary operative is a non-six-trained, former bobby? I mean, risky, no? You'd think they'd have enough sense to involve me, Marissa."

"You've been talking to Tillman?" Glass raised his eyebrows but said nothing. Marissa frowned. "Come on, Henry. You think we don't monitor every call within a thousand metres of this building? You really haven't been here for a while."

"Yes, well," he said, searching her eyes, "I like it that way."

"Don't I know it," she said. "Don't worry, though. Mason's no clue of your little sidebar with Tillman. Suppose it would be courteous of me to inform him. But to be honest, I don't think it's relevant."

"Thanks ... I ... "Glass ran a hand through his fine, floppy grey-blond bangs. "Sorry—this is terribly awkward, isn't it?"

Marissa gnawed her lower lip and looked away. Glass studied

her features more closely. She'd aged, yes—but looked so very much the same. Thin arms. Long, regal neck. Jet black hair. Eyes, glacier blue. And there was that red lipstick she'd always worn— so juicy—so irreverently French. He wondered: what were her breasts like beneath the power suit? Had they lost anything? Had they sunken, a spate of child rearing to blame? He hadn't heard of her marrying. But he'd been so far afield, news of such things rarely reached him.

"Come to dinner with me."

Marissa drew back in her seat. "What?"

"Yes, dinner. Place of your choosing. Haven't been in town for a spell, and I figure it'd do me some good to get back to my roots. We can catch up."

After an uncomfortable laugh, Marissa said, "London isn't quite as you remember it, Henry."

"Is anything?"

"Depends on the way you look at things, Chap."

Chap ...

Glass froze, chest aching as it echoed through his head.

Chap ...

And there he was in Cairo, again—shirtless, leaning out the window, listening to the sirens. And there was Marissa—stark naked, smoking, waltzing about the room as if the whole city weren't burning.

Chap ...

"Fair point," he said, finally. "How about for old times' sake?"

CINCO

Neither James nor Cristina took the news quite as he'd expected, but the outward indifference with which the boy received it bothered Amir. What the fuck. Kid's ten. Damn young for adolescent reticence. Did he really not give a shit that his dad had to up and leave for two whole weeks? Maybe he'd have shown more concern if he knew where Amir was really off to.

"You okay, buddy?"

"Yes, Papi—what's the big deal?"

Cristina, fixing breakfast, glanced over her shoulder. "What's so important that they need you to go all the way to London?"

"Who the hell knows ... management issues, I guess. James, you're sure everything is alright?"

"He'll be just fine, Amir," Cristina said with a shake of the head. She shut the burner off and turned toward the table where Amir and James sat. "Are *you* okay?"

"Yeah, why?"

"Are you anxious about travelling?" she asked, leaning to place James's plate on the table.

Amir watched James closely for a moment. When the boy picked up his fork without speaking, Amir said, "*Chico*—are you kidding me? The woman isn't your servant."

"What?" the boy said, voice squeaky as a rubber duck.

"*What? Thank you* would be the words you're looking for."

"Oh," James said, words garbled by a mouthful of eggs. "*Gracias*, Cristina."

"Jesus. I hope it's not like this when I'm gone."

Cristina looked at Amir with great intensity. "You're in one hell of a mood."

Amir pushed his uneaten breakfast to the centre of the table, rose from his chair, and left for the living room. A minute later, he returned with a small luggage bag around his shoulder. "As I said, you won't be able to reach me for at least a few days, so you might want to be in touch with Brit if you need anything ... if anyone cares, that is."

Before Cristina could address the remark, James asked, "Will you take pictures?"

"I'm not sure I'll have the time."

"I wish I could go," the boy said, in between bites. Suddenly, James hopped up from his seat, scampered over, and tossed his arms around Amir's torso.

Amir placed a hand on the crown of the boy's head. "*Yo tambien, mi amor.*"

Cristina smiled, shaking her head as she walked to them. "We'll miss you," she said and leaned over to kiss him.

"I know."

"*Do* you, though?" she said, needling. "You should have fun, baby. Who gets to fly to London? I can barely remember last time I was outside the wall."

The boy looked up at his dad. "I've never even been outside the city."

"One day, buddy," Amir said, giving the boy a final squeeze. He then placed a kiss on Cristina's lips and said, "*Los amo.*"

Then Amir was off, bounding down the stairs to the landing below, where the diurnal patina of the rising sun glimmered on the tiles of the foyer floor. In the wash of light at the foot of the steps, he opened his bag, withdrew his nine, and holstered it on his thigh. Returning the luggage to his shoulder, he paused for a moment and listened to Paco's high bark bounce sharply through the tetragonal cavern of the stairwell above.

I'll miss you too, you furry little maniac.

Amir reached for the knob and abruptly paused. Fingers resting loosely over the faded brass handle, he leaned forward until his face was no more than a few centimetres from the door's plate glass window. The winding cobblestone road outside looked much as it always did, perhaps a bit cleaner, a bit quainter. He drew a deep breath and reached for the pack of smokes in his back pocket, hoping a dose of nicotine might quiet his plaintive heart. Lighter raised, the flame's reflection jumped in the dusty glass. A view of Amir's own reflection soon emerged—wavy black hair, dark stubble, and deep green eyes showing more prominently than the rest of him.

It was an odd sight: features only half there. A ghost in the light, conjured through the thin medium of reconstituted sand. The Arab was on spectral display, the Spaniard adrift somewhere outside in the morning sun. As Amir opened the door, he thought of Jeddo. Again, the impulse to pray returned. Though he wasn't sure if he had the time. *Make time*, Amir thought, stepping out onto the street.

You'll need it where you're going.

***

"Strangest thing about the British," Jeddo once said, "is their interminable restlessness. And I don't just mean those twitchy brutes you see standing around checkpoints with rifles, smoking cigarettes, jibber-jabbering about god knows what. I'm talking about the British *people*. All of them. Look at their history, their culture—they can't sit still."

It was an early morning not long after the PAF had taken the city. The boy and his grandfather were sitting on the garden terrace of the Gran Mezquita, chatting after prayer.

"Remember this, Amir—don't trust anyone who can't sit still."

Amir wasn't quite sure how to respond, except to, well, try and sit still. But after a while, he stood up, stretched his wiry arms, and said with a yawn, "I like being here in the morning. So quiet compared to the afternoon."

"It's fine, I suppose."

On balance, the grounds of the Mosque offered one of Granada's most stunning views. A panoramic sweep of the entire city—foreground bejewelled with the red tiled rooftops and white washed walls of the sloping Albaicin. On the horizon, past the sprawl of the valley, the green peaks of the Sierra rolled upward to meet the sky.

"That's where we belong," Jeddo said, with a sluggish nod in the direction of the Alhambra.

"At least we've got a great view of it," the boy said. "I wonder what they're doing in there."

Jeddo let out a huff. "Desecrating it … some way or other."

He dared not comment, but the boy found Jeddo's dissatisfaction in the matter mildly ironic, given the very worthy replacement they'd selected. In some ways, the grand Mosque actually made more sense. It was, after all, the formal place of worship for Granada's Muslim community. And frankly, it was a nice change of pace.

"Are they so dissatisfied with island life, they can't control the urge to meddle in the rest of the world's business?" The old man was still seated, hands resting on his knees. "It's as if nothing is sacred to them," he'd told Amir.

"They did protect us, Jeddo."

"Yes, well, they may have come here under the banner of salvation, Amir. But don't be fooled. They really came here to get away from England."

"Really?"

"It's true," the old man said. "They saved us from the Red Death. For that, I suppose we should be grateful. But look at what they're doing now. Building a big wall around Granada? Shameful."

"Isn't it to protect us?"

Jeddo gave the boy a harsh look. "Know why they're really here? They want to make us islanders just like them. Difference though, is that they own *our* island. And a bunch of others, too. You know what they've done? They've created an entire archipelago. And while we are captives on this island, they come and go as they please—bouncing around from one to the next, island hopping as it were."

***

Gun on hip, travel bag heavy on shoulder, Amir strode past the grandiose facade of El Palacio de Carlos V with Jeddo's voice echoing in his head. As a group of armoured grunts marched out from the palace doors, Amir debated the best place to pray. But there was really only one suitable location given the circumstances. And who gave a shit if a handful of jarheads saw him kneeling there.

John Ward

Make the old man happy, he told himself.

Amir descended the plaza steps, skirted a wall of landscaped hedges and sauntered to the centre of El Patio de Machuca. Save the soldiers milling past, the Moorish terrace hadn't changed much in thirty years. Hemmed in by tan arches and manicured green. A startling vista of Granada just beyond it. Amir unzipped his pack, removed his compressed sleeping bag, and unfurled it over the sandstone floor. He then unlaced his boots, pulled them free, and set about his prayers with maximum concentration.

It was nearly 9:30 when he finished. And though very late for briefing, Amir felt calmer for having made the time. As he wrapped his things back up, his cell buzzed.

"Yup?"

"Amir," Brit said haughtily, "what are you *doing* down there?"

"I'm on my way up right now."

"Bloody better be. I've had London on the line for the last half hour. As you can imagine, they're pissed."

"London?" Amir asked. "Who—Glass?"

"No. Mason."

"Who the fuck is Mason?"

"He's my boss, Duran. Jesus."

"Oh, yeah—*Mason*. Isn't he a bit senior for this sort of shit?"

"It's a critical op," Brit growled.

Several metres from the palace entrance, Amir nodded to another agent and said, "Tell him I'll be there in three minutes."

"*Fucking Christ.*" Brit ended the call.

Amir hung up, feeling slightly amused. What would they do, fire him? Might be nice to get back to policing.

Crossing the arena-like courtyard of the palace's open-air interior, Amir's eyes traced the circular contours of the second-floor balcony. Fight a bull in here, he mused. Or another man. All you'd need is a sword and shield. Maybe some leather sandals and skirt. Strange how matadors and gladiators both dressed a bit like women. *Thumbs down*, Amir thought with a chuckle.

Rather use a Glock.

When he reached the briefing room, Brit was standing next to a tall uniformed kid with a red beard and an RAF patch sewn to his sleeve. On the coms panel above, a close-up of Mason's face dominated the live feed from London.

"That's Duran, in the background, I presume?"

Brit waved for Amir to join them at the panel and said, "Yes, sir. He's just arrived."

Amir placed his pack on the desk behind him and turned to face the screen. "Morning, sir."

"I don't even want to know why you were so fucking late, so save it," Mason said. "This is Sparrow, he'll be flying you down." Amir suppressed a laugh and shook the airman's hand. The pilot cocked his head back and smirked. "We've no time to waste," Mason said, "so I'll move through this rather quickly, *comprende*?"

"*Comprendo*," Amir said with an exaggerated accent.

Mason went on. "General Tillman knows the plan A to Z, but I want you to hear from me directly, so there'll be no confusion. First things first. You and Sparrow will chopper out to a little airstrip down on the coast, outside an old resort called San Jose in Cabo de Gata."

"I know the area," Amir said. "Used to go on holiday as a kid."

"Well, it's nothing like it used to be," Mason said. "Once there, you'll be taking the quickest, quietest twin prop known to man. Sparrow's a surgeon with it, so you'll be coasting below radar nearly the entire time. After a brief refuel in Chad, it's on to the coast of Tanzania. From there, a local will take you over by boat. Name's Jeff."

Amir gave Mason a sceptical grin. "Jeff?"

"Yes, Jeff. The handler hasn't received the assigned name as of yet, but will. If anybody but Jeff receives you, kill them. Sparrow will be the stand in if necessary."

Amir looked at Sparrow. The airman leered back. "Then what?" Amir asked.

"Just listen," Brit said.

"Then you arrive by boat to Stone Town."

"Stone Town?" Amir said, ignoring Brit's directive.

"Waterfront neighbourhood in Zanzibar City," Mason said. "By the time you've reached the harbour, Jeff will have updated you regarding any developments on the ground."

"Specifically?"

"Specifically, the boy's location. Once docked, you'll immediately move on the target and bring him back to the handler's safe house. Move quickly—no time for mucking about. When you've returned, contact us and we'll provide instructions regarding exfiltration. If all goes to plan, you'll be in and out in twelve hours. No fuss."

Twelve hours ... *no fuss*? Amir studied Mason's oversized head. "Sir, what should I expect to run up against down there?"

"Right," Mason said. "The Reds and Japs'll definitely be in play. But if I were you, I wouldn't complicate this. Get the boy and bring him back. Encounter resistance, employ some of that scrappiness I've heard so much about."

Amir said nothing, though he found Mason's antiquated reference to the Russians bizarre. Not a communist left in that hell hole.

"Well, Agent Duran, that's all I have for you," Mason said. "The basic itinerary is loaded into your GPS, so protect that device with your life. It's a matter of national security, old boy. Plus, you won't be able to get home without it."

Not my nation, thought Amir. *And don't call me old boy, you presumptuous prick.*

Шесть

In the privacy of the Africa House's most opulent chambers, Sattar Ebrahimi flouted parochial mores with great zeal.

"I'm having a touch to drink," Ebrahimi said to his guests. Facing the wet bar, he loosened the tie of his silk robe. "Would either of you like one? I know it's still early and all."

The boy at the foot of the bed looked to his elder for guidance. She was perhaps nineteen or twenty and while her cocoa skin was lineless and radiant, her dark eyes were gaping and hollow as death. After a good ten seconds she shrugged and said, "Sure."

A pleasant smile came to Ebrahimi's lips. "Good then. While I'm fixing them, please disrobe." As the girl unbuttoned her shirt, Ebrahimi abruptly turned from his work at the bar. "No," he said, pointing at the girl, "you take his clothes off first. When you've finished, take your own shirt off. Then get on your knees and suck his cock."

The girl went to it without hesitation. Ebrahimi stirred the martinis and glanced over his shoulder every few seconds for a good look. When he finished mixing, he placed the glasses down on the night stand next to the bed and began to fondle himself.

"So beautiful," he said. "You're both so very beautiful. Young man, would you mind helping me out of my—"

A loud knock sounded from outside. The boy and girl scrambled for cover in the bathroom. Then came another knock and muffled barrage of angry Russian.

"Fucking Kamkin," Ebrahimi grumbled. "Damn you!" He stomped over to the entrance of the suite and whipped the double doors inward with both hands. The rush of air drew his robe wide open, and Ebrahimi's flaccid penis swung wildly for Kamkin to see.

The exposure prompted laughter, followed by a flurry of more swears. Eyes ablaze, Kamkin jammed her index finger into the Persian's chest. "I am not paying you to fuck whores all day, you piece of shit. Now put your fucking clothes on and get going!"

Shouldering past him, she announced the cancellation of the party. "Hello—whores! Come out, out, wherever you be." She'd said the last bit in English. Despite her false linguistic assumptions and syntactical inaccuracies, Kamkin's tone was interpreted as intended. The boy walked out first, his sinewy brown frame on full display, genitals a sizable contrast to Ebrahimi's withered manhood. The girl came next, forearm raised over her breasts.

"You swine," Kamkin said in a boiling roar. "They're children!" Disgust had sharpened the accuracy of her Farsi.

"Oh, fuck you," Ebrahimi said in Russian, and walked toward the nightstand to retrieve his cocktail.

"Pay them and get dressed."

"For what? I didn't even—"

Kamkin dug a pistol from her sport coat and pointed at the door. "I said pay them and get them the fuck out!"

Ebrahimi stormed across the room toward a small painting mounted on the far wall at eye level. In a fluster he tore the artwork free from its metal hanger, tossed it to the carpet. He then spun the lock dial of the exposed safe, popped the door and withdrew a meagre sum.

The young whores collected their fees and fled.

"You really need to get your shit together," Kamkin said. "We're relying on you to deliver. Lotto is down at the port. If you're not there in ten minutes with a damn good sales pitch, I'll intervene. Which will be bad news for him, and for you."

Ebrahimi took a big swig from the martini and drew the back of his hand roughly across his mouth as he swallowed. After a second gulp, he raised his eyes to Kamkin and shook his head.

"*What*?" she said. "What about this situation is so fucking hard for you to understand? We're on a fucking timeline. It's a goddamn wonder the Japanese and British haven't already snatched the boy. It'd surprise me if they weren't already here, in fact."

"Well *are* they here, or aren't they?"

"For your sake, let's hope not."

***

From the open bay of the old Puma, the desert mountains of Cabo de Gata looked much as Amir remembered. Low and brown, rolling south-eastward toward the cerulean plane of the Mediterranean.

The sun-boiled flat of the valley was a different story. Where there'd once been an intricate patchwork of plastic hothouses stretching in all directions, a vast expanse of scrubby overgrowth now sprouted from the desert floor. A few relics remained. Some twisted sections of chain-link. The occasional apex of an aluminium A-frame peeking up from the gnarled bush. Sparing the chop of the Puma's blades, nature's silent re-conquest was all but complete.

A few kilometres south, Amir caught his first glimpse of the seaside San Jose. And praise Allah, it appeared not to have suffered the same fate as the farms. *So fucking surreal*, thought Amir. To see the things just as they were. To know some things never change. Of course, it was all from a distance.

But even at a distance San Jose made Amir's heart flutter. The pink pop of flowering bushes. The bleach-white villas dashing down twin coastal peaks like a pinch of sprinkled salt. The yellow crescent of the beach, flat and sharp against the shimmering blue. It all looked both solid and fluid. Hauntingly real yet other-worldly. Remote yet intimate.

Yeah, it was just as he'd left it. And he was fine with the distance.

Down to the east, the boulders of Monsul rose up from the coast with Martian grandeur. Generations prior, Monsul served as a cinematic backdrop to countless Westerns and adventure epics. O'Toole had dawned the white turban nearby. But Amir's fondness for the place grew from his boyhood affinity for American bad-arses. The cigar chewing Eastwood. The whip-wielding Ford. Each had memorable performances there. And as a kid on holiday, Amir re-enacted the scenes over and over, while his mother sat under an umbrella, reading her magazines.

Amir smiled. When this whole thing was over, he'd dig Jeddo's old movies out of the closet.

Contrary to Mason's briefing, Sparrow took the chopper down right in town. Why, Amir wasn't quite certain. They'd passed a

John Ward

small runway several miles inland. He'd figured they were circling round as a precaution. Perhaps surveying the surrounding landscape for any potential interference. But that clearly wasn't the case. Safely grounded in the village beach, Sparrow leaned his head back toward Amir and motioned for him to get out.

It was the first time Amir had set foot in one of the earth's hundred million ghost towns. All that beautiful distance suddenly vanished.

Crouching to avoid the rotor wash, Amir jogged forward with a hand on his brow and surveyed the deserted architecture. Sparrow came around from the other side, and joined him on a patch of beach roughly thirty metres from the heli.

"What are we doing here?" Amir said, voice strained over the sound of the turbines.

"Getting you tooled up," Sparrow said. The pilot's eyes were drawn toward one building in particular. A former Italian pizzeria, if Amir remembered correctly.

Amir squinted, sand still whirling about. "I don't follow. I've got what I need. My own strap, plus a smaller piece and silencer." Sparrow didn't say anything, just kept looking over toward the building. "Hey," Amir said, placing a hand on Sparrow's shoulder. "What the fuck?"

Sparrow pointed. "There he is."

From the door of the pizzeria, a plain-clothed man trotted toward them, large black duffle bag bouncing at his side.

"Who the fuck is that?"

"That's Father Christmas," the pilot said. "Been a good boy?"

"Mason didn't say anything about this."

"Sensitive ops require discretion in mixed company."

Amir took that to mean Tillman—which worried him.

When the man with the bag arrived, he nodded to Amir, saluted Sparrow, and dropped the big, black canvas duffle at their feet. Then he trotted back in the direction from which he came, without so much as a word.

Amir reached down and lifted the bag by its handles. It was heavy, cumbersome, rigid contents shifting as he hoisted it onto his shoulder. Sparrow set off a few paces in front of him toward the chopper. Amir took one last, long look around at the erst-while resort, then trudged through the sand after Sparrow.

When Amir got into the helicopter, he sat down and immediately unzipped the bag at his feet. "*Puta Mierda.*"

Sparrow flipped some switches on the overhead panel and turned back toward Amir. "Nice little arsenal, eh?"

Amir looked up at Sparrow but remained quiet. As the rotors accelerated he listened to the slap and slash of the blades in the ocean air. Sparrow returned to the controls and put his helmet on. Before taking the throttle, he motioned to Amir. "Put your fucking headset on—won't be able to talk without it."

Amir pulled on the earphones and adjusted the position of the mic. "Sparrow, what is all this?"

"Hold on," the pilot said, "lifting off."

They ascended rapidly, keeling in a broad curve along the coast and back inland. As the Puma's course steadied, Sparrow's voice came in, thin and crunchy over the headphones. "Gear suit you?"

Amir glanced down at the open bag. "You tell me. Seems a bit excessive, no?" Sparrow laughed. Amir grimaced. "No, really, Captain. Fuck do I need an AR for—let alone a grenade launcher? Mason expect me to use this stuff?"

"Relax," Sparrow said. "Better overdone than underprepared, right?"

"Don't bullshit me—fuck am I up against?"

"You'll be fine," the pilot said. "Just precautionary."

Amir watched the coastline vanish as they passed over a cluster of mountains. A minute later, they descended toward the flight strip. As the Puma reared up and began its slow hover downward, Amir spotted the sporty looking prop.

Briefly, he considered demanding Sparrow fly him back to Granada. But that was a foolish proposition. *Be a man about it*, he told himself. *Whatever comes your way, deal with it.*

On the narrow Tarmac, Amir and Sparrow loaded the plane in silence. When all was packed, Amir lit a smoke and wandered a few metres away. With the sun beating down, he pondered Eastwood and the celluloid cowboys of the Almerian waste.

One, slumping in the saddle of a broken-down steed, wandering

John Ward

the barren plain in search of water. One, feverishly digging in the rattler-teeming scrub for buried plunder. One, back to a rock, gut-shot and fading, a bottle of hooch his only consolation. Amir thought about the villain. His orange-brown face wearing a look of exaggerated cruelty. His moustache thick and oily. Then there was the desperado protagonist. So lightning quick with the side-piece. So fast with loose women. In the end, it seemed, the hard-hearted hero always fell for some black-haired beauty in grave distress.

"Time to fly," shouted Sparrow.

Amir threw the butt down, snubbed it out with his boot. Then he wiped the sweat from his brow, put sunglasses on, and swaggered across the runway toward the plane. Reaching for the door, he stopped for a moment, hawked a wad of spit onto the asphalt, and hopped in the plane.

Time to cowboy up.

***

A good, strong lanyard wind rippled the baggy fabric of Ebrahimi's tan trousers. Ruffled linen aside, the breeze rendered little effect. The high-set sun had conspired with a hundred percent humidity to drain the Persian's pores of all they contained.

As he trudged toward the harbour he dabbed the base of his skull with a white handkerchief and mumbled profanities. "Fucking Russian bitch. Ordering me around like hired help." A woman pushing a stroller gave Ebrahimi a suspicious look. Ebrahimi was undaunted. "Ignorant cunt. Thirty years ago, I'd have bought her on the black market like the whore she is."

The schizophrenic tirade ended when Ebrahimi arrived at the docks. Not more than fifty metres away, Abasi Lotto stood perched on the bow of a big, storm-battered trawler. A lanky, dark man in a grease-stained jumpsuit stood beside him, clutching a wrench.

Ebrahimi turned onto the nearest mooring and slipped behind the cover a small fishing boat. He tucked his shirt in properly, then withdrew a pair of reading glasses from his sport coat. Looking both benign and important, Ebrahimi moseyed over to his mark.

"Ahoy," he said. Then in Swahili offered, "Fancy seeing you again!"

Abasi peered over the edge of the deck to catch a glimpse. "Mr Ebrahimi." There was an awkward pause. "How are you?"

"Fine, just fine. Out for a stroll when I saw you up there—thought I'd say hello." Abasi nodded but said nothing. Ebrahimi pressed on. "Having engine issues?"

"Among other things."

"Looks like she's been at it for a while," Ebrahimi said. "How old?"

"Fifty or sixty, if I had to guess. No way of knowing, really. My father bought it years ago from a Greek company."

"Amazing she's still going."

"Yet to be seen," Abasi said. "Right now, it's not looking so good. But yes, overall, she's served me well. Probably served you well too, given how much gas the old rig guzzles."

"And the rest of your fleet, how is it on fuel?"

"Fine, I suppose. Frankly, the other ships are in need of serious work also."

"You know, I could help with that," Ebrahimi said, affecting a more serious expression.

"In what sense?"

"My reach isn't limited to commodities, Lotto. I can access virtually any existing manufacturing market as well."

"Good of you to offer, but I'm in no position to invest in a new boat."

"Completely understand," Ebrahimi said. Then he gave a big smile. "I'm familiar with the industry. Margins vary greatly depending on the season. Overhead is substantial. Trust me, you're not the first man to deal with such burdens. Consider this, though—you don't always need up-front capital for a large purchase like that. There are other ways of doing it."

"Not sure I follow," Abasi said, who now leaned over the rail.

"Well, there's credit, there's collateral … and a million other ways to structure debt."

Abasi's brows tightened. "I'm not putting my business at risk, if that's what you're getting at."

John Ward

"No, no, I wouldn't ask you to do that," Ebrahimi said with a slow shake of his head. "Tell you what, I'm about to have some lunch—join me. We can talk more. These sorts of things are complicated, I know. But an aging fleet can really compromise productivity. It's worth sorting through your options, at least."

Abasi glanced over his shoulder. The mechanic was oblivious, standing above the engine hatch, laughing loudly into his cell phone and smoking a cigarette. After a moment, Abasi took a rag from the railing and wiped his hands. "Okay. Give me a minute, and I'll be down."

***

The café was a typical Stone Town affair—tight and homey—one old waitress both serving and bussing the scatter of plastic tables.

"No booze in here, unfortunately," Ebrahimi said.

"It's okay, I need to get back soon," Abasi said, menu hiding his eyes.

"Do you sell to this place?"

"Not this place, no. Tend to stay away from anywhere without substantial monthly purchase orders."

"Right," Ebrahimi said. "I can relate to that. Not enough profit for the hassle involved."

"Exactly."

"So—back to the fleet—what are your needs, precisely?"

"Well, two of the four ships are on their last leg—one of which you saw today. The other two need work, but they will probably last another ten years if maintained correctly."

"Must worry you," Ebrahimi said, head turning toward the approaching waitress. "Hello," he said to her. "How are you this afternoon?"

"Fine," she said, "what will you have?"

Ebrahimi looked at Abasi, who then said, "How's the grouper?"

"It's grouper," the waitress said.

"Okay," Abasi said. "I'll take it, I guess."

She looked at Ebrahimi blankly, as if she were speaking to the wall behind him. "And you?"

"What's fresh?"

"It's all fresh."

Ebrahimi smiled. "*Is* it though? I'll have the shark. And cooked thoroughly. I don't want any pesky parasites dancing around my belly this afternoon." She nodded and walked away. "Pleasant little lady," Ebrahimi said.

Abasi smiled. "My guess is she's been at this since we were in diapers."

"My guess is you're right. Anyway, it sounds as though you're in desperate need of an upgrade."

"I don't know about *desperate*."

Ebrahimi leaned forward and folded his hands on the table. "Mr Lotto, I want to talk about your nephew."

Abasi flung back from the table as if hit by a bullet. "Excuse me?"

"I know. I apologize for the abrupt and rather surprising shift in direction. But I haven't much time here, so I need to cut to the chase. As you can imagine, there is a great deal of interest in Darweshi's condition. I know some very important people who can help the child."

Abasi's face had gone sallow. "Help? He doesn't need any help."

"Please," Ebrahimi said. "Keep your voice lowered. You don't know it, of course, but your nephew is in grave danger. I can keep him safe."

Abasi started to rise from his seat, balance unsteady. Ebrahimi reached across the table and took hold of his forearm and pulled him back down.

"Let go of me," Abasi said, hissing like a trampled snake.

"You need to listen. Your life depends on it. And the boy's. Now sit and hear me out." Abasi plopped down again, eyes shooting around the café. "I'm here to propose a deal," Ebrahimi said. "The people I represent are hell-bent on taking Darweshi one way or the other. So I want to make sure that you and your family benefit as much as possible from the boy's participation."

"Participation—what the fuck are you talking about?"

"The boy is *immune*," Ebrahimi said, tone raw with agitation. "What'd you *expect* would happen when people found out?

Now listen to me and stop acting like a fucking infant. Here's the deal—I can offer you a large sum of money for the boy's participation. A new fleet even. Frankly, I don't care—it's not my money. Name the price, I'm sure my clients will meet it."

"I don't want your fucking money."

Ebrahimi tilted his head back. The waitress came over, slapped their plates down, and returned to the kitchen. He looked down at his dish, leaned over to smell it, then pushed it aside. "Clearly, you don't fully grasp what I'm telling you. I know it's a lot to think about. So, let me make this simple as possible. Hand the boy over, you get paid. Refuse, I can assure you of some very harsh consequences—for your entire family. I wish it weren't the case, but it is. These people don't play nice."

"Who the hell are you talking about," Abasi said in a whisper, drawing both palms down his cheeks in a sort of exasperated confusion.

"If I could tell you that, I would. Trust me, I appreciate your concern."

"My concern? You don't have a fucking clue about my concerns." Abasi shook his head, eyes wild. "I knew something was off with you—"

"Mr Lotto, believe it or not, I haven't lied to you once. Everything I said is true. Zanzibar has been my home for two decades. I'm a business man. I own many companies—"

"Fuck you and your companies! And fuck your clients." Abasi again shot up from his flimsy chair, this time knocking it backward and to the ground. Several other patrons turned toward the commotion. In a frenzy, Abasi pulled some cash from his pocket, threw it on the table, and rushed off through the open door onto the promenade outside.

Ebrahimi looked round the restaurant at the gawking patrons, took a pack of smokes from his jacket, lit one, and stared at the uneaten food. "Fuck."

SEVEN

Mason stood in the men's room of the Lanesborough's Library Bar straightening his pocket square. Like the bar itself—and the hotel that housed it—the bathroom was a pretentious configuration of polished surfaces. It even came with a clean-shaven Pakistani who attended to each patron's needs, aesthetic or otherwise.

"Big day, sir?"

Mason kept his eyes on the mirror and adjusted the knot of his tie. "*Big day*. Yes, I suppose so. But then again, every day comes with new challenges and opportunities, doesn't it?"

"I heard Arsenal are trying to acquire Vivaldi."

"You don't say."

The kid's mouth bunched up. "You didn't hear that?"

Mason leaned forward over the sink and began smoothing his eyebrows. "Danny—if I worried what other clubs were doing or not doing all the time, I'd drive myself mad."

"Right," Danny said, fixing some towels. "I just thought Chelsea was looking to sign him, too. That's what I read, at least."

"Don't believe everything you read, Danny. Most of it's poppycock." Mason clenched his jaw, spread his lips and examined his teeth. "Best thing about my job, I'm able to maintain a level of clinical distance. All *I* really worry about is the bottom line: are we making money or are we not. Frankly, doesn't even matter if Chelsea wins. Long as seats are filled and merch is moving, I'm a happy man. I'll tell you Danny—ownership stake—you should try it sometime."

A sad smile appeared on Danny's face. "You really don't care if they win?"

Mason turned around from the mirror without washing his hands and took a steamed towel from a small box next to the kid. "Ever get bored, Danny?"

Danny's deep brown eyes darted around the restroom and came back to Mason. With a shrug, he said, "I don't know."

Mason tossed the towel into a chrome barrel and balanced a

hand on the kid's shoulder. "Be honest," he said. Danny shrugged again. Mason smiled. "Don't worry, lad—I'm not in the habit of sharing secrets. Won't go report you to management, if that's what you're worried about." The kid said nothing. "See, here's the thing, my boy—life is short. Don't settle for mediocrity. Long as I've been coming to this place—chatting football with you and the like—it's struck me that you're a good, young man, but highly dissatisfied. You should really consider making a change. Otherwise, you see, one day you'll wake up, old and grey, and ask yourself, 'why did I waste my life serving others?' Me? I made a decision long ago to look out for my own interests. It's a dog-eat-dog world, Danny. To victor go the spoils." Mason slapped the side of the kid's shoulder and smiled again. "Now stop feeling sorry for yourself, get out there, and have some fun."

***

Glass hadn't tailed someone since his days in the Middle East. And this afternoon's surreptitious mission was a thrilling reminder of why he'd loved fieldwork so much in the first place. It made his blood rush. Made him feel more alive.

Of course, it was a bold move, following Mason to the Lanesborough. Downright risky, really. If blown, Glass would have some serious explaining to do. But surveillance, it turned out, was a bit like riding a bike. And Glass hadn't lost his knack for it. Not the basics. He'd maintained balance. He'd minded his pace. Pedalled hard here. Pumped the breaks there. Kept his eyes and ears open. Let his mark do what marks do best: mosey around enjoying a false sense of security.

Tony Mason, the fucking dimwit, was the definition of a perfect mark. Myopic, indiscreet, and so bloody self-consumed. In the men's room, Mason must've been glued to the mirror for a good fifteen minutes, completely ignorant to the goings-on around him. Only thing that had pulled Mason away from his own reflection was an opportunity to patronise that poor Pakistani kid. And that bizarre ruse he'd concocted about owning a stake in Chelsea? What a piss-poor cover. Indulgent, really.

Lucky for Glass, Mason's vanity wasn't confined to the men's room. The fool had taken a table smack dab in the middle of the Library Bar's dining area. Glass could've posted up anywhere, but decided to press his luck given Mason's obliviousness. Now, from a seat immediately parallel to Mason's turned back, Glass had a direct view of the agent's lunch companions and could hear virtually every exchange.

So far, the older man and young woman Mason dined with hadn't much to say. Just simple pleasantries and lunch suggestions. It got interesting, though, after the waiter placed the table's drinks down. Mason leaned forward and abruptly inquired, "I'm confused—why hasn't it been executed?"

After a bit of silence, the older man allowed the young woman to explain. "Thing is, Mr Mason—"

"Call me Tony, dear."

"Right. Tony. Sir, thing is, we'll need paperwork. It's the only guarantee of compliance on your end."

Again, there was a pause in the discussion. Mason then said, "Compliance? Things are in progress. I have two men in the air right now. What more do you need?"

"Yes," the older gentleman said, "but how do we really know that? It would be helpful to offer something in the way of confirmation. We believe a signature fulfils that requirement, at least by way of providing … how do I say this without sounding crude … collateral is what we're looking for."

In a near whisper, Mason said something to the effect of, "Don't fuck me about, Mr Matthews. I'm out on a very thin limb, here. This meeting? Out in the bloody open?"

"We appreciate your position," the young woman said. "We, too, are taking quite a risk."

Come on, dear, tell me what you're risking, thought Glass. A waiter suddenly appeared at Glass's side. Glass, deferring to the rules of tradecraft, ordered a bottle of something or other—chilled—and dismissed the man with a brusque, "Thank you, that'll be all."

The waiter had interrupted at just the wrong time. Glass flashed his eyes at Mason's table to find everyone silently reviewing said documents. Fuck. The hush persisted for another minute or so and Glass did his damnedest to home in solely on the sound of Mason's movements. But with a view of Mason's back it was impossible to discern whether he'd indeed signed the papers.

Things got particularly annoying when a group of blustery business types took a table just behind Glass and proceeded to upstage the Mason affair with raucous talk of a good quarter. Fuck, Glass again thought. You fucking morons.

When Glass's bottle arrived, he thanked the waiter and was pissed to find Mason rising from the table. Fuck all! The other two rose with him and took turns shaking Mason's hand. Well, that's a sign of some accord, no?

After Mason departed, the geezer and girl went about their whitefish and salad. In a moment of hasty analysis, Glass considered his options and decided to stay put. Perhaps his reasoning wasn't bulletproof, but a snap judgement was necessary. Following Mason back to Vauxhall would likely produce nothing, and though Glass's poor attendance at the liaison retreat now bordered on full-blown truancy, he'd have no other way of identifying who Mason's cohorts were. Glass slugged down his mediocre Chablis and ruminated on the scenario. Thanks to the bankers next door, listening had become impossible. Might as well glean what he could from good old line-of-sight snooping.

The woman was quite young it seemed, dressed in a kind of typical junior executive get-up: white blouse, grey slacks, conservative earrings. The man, clearly of Glass's generation—perhaps slightly older—wore the sort of dignified three-piece suit you just didn't see much anymore. His hair was a bit longish and white. His face, thin but droopy, was ruddy from what Glass made for a rather expensive Scotch habit.

Glass's options were limited, and he knew it. Following them would require a significant time commitment. And depending on their mode of transportation, things could get dicey. Approaching them outright was perhaps the riskiest play and threatened to undermine what little op sec he'd maintained on this unapproved mission. So he went with the third, even though it hinged heavily on the working assumption that his marks retained a level of civilian obliviousness, and that the old man hadn't the presence of mind to pay in cash.

After he, by the skin of his teeth, pulled off what he'd intended to do, Glass walked out of The Library Bar, took out his personal cell, and immediately dialled Tillman.

"Henry," Brit said.

"I thought you were going to ring me."

"Apologies—caught up in meetings."

"Fine," Glass said. "Are you in the office?"

"In fact, I am."

"Good," he said. "Do me a favour and log on if you're not already in the network. Need you to run a name for me."

"What is this about?"

"Please just do it, dear.

"Okay, go ahead."

"GLogiX, with an X. All one word—G, L, and X in caps. Tell me about the company."

"Um, hold on."

"And Felix Matthews—what's his role?"

"Give me a minute, Henry."

"Yes, fine," he said, walking and lighting a smoke.

"Well, it's biotech."

"Uh-huh."

"*Providing innovative, research-based pharmaceutical solutions to the world's most pressing public health threats*, is the official line. Seems they're a top 50 corp. Last three quarters of revenue have dipped precipitously, though." Brit paused, reading. "This bit's interesting: their contract with the Government is up for renewal in one month."

"*Really*," Glass said. "And what are they working on for us?"

"I'll give you three guesses."

"Holy Grail?"

"Bingo," she said. "Vaccine for the big E. Synthetic, though."

"Clever buggers. And where are they in the process?"

"Doesn't say."

"And Felix Matthews?"

"Board member. Former COO and before that, head of research."

"Well, well."

"Okay," Brit said. "Your turn. What's it about?"

"Not so fast, Brit. How did the briefing with Duran go?"

She filled him in and then demanded reciprocity. He told her about Mason and the meeting, and she was shocked Glass had gone so damn rogue based on a hunch.

"Yes, but tell me you're not a bit dubious of Duran's extraction op given what you now know," said Glass.

"What *do* I know, other than Mason had a meeting with biotech executive whom we do business with? Come on, Henry, I know you don't like the man, but you're assuming quite a lot. Although, I'm still unclear what the theory is here."

"Listen," he said, "I'm not quite sure what he's playing at—but I'm sorry, I've been in this business a long time, dear, and I've learnt to trust my gut. Need I remind you of the mess I predicted last year?"

"Save your breath, Henry. You've been reminding me for the past twelve months."

"Well, what must it take for people to listen to me around here?"

"I've *been* listening, Henry. Don't paint me as unsympathetic. I tell you just about everything."

"And what have you been leaving out?"

"Oh, spare me," Brit said. "*Really*. You'd be bored to death with the minutia."

"I wouldn't call a naked op in Zanzibar a minor detail, Brit."

"Have I held anything back from you on this?"

"You tell me."

"Christ," Brit said, "are you so paranoid, you think I'm complicit in whatever crazy conspiracy you've worked up in your head? Come on, Henry, I need to go."

"Wait," he said, regretting his puerile insinuation. "I know you're on my side. But something is going on here. Trust me."

"It isn't about sides, Henry. Why do you always make it about that? I need to go."

"Okay, get back to it then. Please be in touch."

They hung up and Glass chucked his half-spent fag to the curb in a fit of frustration. *Isn't about sides*. What a load of shite. It's always about sides in this business. Brit was just too young and green to know it.

ثمان ي

From a thousand metres, it appeared as nothing more than a long, brown line. There was no pavement, no hanger, no ground crew scurrying about. Only the rectangular red speck of an idling gasoline tanker distinguished the flight strip from a natural feature of the barren flats.

Islands, Jeddo had said.

And Amir was starting to get the idea. As he leaned for a better look, he felt vaguely like a stowaway, the scorched desolation of the Sahel stretching out beneath him like an endless yellow ocean. Far as he could see, there were no roads in, no roads out. No fresh water to navigate or drink from. No trees to provide shade. How did anyone survive out here? Let alone transport fuel from one place to the next. The place made Cabo de Gata seem like an oasis.

"Someone's down there?"

"Better be," Sparrow said, tipping the throttle gently forward. "Hold on, this'll be a little rough."

As predicted, the plane thumped down hard, wheels skipping and jumping along the runway's pocked surface. Sparrow applied the brakes and fought for stability as plumes of dust billowed from the landing gear. Amir planted his outstretched arms against the headrest in front of him. Nearly twenty-five years since his last plane ride, and this was one hell of a fucking re-acquaintance with the miracle of modern aviation. Felt like a fucking earthquake.

When the shaking ceased, they performed a tight U-turn, and the tanker truck accelerated toward them in reverse. Sparrow brought the prop to a halt soon thereafter, flipped some switches, removed his headset and seatbelt, and started down the aisle toward the door.

"Stay here," he said to Amir. The pilot then drew his pistol, cocked a round into the chamber and unsealed the hatch. As the steps unfolded outward, blinding light flooded the cabin.

Sparrow tucked the Barretta M9 behind his flight vest and added, "Strictly precautionary."

"Sure you don't want another gun down there?"

"No, remain inside. This should take all of ten minutes."

Sparrow descended the steps, and Amir rose from his seat to stand in the open door. Watching Sparrow round the tail of the aircraft, he realized the tanker had pulled parallel with the other side of the fuselage. Amir crossed the aisle, leaned over the seats, and lifted a window shade to catch a glimpse.

What a bizarre and vivid glimpse it was: two men—or what appeared to be men—shoulder to shoulder at the rear of the truck, patterned robes swelling in the wind, bony black hands gripping Kalashnikovs, faces concealed beneath alienesque gas masks, and crowned with headdresses of speckled feathers.

Sparrow seemed unimpressed. He kept pointing at the tanker behind them, as if the greeting party's wild garb demanded no more attention than last fall's collection. But there was nothing passé about these cynosures of post-apocalyptic fashion, was there? Indeed, they radiated the Darwinian precariousness of the present—vibrant colours on maladaptive display like a pair of endangered birds.

To be thin, thought Amir, *flaunt any look you want.*

The enjoyable novelty was short lived. Things below had grown testy. Sparrow now gestured angrily with both hands. The Africans jutted their rifles toward the plane, ornamented heads bobbing with anger.

And so it begins.

Amir popped the standard rounds from his Glock, replaced them with a cartridge of hollow points and scrambled down the aisle. With the furious Chadian sun beating on his face, Amir cocked a slug into the chamber, disengaged the safety, bounded down the steps two at a time, and hit the strip at a full sprint. When he rounded the plane's nose, he made a beeline toward the rear of the tanker, and dipped even with its wheel base.

Concealed from view at the rear of the truck, Amir called in a projected whisper. "Sparrow—what's the fucking deal?"

The Africans went quiet as Sparrow backpedalled several steps.

"Seems we're having a difference of opinion regarding payment," said Sparrow, extending his right index finger upward and subtly moving it in a tight circle. "I keep telling them the fuel was already taken care of. They need to take it up with their bosses. We're not paying anymore!"

Following Sparrow's cue, Amir reversed course, jogged back to the cab and edged around it, weapon raised. Oddly, his advance went unnoticed. Who'd they think Sparrow was talking to? Lost in translation, apparently.

With the argument resumed, Amir crept toward the Africans, nine extended. Halfway, he halted in his tracks. A small, beige cloud had emerged from the horizon. At first, Amir wasn't sure what to make of it and attempted to refocus on the foreground. But as the dust cloud swelled, the threat became obvious.

Amir's sudden pause prompted Sparrow to flash his head around for a look. The black pick-up was gaining ground, a gang of armed tribesman bouncing in its payload. Without a second's hesitation, Sparrow drew his piece, ducked laterally and clapped off a single round. The taller African's masked head snapped back and his body collapsed in a heap.

As the other fumbled at his AK, Amir shot twice. One hollow tip tore through the man's upper back, shattering his spine with a snap. The other pierced the base of his skull and exploded out through the visor of his mask.

"Go!"

"Where?" Amir said, one questioning palm in the air.

"Take the valve handle," Sparrow said, uncoiling the fuel hose from the side of the tanker and pulling its nozzle toward the belly of the plane.

"Then what?"

"Turn it on," Sparrow said. "The other direction, you fucking idiot! All the way to the right!" There was a mechanical groan when Amir cranked the handle, followed by a loud rush of gurgling chugs. Sparrow flicked his gun toward the turbo prop. "Get in the plane!"

"What about the—"

"Leave it!"

Back inside, Amir sucked wind, watching Sparrow rip the fuel line from the plane and toss the hose to the ground. Gas spewed onto the packed dirt of the runway and pooled beneath the tanker. Within seconds, the pilot was pulling up the stairs and locking the hatch.

"What the fuck was that?" Amir said as Sparrow took his seat in the cockpit.

"Sit down and put your belt on," Sparrow said. Amir repeated the question and was answered with a growl. "I said sit down and strap in. You're going to fucking hurt yourself."

The prop gunned forward to the pop of Kalashnikov rounds gauging its carbon fibre body. As the ground dropped out beneath them, the thud of bullets faded in frequency, and Amir closed his eyes. It'd been a good while since he'd killed a man. And the chaos of the past few minutes had his heart banging so furiously it reminded him of the first time he put bullet in someone's head.

***

They sat in silence for a while, cruising low, but fast.

Sparrow spent a good part of it methodically checking the gauges for signs of damage. Amir stared out the window, watching the desert drift by, psyche searching for refuge in faraway things. Home. Family. Good food. The pup. But with the acrid scent of gunpowder still fresh on his wrist, calm evaded him.

"Well done back there, Duran."

"What?"

Sparrow turned from the controls. "I said, good shooting back there. Whole thing would've gone to shit had it not been for your quick thinking."

"My quick thinking?"

"Damn right. I'd have been dead in the water out there alone."

Dead in the water … every man, an island.

"Yeah," Amir said. "So what the fuck was that? Honestly."

"Tried to rip us off."

"Why?"

"Why *not*? They almost got away with it, too. Never been wild about working with those blokes. Shifty lot."

"Where the do they live?"

Sparrow chuckled and said, "Somewhere out there in the fucking sand."

Amir thought about it. "How often do you fly down here?"

"Been a bit, actually." The pilot went quiet for a minute and then said, "First time round, I almost shit myself, trying to land. Had to take a couple passes at it. Still one of my least favourite places to put a plane down. You'd think the desert would be easy—clear sight lines, no fog. Quite the opposite. Vicious fucking sandstorms around here. Basically swallows everything whole. Every few months or so, they send a team to clear the strip."

"The RAF?"

"Engineer corps too. Quite a process. Have to fly a bulldozer in by harrier. You know, one of those huge Condor 380 jobs. Fucking massive, man … ever been in one?"

"No," Amir said, peering out the window again.

"Something troubling you, Agent Duran?"

"No."

"Could've fooled me."

"What do you want me to say?"

Sparrow let it be. Amir was back to his own thoughts until lingering questions chipped away at his silence. "So what's your deal, Sparrow?"

"What do you mean?"

"I mean what's your story—you do this sort of thing a lot?" For all Amir had learnt in the past twelve months about the complicated world beyond Granada, that which didn't affect local ops remained almost entirely abstract. Until now.

"What," Sparrow said, "insert and exfil? Sure. That's my job."

"How often?"

"Well, I can't give you specifics, obviously … but enough."

"What's enough?"

Sparrow shot a look back at Amir. "What are you getting at?"

"You're handy with a piece."

"*And?*"

The discomfort in Sparrow's tone made Amir feel more in

control. "So, they train you for that sort of thing? Are all the pilots that adept with a firearm?"

"Listen—one needs to handle one's business," Sparrow said, cockney leaping like flame from behind that controlled tenor of institutional grooming. "Don't know what Spain is like, but out here you can't sit around wanking your todger all day—you'd get clipped in a fuckin' heartbeat."

Amir glared at the pilot. "I'm aware."

"Oh? *Are you*? And what sort of training have you had? Aren't you a fucking cop or something?" The pilot forced an insecure, bravado-tinged laugh. "That how you learnt to shoot someone in the back?"

It had become a pissing match for sure. One Amir had arguably invited. But getting a rise out of this kid suddenly felt cheap. And where Amir might have previously driven a fist into someone's eye for a comment like that, he was surprised to instead feel some compassion for the pilot.

"Captain," Amir said, "how old are you?"

"What?"

"How old are you?" Amir repeated in brusque staccato.

"Why?"

"I don't know…just wondering."

"Twenty-seven in August."

Young buck, thought Amir. Then he contemplated the ease at which the pilot put that gunmen on the runway down. Clearly not the kid's first kill. Amir's was at twenty-four. By twenty-seven he'd had … four more? Maybe five. Now what would this last one make? Sixteen? Seventeen? No—more. He never remembered the two Africans out in the parking lot at Munoz Farms. Been so focused on stopping Abdul, they sort of became an afterthought.

How strange that killing can become an afterthought. That a life—two even—can fade into the realm of forgotten things. He'd even been the one to notify their surviving relatives. Amir shook his head, contemplating those two desperate, out-of-work lackeys. They'd fallen under the influence of a madman, simply for a pay check.

And what had those wildly-clad tribesmen on the airstrip

expected of today? Certainly not death. Then again, who's to know how they lived down there in the desert? Maybe they spent every waking hour preparing for a showdown, taking target practice amidst the tumble brush, settling in at night on some rough bed, fucking their women every evening like it was the last time they'd lay their hands on female flesh.

Hope they got some action at last.

"Agent Duran."

"What," Amir said, still lost in thought.

"I've seen more action than you think."

"Yes, I'm sure you have."

"Trust me."

"I do."

"Yeah, well," Sparrow said, voice trailing off, eyes straight ahead.

"Fancy footwork, too," Amir said, breaking the ice.

After a few seconds, the pilot flicked his eyes back. "Attribute it to a short stint in the Aston Villa system."

"You're kidding."

"No, *señor*, I'm not. Didn't last long though. Hamstring— multiple surgeries and everything."

"Christ," Amir said. "Must've been rough."

"Bloody right." Sparrow paused. "To be honest, I wouldn't have made it anyway. You get up to U-19 and the game's a goddamn blur."

"Still—I'm impressed."

"You played?"

"I did," Amir said. "Centre-mid."

"Ah," Sparrow said, face losing all its hardness. "Fucking workhorse like me self! Everyone makes so much of the skill involved in striking. I'm biased of course—but I remind them—ball doesn't move without a talented midfield."

"Agreed. I always found it funny watching the forwards wandering around until play moved past the half line. The fucking luxury, can you imagine?"

Sparrow grinned. "Were you good?"

"First selection, all city. Golden Boot, final two years. Whatever the fuck that means."

"You weren't recruited into development?"

"By who?" Amir said.

"Right … must've been bloody weird." They were quiet for a minute after that. Then Sparrow came back with, "So what pro club did you did you root for?"

"When things were still normal, Granada of course. But, I always loved Real, too. Such high-calibre talent, every fucking season. As a kid, I was even obsessed with the history of the club. Knew all the stats going back, like, fifty years. After the invasion, I adopted Man City. Watched Premier on BBC rebroadcasts."

"A true fanatic."

"Nothing less," Amir said, watching the brown below slowly give way to green and imagining the bounce of perfectly mani- cured turf beneath his spikes. Hadn't been on a nice pitch for two decades. The first wave of immigration nearly destroyed all the city's decent fields. The second did them in completely. He remembered that feeling of utter injustice when Jeddo told him the PAF were corralling the blacks and Arabs in stadiums, sorting them out by country of origin. Not for the poor immigrants, but for his precious football pitch. He was young.

"What about players?" Sparrow asked.

"My favourite?"

"Yeah. I'm partial to McAdams. Massive left foot. Generally not a huge fan of the Irish style, but he was special. Grew up watching him absolutely terrorise keepers—picking the top ninety even from a good fifteen metres beyond the box."

"He was damn good."

"Ever wonder what it must have been like during the heyday? Pre all this Red Death shit we grew up with?"

"I saw it with my own eyes," Amir said. "Until I was thirteen, at least."

"Right."

"Saw La Liga at its best." Amir paused, reconsidering. "Well, not its best. Nothing really compares to the quality of play in the early part of the century. You look at those stats from the first two decades and they're fucking mind-blowing. Messi, Ronaldo, Pique … Neymar, Suarez, James … the list goes on. I mean—I never got to see those guys in person, obviously."

John Ward

"Certainly know your shit, though.

"Football's a religion in Granada. You take the tradition seriously—old timers make sure of it."

"Don't know about all the other ones, but I recognize Messi and Ronaldo."

"You're young," Amir said. "And English."

"Not that young," Sparrow said defensively.

Amir thought about the costumed dead men on the runway and said, "No, not that young."

In the wake of the comment, a cathartic stillness entered the cabin. Only the buzzing whir of the props and a slight whisper of circulating oxygen could be heard. There weren't more than a few hours to go now; a solid tailwind lending a hand to Sparrow's work. The pilot wore a look of concentration. Amir draped a coat over his chest and shoulders and began to drift. Below, the vast, sweltering grasslands reached over the curve of the earth and toward the coast. Somewhere just beyond, the Island of Zanzibar lay in wait.

NUEVE

Amir awoke to the sound of Sparrow's cackle. The pilot had his headset on and was yapping into its mouthpiece. The subject of conversation was difficult to discern, all of it seeming intentionally veiled in idiomatic vagaries. Perhaps he was reviewing their earlier troubles on the flight strip.

"What can you do," the pilot said. "Comes with the territory … oh, just fine. Settling in."

Amir closed his eyes again, feigning sleep. Every few seconds, he cracked a lid for a quick look at his pilot. "Will do, sir. Will do. Shouldn't be too much longer … yes, notify you at once … copy." With that, Sparrow glanced back at Amir, removed the headphones, then stretched his arms.

Sparrow was down to a tee shirt, now—the fatigue-green type PAF marines sweat through during morning laps around Alhambra. Maybe the odour of spilt gasoline on the pilot's nylon flight jacket grew too much to bear.

Whatever the case, Amir could now see the dark surface of Sparrow's exposed right arm. The intricate mural stretched wrist to shoulder; every inch inked in black. Naked women straddled the pilot's bicep. Below them, a weeping Christ wore angel wings. Two broken hearts shed blood—or tears—onto his elbow. A grinning jester unfurled a scroll of androgynous names down his forearm.

Once a footballer, always a footballer, Amir thought.

"I see you back there, clever bugger. Eavesdropping, were we?"

"Yeah," Amir said. "No fucking clue what you were talking about though."

"Just Mason checking in."

Amir looked out through his window at the endless savannah beneath. "Can I ask you something, Sparrow?"

"By all means."

"Why do you think Mason wanted me for this?"

"Shit, I asked him that my bloody self—no offense, obviously."

"None taken." Amir's eyes rose to the cloud cover. "I don't get it."

"I don't either. I mean, I'm sure you're damn good at what you do and everything. Tell that by the way you handled yourself back in Chad. But couldn't they've sent in a spec ops team, plain and simple?"

"Exactly. Though Tillman told me they were looking for the lightest possible touch."

"Come on—SIS black ops? Those blokes are fucking ghosts, man. Real bad boys. They'd be in and out in the blink of an eye."

"So fucking risky like this," Amir said. "I mean, no back up? Sorry—doesn't scan."

"I'm with you. Op like this shouldn't be a one-man show. Deserves more planning, far as I'm concerned."

Sparrow was making sense; echoing all of Amir's own doubts. Maybe the kid wasn't telling him something. Which was a distinct possibility. For all that Wild West shit, Sparrow still struck Amir as something of a smooth operator. Who the fuck knows. The Brits were crafty.

"Sparrow—ever question the basic fucking morality of what we're doing?"

"No. I mean … what? Snatching this kid? No—god no. Are you kidding? A cure? It would be wrong not to do it, for Christ's sake. Need that kid back in London."

"I mean *all* of it."

"Feeling a bit philosophical, are we?"

"I'm serious. The boy's a perfect example. Taking him from his home, his family?"

"I don't know, Duran. Jesus. I'd say it's worth it. Wouldn't you?"

Amir eyed the names etched into the pilot's arm and said: "You have any kids?"

"Proud father of none," Sparrow said. "Nice to come home to a quiet flat and have a few pints to me self. Plus, get to go out and tear it up with me mates when I please."

"Can't argue with that."

"I'd like to keep it that way," Sparrow said. "For a while, at least. You got kids?"

"Yeah."

Sparrow turned. "How many?"

"One boy. Just turned ten."

"Name?"

"James."

"Well that's awfully English of you, Agent Duran. PAF make you do that?"

"Fuck no. Named after the footballer. The Colombian."

Sparrow laughed again. "Told you—much as I love the sport, I'm no historian of it. Does your boy play?"

"Yup."

"Good?"

"Too good."

"Ha! No such thing!"

"In Granada there is."

"Well, not in bloody old England, man."

"Maybe not."

"Definitely not. Blokes fight tooth and nail for a roster spot at any level. The money in football? Unreal. For that reason alone, I wish I'd made it. Be damn fucking rich. Big estate. Top line Aston Martin. Different bird every night. Whole shebang. God, that'd be the balls. No more midnight flights with your lot!" The kid was really amusing himself now, cockney accent back with gusto.

"Believe me," Amir said, "I've thought about it myself a few times."

And there was silence once more. The stubborn kind that sits down and refuses to budge. Like a tired elephant, squatting in the dust.

The dust. It was everywhere. Granada, San Jose, Chad. Amir couldn't get away from it. Maybe Zanzibar would provide some relief.

***

Sweat beads gathered on Kesi's nose and brow as thick drafts of steam rose from the stew beneath her. "At least crack a window," she said, a bit of desperation in her tone.

"No," Abasi said.

"Are you trying to give us heat stroke?"

"Stop being dramatic."

"Dramatic? It's hotter than hell in here. Your father will have a goddamn heart attack!"

"Stop with the crude language already," Abasi said. "Sound like a dock worker … I thought you'd called for the repair man."

"He can't come for another day," she said, walking to the kitchen window, unlatching the lock and boosting it open fully.

"Do not do that," Abasi said. His outburst drew the attention of the kids in the living room.

Kesi leaned toward Abasi and lowered her voice. "What has gotten into you?"

To that, he had no reply. The children's attention returned to their card game. Only Darweshi's big eyes remained raised toward the kitchen.

"Darweshi, son, is everything alright?" Abasi asked. The boy nodded and looked back down at his hand.

"Better question, what is wrong with *you*?" Kesi said.

"Nothing. I'm calling that bum repairman myself. Where's my phone?"

"Wherever you left it," she said, turning back to the stove and stirring the pot. "It's supper time. Leave the man be."

Abasi marched from the kitchen to the living room and plopped down on the couch with a huff.

Babu slowly emerged from his room down the hall and staggered over to his grandchildren. "Who's winning—Darweshi, is it you? Watch it, kids, Darweshi's a real shark at this game." Darweshi smiled. As the old man limped past the kids, cane clacking against the ceramic tiles of the floor, he looked at Abasi and said, "What's wrong with you … bad day at the office?" Then he pulled a handkerchief from his back pocket and dabbed his brow. "Hot as hell in here. Why's the front door shut?"

Abasi shot up, stormed over to the door and flung it open.

"There," he said. "Is everyone satisfied? Enjoy!" Stepping onto the porch, he scanned the yard. The sun dipped low and long shadows leaned out from the trees onto the patchy crab grass. As he shuffled back into house, the neighbour's mutt sounded off in abrupt, piercing intervals.

"Tell you why I hate leaving the windows open," Abasi said. "That fucking dog!"

Kesi flung the wooden spoon into the pot. "Abasi!"

"It's true," he said. "Won't shut up."

"Are you losing your mind?" she whispered, eyes boring into him as he reached for the cabinet below the countertop.

Finding it empty, he said, "What does one have to do to get a drink around here?"

"You're looking for liqueur?" she said, tone strained with concern. Abasi wouldn't grant a response. "I'm talking to you, Abasi. Stop ignoring me."

Abasi rose from the cabinet and stared back at her. He was breathing heavily, trembling a bit. "What did you do with it? I had some here."

"You finished it. I need to speak with you—privately."

There was a knock on the frame of the open front door. A plump brown hand reached inward and waved. "Hello? Mr Lotto?" Before Abasi could answer, Ebrahimi was over the threshold and addressing the family. "Hello! I hope I'm not disturbing you."

Abasi stormed over to the smiling Persian. "What are you doing here? Get out!"

"Abasi," Kesi said, "who is this?"

"My name is Sattar Ebrahimi, ma'am. I'm a friend of your husband's—we had lunch earlier today, actually."

In a flurry, Abasi grabbed a fistful of Ebrahimi's collar and pushed him backward toward the door. "I said get out of my house!"

But as the men tumbled out, Ebrahimi's shoulders were met from behind with the countervailing force of another man's raised and rigid forearm. The force of it drove Ebrahimi back against Abasi and into the home. Abasi stumbled, heels catching on Ebrahimi's ankles and fell to the floor. Abasi's wife cried out as Ebrahimi fought to maintain balance.

Suzuki leapt forward, thrust the blade of his Hissatsu over Ebrahimi's shoulder and ripped it inward across the soft flesh

John Ward

of the Persian's neck. Blood burst outward from the wound and rained down over Abasi. Ebrahimi's corpulent body crumbled at Suzuki's feet. Suzuki calmly wiped the Hissatsu against his pant leg and withdrew a pistol. "Which is Darweshi?"

When Suzuki received no response, he repeated his demand in broken English and flicked the gun toward the living room. Kesi, eyes wild with fear, thrust a finger toward the boy and screamed, "There! He's that one!"

Abasi scrambled to his feet and lunged toward the Japanese assassin. "No! Get away!"

The butt of Sazuki's pistol met Abasi's forehead with a dull thump and he fell back to the floor quicker than he rose. The children shrieked. The old man impotently punched at the intruder as he crossed the living room toward Darweshi. Most of the blows met the assassin's chest and shoulders. By pure chance, one struck Suzuki in the chin. Stride unbroken, he repelled the old man with no more force than one might use to swat away a fly. The old man tumbled to the tiles.

As Abasi squinted, pupils fighting for focus, Suzuki dragged the boy across the floor to the open door and out into the falling darkness. Again, Abasi attempted to gain his feet, daughter pulling at his shirt to help. Propped on one elbow, he turned toward his wife. "What," he said, tears welling, "did you do?"

PART TWO

KUMI

Ten minutes had passed according to the dash clock. But it was a wonky, old, American piece of crap and Kamkin's cell measured twelve and a half. Either way, the portly Persian was overdue by at least five.

Before he'd sauntered off for the Lotto's yard, he'd decried the timeframe as unrealistic. She'd told him tough. Moscow was so far up her ass she'd gotten a stomach ache. He'd smiled and quipped that he enjoyed the imagery of it. Kamkin slapped his fat face and kicked him out of the car.

She hadn't been exaggerating about Moscow, either. Ovechkin, her superior, had texted her every hour on the hour for the past twenty-four demanding an update. With news of Ebrahimi's glacial progress, he'd labelled the businessman a useless slob. Which was ironic, given Kamkin had lobbied so aggressively to do it all herself. But the boys at the Kremlin wouldn't budge. Ebrahimi owed them favours. And besides—this way was quieter.

"Arrogant bastards," Kamkin whispered. "This is what happens when you send a man to do a woman's job." She screwed the silencer onto her pistol and checked the time again. "Fuck it," she said, tossing the gun onto the passenger's seat and jerking the shift into drive.

As Kamkin pulled around the corner, the sudden scream of a siren drew her eyes immediately north toward the front of the Lotto's property.

She slammed the brakes. Two blue jeeps lurched to a halt in front of the house, a uniformed cop hopping out of each. One lit a smoke and casually strode down the Lotto's front walk. The other lingered with a cell pressed to his ear.

After another minute, an ambulance arrived. It was a dinky, turn-of-the-century rig with flashing red lights. Two skinny kids leapt from the cab. They talked to the cop, unpacked a stretcher, and carried it out of Kamkin's view. With the engine cut and the lights off, she waited there, swearing, furiously pumping out texts to Ebrahimi.

No reply.

After five minutes, the med techs—or whatever the third-world equivalent was—marched from the yard, one on each end of the stretcher, wind rippling the white sheet draped over the corpse they lugged.

The bulging midsection of the dead man beneath was unmistakable.

Kamkin beat her palms against the steering wheel. "You can't be fucking serious!"

Next, Abasi Lotto emerged from the yard, flailing his hands and shouting at the police. Within seconds, Kamkin's engine was redlining, loose gravel firing laterally from the truck's reversing tyres. Left hand on the wheel, right pinching the phone to her ear, Kamkin craned over the passenger's seat for a view of the road behind her.

"The boy's gone," she said.

"What do you mean, *gone*?" Ovechkin asked.

"He's been taken!"

"Where is Ebrahimi?"

"He's fucking dead," Kamkin said, cutting the wheel as she hit the intersection and shoving the vehicle into drive. "Get eyes on the grid—scan the small neighbourhood just west of Stone Town for anything moving fast."

When she gave him approximate coordinates for the satellite, Ovechkin asked, "Where exactly are you?"

"Oh, fuck you—you think I'm bullshitting you about this? I'm three blocks east of the Lotto's villa, heading back to the Africa House. Getting my things. I need an immediate lock—a vector—on anything moving and its destination."

"How long has it been?"

"I don't know—fifteen minutes tops."

"They could be anywhere by now. We don't even know who—"

"*Get* me the location," she said.

"Watch your tone!"

"Fuck you!" she said, seething. "This is your fucking fault. All the pussyfooting."

"I said watch your tone! Just get back to the Africa House and tool up." There was a pause. "Think it was the British?"

"I told you, I don't know who it was. If I did, I'd be after them."

"Alright, I'll be back to you shortly."

"Send a team in."

"I'm not sending a team in to clean up your mess," Ovechkin said.

"*My* mess?"

ELEVEN

As a young agent, Glass had experienced extended periods of anxiety. But none so prolonged or acute as the days directly preceding his first encounter with Marissa.

And it wasn't just him. That fall, all of Cairo had quavered with the tension of an overstretched elastic. Parliamentary elections were just around the corner, and the prospect of maintaining a moderate majority had been diminishing by the day. To have called the situation unsustainable would have been an understatement. Looking back on it, it was hard to believe he'd made it out alive.

What a total fuck-show. Unemployment held steady at thirty-six percent. Demonstrations had become frequent and increasingly violent. Black flags hung from the windows of every dilapidated tenement in the city. And Tahrir Square was a daily sea of burning red, white and blue. Old Glory had bared most of the kerosene-fuelled brunt. The Union Jack doubled as reliable kindling.

Per usual, The West hadn't any good plays—stuck between a rock and a hard place, as it were. At best, an electoral victory rested on razor-thin margins, and would inevitably provoke a full-scale uprising. At worst, the Islamic hardliners were set to retake the government in sweeping fashion, drawing the country to the brink of war with Israel. Either way, Egypt lurched ever closer to revolution, the MI6 and CIA-backed military poised to reassert its bloody control.

It was one hell of a bad time to dry out. But Glass had been doing his best. Abstinence was a wholly unappealing concept, but his liquid dinners had inched toward lunch, and were beginning to take a toll. He'd felt the booze clouding him, weakening his concentration, dulling his instincts, and worst of all, sapping his motivation.

Not that he'd been getting anywhere, anyway—sneaking around at night, futilely pleading with 'moderate' elements of the

Neo Brotherhood to consider foregoing party loyalty for more centrist affiliations.

Democracy is about compromise!

Crickets. *Why compromise with the Devil*, one of them once declared over tea and cigarettes. To that, he'd no good answer. Though Glass had been tempted to delineate the variety of satanic responses MI6 reserved for uncooperative arseholes. But why press the point. If the man wanted punishment, let him have it.

Oh, the Middle fucking East.

Only thing that had exceeded the volume of petroleum beneath its sand was the suicidal hubris of its men. Infinite supply, arrogance by the barrel. Of course, it would all end very badly for those avowed to the theocratic cause. Much as it had for their fathers—the brave sons of the Arab Spring.

But hey, martyrdom's a bitch.

Particularly when it involved certain means of forced confession. Amazing, how committed the Egyptian Army were to time-honoured methods. A few finger nails here, a little bit of shabeh there. Nice long stay in a wet hole and then bang! The firing squad to cap it off.

Thinking of it now made Glass's stomach turn. All of that bloodshed and torture. For what? The Red Death had eventually done them all in anyway. Politicians and paupers, the innocents and the implicated, secular or devout. It spared none.

Why his chest ached when he thought of those days was a different story.

Two weeks before the revolution began—the brazen assassination of Imam Hussein al-Hosseini during Friday prayers at the venerable Mosque of Mohamed Ali, marking its official start—Glass had been working hard to turn the allegiance of a particular parliamentarian. A young businessman and Brotherhood partisan named Hamza Salim, if his memory served him. Things weren't going so well with Salim. And one evening after a maddening round of late night horse-trading with the manipulative real estate broker, Glass's commitment to sobriety wavered.

Around 1:30 am, Glass stormed up to the bar counter at the Crescent Moon and demanded a gin and tonic. *Extra lime*, he'd told the bartender. *And don't skimp on the Tanqueray. Had one a month ago, tasted like bloody Sprite.*

A lesser known joint tucked a few blocks back from the embassy, the Moon had only two types of patrons: frustrated journalists chomping at the bit for their next assignment, and young American foreign service officers attempting to avoid the scrutiny of married colleagues over their burgeoning infidelities.

The Moon wasn't a very British place—no football on the tele, no chips, and a bloody piss-poor beer selection. So it was a surprise then, when Glass saw Marissa White—the young and alluring new analyst from his division—saunter up to the service counter and order a scotch, neat, and take out a pack of Turkish smokes from her white and gold Channel clutch.

She'd clearly felt his eyes on her, and being the precocious, budding careerist she was, didn't pass up the opportunity to flirt with a senior agent.

"Fancy a fag, chap?"

Chap, he'd thought—how bold. Plus, fag? How wonderfully antiquated and un-PC.

"Love one. It's Ms White, correct?"

"Why yes, sir," she said, some cheekiness in her tone. "That is correct. Call me Marissa."

"Didn't expect to find anyone from the office in this dump."

The bartender had raised his eyebrows and sighed.

"I quite like the place," Marissa had said. "Very—I don't know—*inconspicuous*." Then she leaned toward him. "Type of establishment you might find spies hanging about."

"Ha! Doubt it," Glass had said with a smile. Then, looking down the bar at a middle-aged man in khaki, he whispered, "More the like the type of place an AP stringer whittles away the hours before the next flight to Aleppo."

Marissa grinned. "The art of killing time."

"It's an art now, is it?"

"A damn fine art, in the right company."

"Cheers to good company," he'd said with a hoist of his gin.

"Good company, indeed." There was a pause in the repartee, a solid meeting of the eyes, and a quick, reflexive look away from one another.

John Ward

"So, what do you think of Cairo, Agent Marissa White—everything you'd hoped for?"

"And *more*," she'd said. "Certainly not a dull moment."

"Dull? No," he said in between puffs. "Could use a bit of healthy monotony frankly."

"Who? You or the city?"

Glass had laughed. "All of the above. Bloody fucking shit show. You'd think they'd tire of all this revolution rubbish."

"Unlikely. Though, I must say—when will these people catch onto the fact that none—literally zero—of these so-called leaders have their best interests at heart? You know what they need? A good woman in charge."

"Now *that* is unlikely."

"You really think so?"

He'd said nothing and let his raised eyebrows do the talking. She'd smiled, in a kind of sad way that surprised Glass, and said, "A girl can always dream."

"Do yourself a favour, Agent White. Measure your expectations round here. It'll work wonders for your sanity should you decide to stay in this business."

"And that's why you've such a rosy outlook, old chap?"

Glass laughed and ordered another round. "So, you come here by yourself often?"

"More often than I'd like to admit," she'd replied. "Can't seem to shake the stress off without a couple stiff ones, I'm afraid."

"Tell me about it," he said, suddenly feeling relieved; the type of consolation one finds in another's vulnerability. That day had been long, and for what it was worth, she'd provided him a touch of unexpected companionship.

Looking around the bar, its low lighting and aging decor had felt almost romantic with her there—by his side—saddled up to the counter, commiserating. He knew the answer to what he'd ask next, but for the sake of sustaining connection said, "Where were you before Cairo?"

"London, actually."

"Really. First whirl at this?"

She'd said, "Sort of. Briefly, I was in Gibraltar and then Casablanca, but went back to Vauxhall for a spell before heading down here."

"Miss it?"

"What, London? No. Not really. Maybe certain comforts—a nice flat and what have you. But it was time for me to spread my wings."

"What's the plan?"

"You mean I have a choice in the matter?" she'd said. "Maybe you know something I don't."

"A talented, young go-getter such as yourself?" He'd been shameless.

"Agent Glass, I'm flattered!"

"Really though—if it were up to you, where would you be in five years?"

"Hmm. Honestly? Not really sure. Back home, all my girl-friends are married—having kids and what have you. For a while, when our betters in London were still sorting out my next job, I considered requesting they keep me local. Thought about settling down and all that. But, you know, the whole hubby and townhouse, two-point-five children and a dog thing never really appealed to me. Guess I'd be happy here for a while. Despite all the chaos, I find Cairo charming. The history, the museums. The Crescent Moon," she said with a laugh.

"The *danger*," Glass said.

"Yes. In theory. But I don't get much of that behind a desk now, do I?"

"White woman in the field doesn't quite much make opera-tional sense now, does it?"

"I suppose not."

"Don't worry," Glass said. "What you're doing is important."

"*Is* it, though?"

And she'd been right. It was obvious where things were headed for Egypt. No amount of keen analysis could change the course of things.

"It is," Glass said anyway.

To that, she'd lit another cigarette and smiled. Such a drop-dead gorgeous smile, too. "I should run. Not exactly getting any safer out there."

John Ward

"Let me walk you back," he'd said, standing from his stool.

"No, please. Don't quit on my account."

"I should really be getting home anyway."

"Well, fine with me then. You know, some of your colleagues would do well to take up after you."

"You've forgotten? Chivalry is dead," he said, helping with her coat. Glass tossed some money down, knocked his knuckles on the bar and waved to the bartender. It had been the first time in ages he'd left a drink unfinished, and since then, probably the last.

That night, they took the long way around, chatting about work, laughing at the absurdity of their lives. They were just two Brits in the Middle East; a couple anonymous colonials failing to bend the arc of history back toward the West. And the Chinese, how fucking crackers are they? Bunch of technologically superior ants, marching round Asia in perfect little columns.

By the time they'd reached her apartment, Glass and Marissa had generated a single, elegantly simple solution for all the world's problems. More alcohol! Everyone would be too pissed to care about all this grandiose geopolitical bollocks.

"Right," she'd said with a giggle, then took her keys out and turned toward him. They lingered for a moment at her door, a dry chill of evening wind wrapping round them. She'd hugged at her torso. He'd zipped his coat collar up higher.

"Where's your—?"

"Oh, just a couple blocks further," he said, in a burst of awkward timing.

"Right. Well, chap, thanks for the drinks. Had a smashing night of it." After hesitating, she'd extended her hand. He took it but didn't shake. Just sort of held on for a while. It was the first time he'd touched her skin. And it was everything he'd imagined—silken and warm, a seductive contrast to the hard world around them. Free of flaws, free of tension.

"Any time," he finally said.

They didn't kiss that evening. That would come a few nights later—at her place—after another round at the Crescent Moon. It had been the beginning of a ritual. One they'd continued even after the uprising.

And it was a profoundly satisfying ritual—dodging wild protests and roving gunmen to claim a piece of the night: a couple of seats at the bar; an hour or two of laughing over hard liquor; ten minutes sidling back through the shadows to her tiny flat.

In Marissa, Glass had found a bit of solace. In her bedroom, a bit of refuge.

The first month of the affair played out to the clattering rhythms of errant gunfire. The second, to the eerie silence of martial law. Late into the night, they'd lay awake after making love with the windows wide open, simply listening. Her hair had stretched out over his chest like an unwound spool of onyx thread. She'd whisper things occasionally. Unforgettable things that made him so much more hopeful than he'd ever been. Things that made him feel different about himself, and life.

And so, his chest now ached as he walked along the leafy edges of The Long Water on his way to meet her. The way he'd left Cairo was so terribly … well … terrible. Such a fucking rush; no solid explanation, another pressing assignment to sort out—the details well above her clearance level.

There'd been promises of course. The kind one makes sincerely, without acknowledging what loomed on the horizon. No talk of barriers, distance—things the heart magically looks past to keep afloat. What is romance, anyway, but a lens through which we find a glimpse of happiness?

Glass had misplaced that lens long ago. Lost it in the shuffle somewhere on the way to Granada.

Then again, maybe he *hadn't* misplaced it. Maybe he'd subconsciously intended to leave it behind … in Cairo, in her flat, in the bedroom, on that rickety old double bed, under a fold of white cotton. When she left—to Ankara, or the Balkans, or wherever came next—had that lens, that perspective, made the journey with her?

Or had she, too, forgotten to pack it, in a blinding haste to answer duty's call? Or perhaps she'd also purposely discarded it. Maybe it was something recyclable—buried in the sheets for someone else to discover, cherish and discard.

Well, suppose I might as well ask her myself, he thought. Once I get a bit of liquid courage in me.

John Ward

***

In the brasserie, Marissa sat at a small table toward the back, aromatic ghosts of Provence wafting from the kitchen, black-clad waiters drifting by at a relaxed, pre-rush pace. She'd ordered a bottle already. The old Bordeaux sat in tandem with a modest floral arrangement at centre. The wine was, by any standard, damn expensive—the dwindling supply appreciating by the day.

When he finally arrived, a good dent had been put in the Bordeaux and her flushed cheeks told the tale of its conspicuous disappearance.

"And here we are again," he said, pulling his chair out from the table.

"Why, yes, here we are. Okay with red?"

"Things haven't changed that much," Glass said, without a smile. "Thanks for meeting me."

She poured his wine and said, "What else is there to do?"

"You know, didn't even consider this ..." Glass paused for a liberal first sip. "But I realise you're technically my boss now. Hope that's not compromising, somehow."

"You *just* realized this?" She shrugged. "Who's to know?"

Glass smiled. "Marissa White, forever the adventurist."

"I've grown far more boring in middle age."

"I *know*—it must be quite dull presiding over MI6."

"I still answer to higher powers, Henry. Daily check-ins with C and the like."

"Yes, that must be excruciatingly tedious," he said with a half-grin.

"I'm not sure tedious is the word. Perhaps a touch stifling."

"Try answering to Tony."

"Is he really such a pain?"

"Immense."

"I put him there, you know."

Glass laughed again, a bit of mischief in it. "I know. It makes me rather question your judgement, Ms White. Placing responsibility in the hands of such a plainly shallow, social-climbing prick?"

"Easy Henry—he's not *that* bad." Now Glass shrugged. Marissa's brow descended. "You act as though the man holds some personal vendetta against you. I've yet to observe any unfairness on his part."

"He doesn't listen, Marissa. Worse, he pays attention to all the wrong things."

"He pays attention to what we tell him to pay attention to. Is he pompous? Sure. A little bit of a dandy? Matter of personal style."

"Well I'm interested what you'll think of this." He took his phone out and handed it to her.

"And what is this supposed to be," she asked, eyes on the illuminated photo.

"It's a receipt."

"So?"

"So, read the billing details."

She leaned over, opened her purse and removed some reading glasses. Peering down at the screen, she said, "Why do you have this?"

"Do you know whose name that is?"

"Yes, Henry, but why do you have a picture of it on your phone?"

"He had lunch with Mason today."

She put the phone on the table and looked directly across at Glass. "And how do you know that?"

"I was there."

"Where?"

"The Library Room—at the Lanesborough. You know the old hotel near—"

"Yes, I know it," she said quickly. "You followed him there? What the fuck are you doing, Henry?"

He refused to be derailed. "I think they were signing some sort of contract, Marissa. I'm almost sure of it. Why is Mason—fucking glorified case officer—meeting with a board member of a government-contracted pharma? You know what GLogiX is working on right?" He stopped to take a huge gulp of Bordeaux.

"I'm aware. Who else was there?"

"Young lady. Probably a corporate colleague—not certain though."

"What were they discussing?" Marissa asked, swiftly refilling her own glass.

"Only caught the beginning of it ... she and this Felix Matthews seemed to be pressuring Mason into signing something. Sounded like a guarantee of compliance. Mason mentioned something about an op being in progress already. He's got to be referring to the Zanzibar thing, no? What other ops is he involved in right now?"

Marissa ran her hands over her face and sat there quietly for a minute, elbows to the table, taking sips from her wine and staring vaguely at the almost empty bottle between them.

"Mind if I?"

"Yes, please," she said, as he reached for the Bordeaux and emptied it. "I'll order another."

She signalled to the waiter. For a good long while, Glass simply looked at her, waiting for more questions. But when none came, he said, "Why is Mason meeting with them, Marissa?"

"Not your business, Henry."

"Maybe not," he said. "But the whole thing—it's not—it doesn't feel right."

"And how *should* it feel," she asked, making eye contact. "Frankly, you shouldn't have any feelings about it. You should be at headquarters, in the conference room, worrying about the business of keeping Granada safe."

"Granada?"

"Yes, Granada. That's your world now, isn't it?"

"We've finished for the day, the liaisons."

"So you've taken it upon yourself to do some extracurricular snooping."

"Snooping? You make it sound like I'm a mother looking through her teenager's diary."

"Why are you doing this then?"

"I told you why I'm here. Mason cuts me out of the equation, goes straight to Tillman. Assigns a local copper to an international black op. Sorry if that rubs me the wrong way, Marissa, but I don't appreciate being left in the dark—particularly on such a wildly risky, high-priority mission. We have operational structures and protocols for a reason. Thought you'd be the first to acknowledge that, given your position."

For several seconds, she remained quiet. Then, looking away to her left, said: "I can't talk about this anymore, Henry."

"You don't even know what's going on here, *do* you?"

"I said I can't discuss it any further."

"Well that's convenient."

"Convenient?" She gave him a disgusted look. "Like up and leaving twenty years ago without as much as a phone call since?" Glass drew back in his seat, stunned. "I'm sorry," she said immediately. "Completely uncalled for."

"No," Glass said, leaning back in. "No, it's okay."

"It's not okay. I didn't come here to hash out the past. Really, it's not alright. Completely un—"

"No, listen. It's fine. You're not wrong to have said it." Glass gulped in a deep breath and looked away. "To be honest ..." Again, he stopped. "You're on my mind every time I come to London. I suppose this situation with Mason finally gave me a good reason to see you. I'm sorry. It's not your fault. It's mine. I'm the one who asked you here."

The waiter came over and uncorked a new bottle, pouring a bit for Marissa to taste.

"It's fine," she said to the waiter, "just leave it."

Glass quickly reached for the wine and filled Marissa's cup.

"I didn't ... there wasn't a day I didn't think of you when I left," he said. "Not a day."

"Not even an email, Henry."

"I couldn't bring myself to. What would I have said? The writing was on the wall. I figured nothing at all was better than some sort of protracted, painful correspondence. I'm not good with that sort of thing, Marissa."

"Well it would've made a difference to me. I'm sorry, I need to go," she suddenly said, raising her arm up for the check.

"No, please," Glass said, reaching for her extended hand. "Please—stay. Please."

As she put her hand down, Glass waved off the approaching waiter. "I'm sorry for making this ... I'm just sorry," Glass said, with a great tension in his voice. "I loved you. More than you knew."

She said nothing, raising a hand to mask the flooding surface of her eyes. "And I loved you," she finally responded. "I would've understood, you know. Not as if I didn't realize where things were headed. I just could've used a bit of … closure."

"You know, I couldn't even bring myself to read your letters."

"What? I figured you just never received them."

"I did," Glass said. "Just never opened them."

"Why?"

"I couldn't … I just couldn't bear it."

"So you threw them away?"

"No," he said, the confessional now in full swing. "I still have them. The whole stack. Wrapped in a rubber band, sitting in a desk drawer in my flat in Granada."

"Jesus, Henry. Why?"

"I don't know." He looked down at his wine, took the glass by the stem, twirled it a bit, and watched the crimson liquid swirl up against the sides. "I've no idea."

"Such is life, I suppose."

He remained silent, not thinking as much as feeling—a strange, potent mix of sorrow, and well, strangely, gratitude suddenly pouring over him. Somehow, this proximity to her felt ripe with opportunity. Not so much for redemption. More for the catharsis that had evaded him for twenty some-odd years. Even the sadness felt soothing, his regret at least being shared, mutually acknowledged.

"I never really stopped, Marissa."

"Stopped what?"

"Loving—"

"Please," she said, a harshness leaping up. "*Don't.*"

"You want me to lie?"

"I don't know what I want. I've been just fine, here, getting on without you."

"And you should be proud of what you've done."

"Don't condescend me."

"I'm not. Look at me! thirty-five plus years at this—still stuck in some Banana Republic."

"London was never for you."

"Well, I never really had a chance to find that out, did I?"

"Yes, you did, Henry. Every time you came up for promotion, you found some way to stay in the field. I've seen your file."

"I don't know if that's fair."

"Well, it's true."

He'd no response but, "More wine?"

"Yes, thank you."

Filling it, he said, "I will say, you still look damn beautiful."

"Ha!" Marissa said, tears and a smile springing up simultaneously. "Henry," she said, wiping at her mascara with the corner of her napkin. "You really know how to show a girl a good time."

"What can I say, *once a charmer*."

"You *were* quite dashing in your day."

He laughed. "My day has passed now, has it?"

"I think we're both a bit long in the tooth for this sort of adolescent foolishness, old chap."

The smile faded from his face, eyes now wearing something of reflective look. "Can't a couple old spies enjoy a quiet bottle of wine?"

"Or two."

"Or three!"

"Don't get crazy now, Henry. We wouldn't want you too pissed to make it out of bed tomorrow."

"Blah. They'll be just fine without me."

"Well then, chap, next bottle on you. Must warn you though, Bordeaux's a bit pricy these days."

"What else am I going to spend my humble salary on?"

She smiled, with some tears again. "Precisely."

TWELVE

Through a charcoal-grey plume, C peered across the room and shook his head.

"What were you thinking? Really, Tony, I'd love to know." But as Mason inched forward on the leather seat, readying a response, the old man pre-empted him. "On second thought, I actually don't give a rat's ass. It's a moot point—damage done."

Mason withdrew, eyes lowered toward his own chest. Slipping a thumb between his buttons, he tugged gently to straighten the pressed surface of his shirt. After a stretch of silence, he finally ventured a modified response. "Hadn't much in the way of options, sir. They threatened to discontinue their involvement."

C took another draw from his pipe and exhaled slowly. "Aren't we beyond excuses at this point? Truly, I'm now wondering if appointing you for this was a mistake. Maybe it requires someone with a bit more—I don't know—discretion."

Mason winced and clenched his jaw as if C had dragged the tip of a dagger across his ribs. "Sir, please," he said. "By no means have you chosen unwisely here."

"So far, there's no indication of that."

"By tomorrow, everything will have worked out quite perfectly."

"Really?" C said. "And if someone should go poking around?"

"Well, with all due respect, sir, who—"

"There's a paper trail now, you bloody fool." Strangely, the old man's tone lacked the hardness of his words. It was as if he were a stand-in at rehearsal, dispassionately reciting someone else's lines.

"I'm sorry, sir. You're right, sir."

"Save it," C said.

Then the old man lit a wooden match, lifted it to the pipe's chamber, and rhythmically stoked little clouds from the tobacco flake. In between rapid puffs, C's tongue flicked out at the corners of his tight little mouth, lapping up the crust of white spittle gathered in the creases.

Watching him, Tony Mason looked much like a child who'd

discovered a colony of invertebrates clinging to the damp under-surface of an overturned stone—eyes pinched, lip curling with primal revulsion.

"Just be sure the operation goes off smoothly," C said.

"I'm feeling …" Mason averted his eyes and took a breath. "Very confident."

"Spare me, Agent Mason. Empires aren't built on feelings, they don't survive on opinions. Reserve that crap for the politicians. I'm looking for results."

"Right," Mason said, face flushing. It was as if he had a flu now, swallowing heavily in between words, sweat bubbling on his brow. "I will be sure … I'll be sure to, um … "

"What? Get on with it."

"No, sorry … results, yes."

"And no more winging it when things get complicated. Run into a snag, inform me immediately. Hell of a lot resting on this one."

"Things are going to plan, according to Sparrow. A bit of trouble in Chad, but nothing they couldn't handle."

C raised his eyebrows. "What sort of trouble?"

"Just a bit of wrangling over price."

"I thought you took care of them in advance."

"There seemed to be some confusion."

"And what came of it?"

Mason squirmed a little and said, "They were able to refuel and make it out just fine."

"You're a shit liar for someone who fashions himself a spy."

"Sir, there's nothing untruthful in what I—"

"I'm interested in what you didn't say, Agent Mason."

"Force was used."

"And?"

"They were set up. They did what they needed to, flew out in a hurry."

"Damage?"

"Yes."

"How extensive?"

"You mean how many men did they kill?"

"No, I mean did anyone have their bloody feelings hurt," C said snidely. "You imbecile, yes! How many of them were killed?"

"Two tribesman," Mason said sharply. "A few others were headed their way but didn't reach the flight strip in time. Though I might add … these tribesman, they were not my contacts. I didn't cultivate that connection. Those were the operators you gave me to work with."

"Ah, yes—*quite*," C said, thin lips wearing a decadent smile. "But now they're your problem, aren't they? Are you aware of how long it took us to build a reliable fuel connection within miles of a viable airstrip in that region? Are you?" For a moment, he paused as if he might actually allow Mason a response, but then quickly added, "Oh, I'm sorry, why would you? You're a bloody case officer … I almost forgot."

"I'm an ops manager, actually. I oversee the entire European—"

"A decade … that's ten years, Agent Mason. Ten."

"I can count."

"Oh, *good*! Is that on your resume? I'll tell you what," C said, an evenness restored to his tone, "there better not be any more cock-ups. Where are they now?"

"Sparrow and Duran?"

"Yes."

"Arriving in Tanzania shortly. Everything arranged as you wanted."

"Fine. Let me know when this Duran character's on his next leg." After a few seconds of silence, C looked up from his desk and said, "That's it. See yourself out."

Mason rose slowly from his chair and walked toward the door.

"Oh, and Mason," C said, just before Mason opened it, "that bit about the airstrip in Chad—I do mean that's your problem to fix. Quickly, too. There won't be time for other arrangements on the return flight."

Mason nodded, staggered into the hallway, and began coughing uncontrollably.

***

"What do we do now?" Amir asked.

Jeddo ceased wailing but remained quiet—prostrate—brow kissing the cold stones. It was just after dawn—an impossibly-radiant dawn—and the old man's lily-white thwab had bloomed into a bundle of rose-pink. As the breeze lapped at the robe's pristine folds, the boy received his first real, significant dose of existential despair.

How, wondered Amir. How is it that the sun can shine so bright on a day like this? Why does the wind blow so soft, when everything inside me feels like a storm? Was it some sort of joke?

Where is Allah?

Jeddo always said God was most evident in the beauty of nature. But Amir just couldn't see it. In fact, he saw quite the opposite—all of it hollow and devoid of meaning, maybe even worse. The blush sky, the fading half-moon, the dew sparkling on the spruce trees at the edge of the terrace. Why? Why was it there? To remind him of things that weren't? To torture him?

When Jeddo finally rose, Amir was sitting on the Mosque steps, crushing pebbles into the rock beneath his sandals. Without a word, Jeddo placed a hand on Amir's shoulder and motioned for them to leave.

"Where are we going?" the boy asked.

Jeddo looked around, eyes bloodshot. "I don't know."

"I'm hungry."

"Let's find you some food, then," Jeddo said, voice nearly a whisper.

Amir stood. "I want to go home."

"No. Let's go somewhere else."

"But I don't want to eat at a restaurant."

"Well, I don't know what to tell you. We've no food at the apartment." And no mother or daughter to cook it was the obvious meaning behind the old man's words. She'd been gone for months, and it was on this morning they'd finally, formally, surrendered to the fact she'd never return.

They'd had a funeral there in the screaming silence of sunrise. But there'd been no body to bury, no offerings for the earth. It was the worst type of funeral. Nothing to address but pain. Nothing to part with but hope.

John Ward

"I want to go home," Amir repeated, tears falling.

The long walk down from the Albaicin was excruciatingly slow and filled with countless shuddering pauses. A passerby had mistaken Jeddo for a limping cripple, crushed and convulsing under gravity's cruel reign.

"Can I help?" the man had asked, leaning toward the Jeddo.

"No," Amir said, taking Jeddo by the arm, protectively.

At the bottom, the boy and his grandfather had no more sense of destination than when they'd departed the grounds of the Grand Mesquita. So they just walked. Walked all day not stopping once for food, winding through the serpentine alleys, down the broad thoroughfares, into the shaded parks, across the sunburnt plazas, along the footpaths abutting the river. Walked. Sometimes shoulder to shoulder, occasionally Amir pacing slightly ahead. Walked until the boy's calves burnt and head ached from dehydration, walked until the chafing created blisters, and the blisters gave way to raw and broken skin. Walked until the sun descended—until the street lamps came alive, hanging like disembodied, glowing souls urging Amir and Jeddo on to the next street—to the next row of closing shops—past the facade of the next lonely chapel, and then finally, home.

At home, Amir got his wish, and the two ate something cold and simple. Something small and forgettable—though the taste of that day's silence lingered on his tongue for decades … .

Sparrow's radio crackled from the cockpit. Amir rubbed his eyes as the pilot chuckled and mentioned something about the coast. Amir's thoughts returned to Granada. The present, though. James … Cristina … he wished to hear their voices. The boys, still little, raspy and hopeful. Hers, a velvet, soft, and sultry delight.

What if he were never to hear them again?

Oh, here's that pussy shit again. Control yourself, Amir. Don't get sucked into that anxious, compulsive spinning. Ain't a damn thing to do about it anyway.

His mind suddenly leapt to the two Africans they'd shot dead on the runway. And instead of feeling remorse, his heart stirred with a strange excitement. Who gets to do this sort of shit anyway? Who but you and Harrison Ford?

You call him Doctor Jones, lady!

Amir briefly wondered if a whip could, in actuality, be an effective weapon. Snap! And now your gun's on the ground, bad man. Snap! And now your knife, too. The Nazi with a look of fear and amazement. Don't do it, asshole, don't charge me—I'll break your fucking jaw. Or maybe I'll just pump a little lead into your chest with this colt revolver, for efficiency's sake. That's right, you fascist fuck—run.

Amir leaned into the aisle, unzipped the huge poly-coated duffle and began sorting through the weapons. Still couldn't get over the grenade launcher. He'd tried one out during police training. Loaded with dummy grenade, of course. Though, he had to admit—the accuracy of the weapon was nothing to sneeze at.

Amir shuffled the bazooka aside and wrapped his palm round the short grip of an amazingly well cared for UZI-UPP9. He'd never shot one of these bad boys. Always wanted to, though. Could never get his hands on one. Talked to a PAF special operator about it once. Fast—impressively stable, the guy had said. Bloody fucking overpowering in tight quarters. We should all have them.

"Knew you'd like that piece," Sparrow said, glancing back at Amir.

"Ever used one?"

"Never leave home without it."

"Where do you guys get them?"

"I requested mine—ordered direct from the armaments section. PAF, though? Fuck if I know. Heard a few rumours that we—well, the RAF—recovered an entire cache from a factory in the Sanai. Shipped them out to the territories."

"The place was intact?"

"Yeah," Sparrow said.

Amir suddenly tossed the gun down.

Sparrow laughed. "Don't worry, man—that one's from the UK. I think the whole story's a bunch of rubbish anyway. Heard it from an old-timer I don't quite trust. Not sure the old bloke had all his marbles. Too many tours. That's funny, though, you thought I armed you with a fucking radioactive machine gun. Ha! That'd be something."

Amir looked out the window. It was night now, though he wasn't sure how late. "Where are we?"

"It'll be soon. Coast is about 50 miles east … you've been out for a while."

"How do you expect this to go down?"

Sparrow returned his gaze to the controls. "You worried?"

"After the last exchange? Yeah—for good reason. Hadn't planned on killing anyone."

"Well you better prepare yourself for the island, mate."

"Hence the fucking arsenal," Amir said.

"Hence the arsenal."

"And yet, Mason made it sound so simple."

"Everything sounds simple in the safety briefing room," the pilot said with a flex of bravado.

"What do you make of that guy?"

"Mason? He's fine. Too bloody institutional for my tastes, but he's looked out for me."

"Looked out for you?"

"Yeah, I mean, puts me on the fun stuff."

This fucking kid, thought Amir, *all balls*. "So what should we expect down there on the coast?"

"I've been given the same info you have. Supposed to be clean. But shit—keep your eyes open, mate."

"Right," Amir said. Then to himself, "eyes *are* open."

"What?"

"Nothing."

"Talking to yourself again?"

"What do you mean," Amir said, brow furrowed.

"Whole last leg, you been rattling on about god knows what in your sleep. Jeddo or something?"

"Oh … sorry."

"What's Jeddo?"

"Jeddo was my grandfather."

"Dreaming about your granddad?" Sparrow couldn't contain a laugh. "Sorry, man, that's fucking hilarious."

If you only knew, thought Amir.

THIRTEEN

For the second time in eight hours, Mason abandoned the climate-controlled terrarium of Vauxhall Cross for the leather fishbowl of the Lanesborough. His blazer still reeked of pipe smoke from his earlier encounter with C and for some reason, his cough still lingered.

As he sunk into a black leather booth seat, he loosened his tie and glanced down at his gilded wristwatch. Five minutes later his martini arrived, and he asked the waitress—a rather busty little Black girl with a pony tail—for the dinner menu and took out his phone.

"Sparrow," he said, taking a sip.

"Everything alright, boss?"

"Yes, quite fine. On the return trip, though—is that strip in Benin still functional?"

"Should be, used it a couple months back."

"Good. Ring them. I'm adjusting your flight plan. When Duran's back on board tomorrow morning, you'll fly him to Spain via Benin and the RAF base in the Canaries. Got it?"

"Copy. Why though, sir, if I might ask?"

"Well, I don't know—maybe that little trigger finger of yours has something to do with it? I mean, be my guest to give Chad a run. My sense is you might find yourself running into a little resistance."

"Copy that, sir. Hope we didn't cock things up too badly for you there, sir."

"Don't worry about me. Worry about finishing the job."

"Copy, sir. Loud and clear, sir."

Mason launched into a coughing fit and slugged down a gulp of vodka.

"Sir?"

"I'm fine," Mason said. And after another wretched burst: "Call me when you've put Duran on the water."

"Copy."

And that was that.

He put the martini down fast.

When the waitress arrived, he made a show of his culinary sophistication, rhetorically inquiring about the provenance of the Lanesborough's parsley, perfect wine pairings and what not. She was nice but didn't give much of a shit.

Waiting for his rabbit, he drained down his second martini, this one, with a touch of vermouth.

***

"Buckle up," Sparrow said. "We're coming in hot."

Amir drew the nylon strap across his lap and dug his fingers into the cushion of the seat like a kid bracing for a dentist's drill. The plane touched down smoother than expected, Sparrow showing real skill as the aircraft drew level with the plane of the runway. But just as Amir's grip loosened, the jarring deceleration sprung him forward in his seat, brakes screaming loud enough to be heard from within the cabin.

When they lurched to a stop, Sparrow tore his headset off, tossed it to side and said with great exuberance, "And that's how you tell naval radar to fuck off!"

"The Russians?" Amir asked, immediately unbuckling.

Sparrow hopped from the cockpit and marched with speed toward the rear of the cabin. "Theirs, ours, everyone's. The Japs, too, for all I know. Ain't a goddamn soul locked onto this bird. Grab your shit."

"Ours?" Amir asked, zipping up the weapons and checking his own nine.

"Oh, yeah—bloody important to keep it dark on our side, too. Don't want something like this circulating among naval command staff. Too fucking risky."

Amir holstered his pistol and eyed the pilot. "Doesn't everyone have drones out here?"

"Not supposed to—not according to the treaty." Sparrow turned back toward Amir with two hazmat masks in hand. "Take this."

Amir caught the mask, studied it for a moment, and watched Sparrow put his own on. "Hate these fucking things," Amir said.

"Hate it or not, you'll need it for the ride out to the coast." Sparrow lifted a small aerosol can from his bag and threw it to Amir. "Oh—and give yourself a good once-over with this shit. Don't want the mosquitos having a feast. Good way to get sick."

After applying a healthy dose of repellent, Amir slipped the mask over his head and grabbed the duffle. Sparrow opened the hatch and pressed a finger to the small button at his temple. "Switch your night vision on. Dark as all hell out here."

On the Tarmac, it was cooler than Amir had expected. The foreign feel of the ocean air another reminder of how far from home he really was. In the moonlight, he could see the airstrip was entirely hemmed in by thin, high trees, no coast in view. But it was clearly close given the unmistakable quality of the breezy, moist wind sweeping across the tarmac.

Following Sparrow toward the trees, Amir was tempted to lift his mask off and spark a smoke. The Red Death. Really? God, it'd been hours since he'd had a nicotine fix. Just wait until you're on the boat, you addict.

As Sparrow faded into the shadows at the edge of the strip, Amir engaged the night vision, and bam! The deserted, silent environs came alive. The world through the infrared lens was nothing normal; everything glowing a spectral green. It was as if the goggles captured more than just light frequencies invisible to the naked eye. As if they'd magically penetrated some sort of astral membrane—objects' truer, stranger nature on full display.

"How do you concentrate with this thing on?"

"You'll get used to it," the pilot said. "Takes a second for the eyes to adjust."

"Jesus," Amir said, watching the pilot drag a large tarp from the top of a truck, folding it up as he went. "That's our ride?"

"That it is," Sparrow said. "Hope it's properly lubed. These old Land Rovers tend to get cranky when the engine hasn't been turned over for a while."

"Couldn't be as bad as the shit box I used to drive."

"You had one?"

"I wish," Amir said. "Had a fucking Mitsubishi, department vehicle. Must've been forty years old."

"The Japs make shit that lasts, I'll give 'em that. Hop in," Sparrow said, opening the driver's side door. "Let's fire the old girl up." In one twist of the ignition, the truck roared to life like a slumbering she-beast shaken awake by her hungry cubs.

"She lives," Sparrow said raising his arms in triumph, and then returning them to the wheel.

"Where's the road out?"

"What road?"

"You're fucking kidding me."

"I *am* kidding you—it's just beyond that patch of vegetation there." Sparrow pointed to a grove of trees across the runway about fifty metres to the north. "See that little clearing there?"

Calling it a clearing was generous, rover stumbling and bouncing over the low scrub as they entered. Once through, the earth flattened onto narrow road buttressed by jungle on both sides.

"I'm telling you, Duran, keep that thing on," the pilot said as Amir removed the pack of cigarettes from his pocket. "Not worth the risk. Things'll fucking kill you, anyway, man. Surprised an athlete such as yourself ever picked up such a deadly habit."

Amir slapped the pack against his palms a few times, slipped it back into his pocket and said, "Death becomes me."

"What?" Sparrow said with a chuckle.

"Spend enough time around corpses, you tend to find way to take the edge off."

"Keep forgetting you were a copper."

"Yeah," Amir said. "Me too."

"Miss it?"

"Not really … sort of, I guess … sometimes."

"Like right now?"

Yeah, like right now, thought Amir, feeling the isolation creep in around them. "So you've never met Jeff?"

"Never even heard of the bloke."

"Somebody's had to have worked with him before."

"I'd assume," Sparrow said. "Don't really leave this sort of thing to chance. Then again, I don't pretend to know how these things work. I'm in transport. That's as far as my logistical expertise goes."

Yet you move like a fucking mercenary, thought Amir. He took his pack of smokes out again and continued to pack them against his quad. "How much further?"

"About a click."

"Do me a favour."

"What's that?"

"Let me do the talking this time."

"Afraid I'm going to shoot someone?" Sparrow said.

Yes, Amir *was*, but said: "No, I want to establish my own report, right from the jump. Given I'll be spending the next twelve hours with this prick, it makes sense."

"Already painted him an arsehole, have we?"

"Whatever he is, I want to be in control as much as possible."

"Not sure it matters, but whatever suits you." Soon, the road tapered and curved, and at the sharpest part of the bend, Sparrow slowed the truck to a stop. "Here we go," he said, cutting the engine. "Through these trees."

Amir hopped out and hoisted the duffle onto his left shoulder. With his right hand, he unholstered his Glock, flicked the safety off, and took a look around. *Fuck*, he thought. *Type of place you find a dead body.*

The woods were dense as hell and Amir hadn't much of a view but Sparrow before him, weaving through the tangled underbrush. A little less than a hundred metres in, though, the jungle thinned and shortened into a scatter of palms. Then suddenly, the moon appeared—low and big through the palm leaves— a pulsing half-orb in the periphery of his infrared vision. The breathy rhythm of the tide grew louder with each step forward. And before long, Amir's boots were sinking into fine sand.

The beach itself was narrow—no more than fifteen metres between the ocean and the tree line. Sparrow had gone to its very edge, waving for Duran to join him. A few steps from the water, Amir dropped the duffle to the sand and turned around in

a full circle, adjusting his grip on the nine, surveying the immediate surroundings. Even through the otherworldly filter of his
infrared visor, he sensed the immaculate, pristine nature of the
place. Shame he couldn't take the foolish fucking thing off and
have a real look.

"See that?" Sparrow said in half-shout, pointing out at the
horizon.

Amir walked forward to the edge of the wet sand and said,
"That's him?"

"Bloody better be."

For the next few minutes, neither Amir nor Sparrow said a word.
In the silence, Amir listened to the waves roll gently in and out and
watched the glimmering light in the distance draw nearer.

As the buzz of the boat's motor grew louder, Sparrow said,
"That's definitely him."

"How can you be sure?"

"See the starboard side?"

"You're talking to a guy that hasn't seen a boat for two decades."

"Right, sorry. You see those dim lights flickering on and off—
look like Christmas bulbs?"

"Yeah, sure."

"That's how we know it's him."

"Jesus," Amir said.

"What's wrong?"

"Been so long since I've been on the water…it's fucking surreal."

Sparrow ignored the comment and faced Amir. "Okay, here we
go, chap. I'll get the bag."

"No, I've got it," Amir said, spell broken, jogging over to the
duffle as the fishing boat eased its pace and drifted silently toward
the shoreline. When Amir returned with the bag, the boat had
coasted to a near stop ten metres parallel to the beach. Behind
the wheel, a slender figure raised a hand and motioned for them
to approach.

"What," Amir said. "Does he want me to get in the water?"

"Only way to do it, my friend. Shouldn't be too deep. Just try
and keep the bag out of it. Grenade launcher doesn't do well with
moisture." With that, Sparrow put his hand on Amir's shoulder

and said, "Good look." Then he looked out toward the boat operator. "Go ahead, give us your bona fidés!"

In high, heavily accented, almost ethereal-sounding English,
the operator called back: "Jeff—two-four-three-nine. Now hurry
on." Sparrow looked at Amir and nodded.

"Cover me," Amir said.

And in he went—mask on, bag of guns above his head—feeling
the ocean's warm weight rise up around his legs, then his waist.
It was a sensation that had long abandoned him. And now it had
returned in such a rush, with such richness, such fullness, that he
had to restrain himself from tossing the weapons aside and diving
under completely.

***

The boy huddled at the far edge of the bed, staring into the dark
corner, eyes glassy as brown marbles.

"You should eat," Suzuki said, pushing a plate of cold rice across
the tightly tucked sheets. It wasn't clear Darweshi spoke French.
But it was the best Suzuki could do. The meal wasn't much either.
But it was all he had to offer. "We may need to leave soon. After
that, it could be a long time before you get food."

Darweshi stayed silent, shock-glazed eyes solemnly mining the
shadows. There was nothing to find but dust. After a few seconds,
Suzuki turned away from the boy, walked through the open door
into the hallway, and tapped his index finger to the surface of his
tracking device. After thirty seconds, its screen remained devoid
of further instructions.

Suzuki grimaced and dipped his head back into the room.
"You should eat," he repeated. Nothing. Not a peep. "Are you
listening?" he said more sternly. The boy slipped a finger beneath
the edge of the plate and flung it upward violently, rice spilling
in clumps over the floor. "Pick it up," Suzuki instructed. "That is
all we have."

Darweshi folded his arms and said, "I'm not hungry," in Swahili.

Suzuki looked up at the ceiling, withdrew the Hissatsu, and
pointed it at the floor. "I said pick it up."

"No!"

"Pick it up!"

"I'm not hungry," Darweshi said, again in his native tongue.

In a rush, Suzuki took the boy by the back of his shirt, dragged him from the bed, and hurled him toward the ground. "Eat it!"

On his hands and knees, Darweshi scrambled to the corner and cowered, forehead pressed to the wall. Suzuki lurched forward, knife angled for a deadly thrust. The boy shrieked and Suzuki's entire body seized up, blade hovering above Darweshi's head.

A hundred times, the killer had driven the Hissatsu into the neck of a recoiling target. A hundred times, the sharp steel had met its mark with nearly automatic precision. But the high, almost delicate pitch of the Darweshi's cry—so different than the shrill scream or awkward bellow of an adult—had paralysed Suzuki in his tracks.

The assassin stumbled backward, lungs heaving. The boy sobbed loudly, his hands chaotically swiping at the corner as if he were some nocturnal creature burrowing to evade an owl. Suzuki sheathed the knife and sat heavily on the bed.

"Stop," he whispered. "I'm not going to hurt you." The boy writhed a little longer, then grew tired and slumped into a foetal position on the hardwood floor. Suzuki closed his eyes. "I'm sorry for scaring you. I won't hurt you, I promise."

Darweshi wouldn't reply.

"Do you drink tea?" Suzuki asked, in the kind of absent, unconsciously benign tone one talks to oneself with. "Let me find some tea."

Suzuki rose from the bed, drifted out of the room and padded down the pitch-black corridor toward the kitchenette near the stairwell. By the light of his homing device, he peeked into the cabinets, opening and closing their thin wooden doors, pinched eyes scanning the deep interior shelves. But the device's blue glow barely pierced the inner darkness and Suzuki swore beneath his breath. Shaking his head, Suzuki lowered his wrist and went for the light switch beside the doorframe.

Under the cool white of the ceiling fixture, he stooped and swung open the lower cabinets beneath the small counter. After several seconds of rummaging he finally found his prize: a small tin, mildly dented, floral-patterned coating peeling at its edges. Still in a squat, he removed the cover and held it to his nose. Suzuki inhaled deeply, and the slightest grin came to his lips.

Upright again, he moved to the rangetop, took the kettle by its handle and filled it in the sink basin. Returning the kettle to the burner, he rotated the stove knob and watched the blue flames jump against the pot's cast iron sides. For nearly ten minutes, Suzuki stood in silence watching the fire do its hasty work.

When the kettle piped up, Suzuki killed the flame, found two cups, and sprinkled a pinch of tea in each mug. Then he poured the boiling water and returned to the boy.

"I've made tea," Suzuki said in French. "I will leave it on the window sill for you." Darweshi was where Suzuki had left him— curled in a ball—head resting on the floor. Darweshi wasn't crying any longer, though his eyes were glassier than before. Instead of putting the cup on the sill, Suzuki knelt down and positioned it on the floor next to the boy, and nodded. "That's for you."

Suzuki then found his own place on the floor, a few feet from Darweshi. Back to the wall, elbows resting on his knees, Suzuki held the mug up with both hands. As the steam rose beneath Suzuki's chin, he studied the boy and made a simple suggestion in Japanese. "You'll need to toughen up."

The boy said nothing but reached for the tea.

John Ward

KUMI NA NNE

The shore receded behind them, black sky and black sea melding into one.

The chop was mild, and the boat bounced only slightly as it carved a path toward the island. But to Amir, it was all remarkable, even with the mask on. The foam spray, the crystalline film coating his forearms and wrists, the cooling headwind wrapping at his soaked shirt. The way the moon hung low like a shimmering coin in the distance. The occasional squawk of passing gull, an invisible reminder that the world was filled with other living things, too.

It was like a dream.

"You can take that off now."

"What?"

"Your mask," the driver said, "it's safe to remove."

Mask pulled free, the scent of the ocean immediately filled Amir's nostrils. "I can smoke?" he asked, digging into his pocket.

The driver turned back to him. "Knock yourself out."

"You're leaving yours on?" he said, raising his voice against the wind and cupping his hands to shelter the flame. Having trouble, he twisted to face the stern. Cigarette lit, he turned back, and was startled to find a woman at the wheel, long hair released from the confines of the mask and blowing wildly in the breeze.

After the shock wore off, it started to make sense, Jeff's high voice and oddly narrow shoulders. Amir had figured it an African thing—the baggy clothes, the guarded affect. Clearly not the case.

Eyes on Jeff, he suddenly felt a bit safer, then quickly reminded himself that danger wasn't necessarily a gendered phenomenon. Most of the time, but not always. Over the years, he'd arrested his fair share of nasty girls. Hookers, thieves. An occasional dealer with a bad man's trigger finger. Amir took a deep draw from the butt and studied her figure. "So, you're *Jeff*."

"And you're Amir Duran," she said, head turned, face in moonlit profile.

Good looking, thought Amir. *I should get out in the field more often.* "So you know my name. What's yours?"

"Just stick with Jeff."

"And what's that?"

"What's *what*?"

"What's—" The boat lurched upward for a split second, then thumped back down as it cleared a cresting wave. Amir lunged toward the closest handhold he could find, and for a moment, his face was uncomfortably close to her thighs.

She smiled. "Finding your sea legs?"

"It's been awhile. I was going to say, what type of name is that—*Jeff*. Indian, Pakistani?"

"Whatever suits you."

Tricky, he thought. "How long have you worked for us?"

She leaned back to watch him re-establish his balance. "Longer than you."

So fluent. "What's the plan?"

"Once ashore, you head straight to them."

"The boy."

"And some company."

"*Company*."

"You've been briefed."

"Right—his family?"

With one hand on the wheel, she pivoted round toward him almost fully. "Family?"

"His family. He's with his family."

"Why would he be with his family?" she asked, brow furrowing.

"Well, who the fuck is he with?"

"He's with the Japanese operative. Mason didn't go over this with you?"

Amir was too confused to be worried yet. "Japanese operative … working for us? Mason didn't mention another player."

She shook her head and faced back toward the bow. "He doesn't work for you. He works for them."

"Who?"

"The *Japanese*—what did you think that big bag was for?"

"What the fuck are you talking about?"

"What did you think the guns were for?" she replied, nodding at the duffle.

Amir paused, thinking about it. "I'm going in *hot*?" Receiving no response, he said, "This wasn't part of the fucking strategy—use of force was a contingency ... not a fucking certainty!"

"Calm down."

"You're telling me Mason knew about this?" he said, the buzz of the boat's twin outboards an angry chorus to his protestations.

"Mason's the one who worked it out. Clearly, you've been kept in the dark. Sometimes it works like this—op sec reasons."

"You've got to be kidding me," Amir said, voice trailing off. He feverishly worked to rekindle his dying smoke, eyes darting around the boat as if there might be a better explanation hiding somewhere on the deck beneath the mess of ropes and old life-jackets.

"Don't worry, you'll have the upper hand. It's all arranged."

"Sure," Amir said, suppressing the urge to tackle her, throw her overboard, head back to the mainland.

"They're at a safe house—you've a floor plan."

"And what, I just shoot my way in? This isn't a plan. It's a fucking disaster in the making."

"He'll be armed, but you'll have the element of surprise."

"He's a pro? What if the boy gets hit?"

"You'll know his precise location. Move in quickly, put him down, take the boy, return to the rendezvous point. Fairly simple."

"*Simple*—than why aren't you doing it?"

"Not my thing."

"Fucking Christ ... *not your thing*."

"No, it's not." Amir shook his head as she continued. "When we make landfall, I'll take you straight there. My suggestion is you choose your hardware now. Leave the bag with me. Also, you should have another mask in there—high-end night vision unit, guidance system built right into the visor. It'll map it all out for you. Just follow the prompts."

Amir glanced at the duffle. He hadn't seen it when he was rifling through the guns earlier, distracted by the grenade launcher. "A mask, again?"

"Trust me, it'll make things easier."

"You've used one?"

"Keep it on when you've collected the boy. It'll take you right back to me. Then we'll call Mason, establish exfiltration details."

Amir gazed off into the darkness of the starboard side. "You seem confident this'll work out."

"Not my first go round."

Feeling the abundance of irony, he wanted to say, *no, but it's mine*. Seemed like everyone involved on the logistics side of this op—Sparrow, and now *Jeff*—were just kids. Too young for regrets. Too fast to feel the dog of mortality nipping at their heels. But it was there though—a few strides behind—waiting for them to trip.

Waiting to pounce.

"How long have you been at this," Amir asked, trying to reel himself back from dangerous assumptions. Everyone had a story.

"Long enough."

"How did you meet them?"

"MI6?"

"Yeah."

"It was quite some time ago," she said.

"Can't be that long."

"I'm older than you think."

Ancient, thought Amir. After a moment, he asked, "How did you work out where they'd be?"

"I assume you're talking about the boy and his captor? It was arranged, I said."

"Wouldn't it have been easier to snag the boy *before*?"

"We didn't have time."

Bullshit, thought Amir—*the Japanese think she's theirs*. He ran a hand through his hair and said, "You know where they are because you put them there."

"Work that out on your own, did you?"

"Doesn't take a genius."

Amir couldn't tell if the boat were picking up speed or whether the open water was simply rougher. Either way, it was getting rocky, harder to brace himself. For a few minutes, they remained quiet, the rumble of combusting gasoline and the slap of the sea against the boat's hull rattling at the edges of Amir's consciousness.

Then Jeff broke the spell in a half-yell. "Don't worry, MI6 pays me enough."

What Amir said next, he knew he'd immediately regret—so he said it as calmly as possible: "I will put a bullet in your fucking head, if I have to. You should know that."

"This is your first op, isn't it?"

"Trust me," he said, "I've done my fair my fair share of killing."

"Wouldn't be here if you hadn't. Still—I can tell it's your first time out." She looked back at him, moonlight sparkling in her eyes. "I know what it's like," she said. "Don't worry. You'll get used to it, dealing with people like me."

"Double agents?"

"Independent contractors."

"That's what you call yourself?"

"That's what I'm called." She hesitated, then, "Down here, things aren't the same. We don't have walls and armies, someone to tuck us in at night."

"What do you know about that?"

"More than you think. I wasn't born … I'm here because I have to—"

"I doubt it," he said, cutting her off midsentence.

Her eyes returned to the water. "Doesn't matter. I won't fuck you. That's all you need to know."

"We'll see," Amir said, lighting another cigarette.

"Trying to kill yourself?"

"I didn't have one the entire way down."

"Making up for lost time, then."

For the rest of the ride, she drove with two hands on the boat's jumpy wheel, vision trained on the horizon. Amir chain-smoked, and sorted through the gear. He tested trigger sensitivities, checked cartridge capacities, devoted some time to the new goggles as well. He had questions for her still—tactical questions—but somehow couldn't bring himself to engage. It seemed unwise to him, going over the details, giving her more authority.

If it went to shit, he needed room to move. Unpredictable angles to strike from.

Thanks, Brit. Appreciate the opportunity, Mason. Not every day a guy gets to risk his life while vying for the fate of mankind.

***

When Moscow called, Kamkin was leaning out the open window, tugging short puffs from a dwindling cigarette. She'd spent the past hour checking her weapons and eventually settled on the PP-90M1. It was a versatile gun—light, powerful, with ungodly muzzle velocity—and especially good in tight quarters. She'd also strapped on her P-96, a handy back-up in close quarter combat.

"Tell me you've found them," she snarled at the laptop screen. It blinked back at her with total indifference. And that's how communication with the Kremlin via computer often went. They could see her, but she couldn't see them. It some ways it wasn't so different than being separated by mirrored interrogation room glass; a disembodied, tinny voice coming in over the intercom.

"We think," was their response.

"What the fuck does that mean?"

"We couldn't isolate a signal and none of the vehicles we tracked panned out."

"So what *did* you find?" She paced around the room, flicking ash on the hardwood floor, voice a near shout. "This better not turn into a wild fucking goose chase."

"Listen, you'll have to live with it. It's a matter of probability at this point. Had to start with some assumptions, then began combing through—"

"I don't give a fuck how you did it—just give me the location."

"Zeroed in on a small hotel. Think it could be the place."

"*Where*, I said."

"Interestingly, not far from you. Half a click from your current location. Sending the coordinates."

"Fine."

"We don't have much on the layout of the place. Couple lights left on—that's how we found it actually."

"I'll figure it out. Just send the longs and lats."

"Kamkin."

"What?"

"It's likely the Japs."

"So?"

"So you might meet serious resistance. Exercise extreme caution."

"How many are there?"

"Just one, we think."

"So, what's the problem?"

"It's Suzuki, Kamkin."

Her left leg buckled slightly, as if something had bumped the back of the knee. "*Suzuki*. How do you know it's him?"

"It stands to reason, given who we now believe is leading it back in Japan."

Kamkin tossed her cigarette to the floor and shook her head. "You assholes better give me a raise after this."

The Kremlin had nothing further. Kamkin switched the feed off and waited for the coordinates to arrive. When they pinged in, she was standing over the machine gun lying on the bedspread and adjusting her holster. Eyeing the screen of her phone, she walked to the window and slammed it shut.

"Don't fuck this one up," she whispered. "It'll be your neck."

FIFTEEN

Unclothed, she was twice as beautiful. Not far from how he'd left her, really. Skin still milky, no looser to the touch. Breasts remarkably buoyant. Waist and thighs a gentle continuity of curves. Incredible what foregoing the miracle of childbirth can accomplish for a woman.

Glass wondered what she thought of him now. He hoped he hadn't disappointed her. It had been so goddamn long.

Even with all the booze, they'd both been a bit shy at first. Incongruously so; years of experience contributing little in the way of immodesty. She had unbuttoned her blouse, standing across the room as if it were a doctor's appointment. Glass had slid into bed, boxers still on. And when they met each other's bodies, it was with a great carefulness—a caution—even though there seemed to be an inevitability to it. As if making love were a foregone conclusion; an accord struck through that first kiss back at the brasserie.

When they finally fell into the rhythm—all of that deferred chemistry flooding back—there was something both cathartic and slightly unsettling about it. Like undressing an itchy wound, and gently scratching at it—doing one's best to avoid drawing blood. Now, they were lying shoulder to shoulder, the past no longer far away. The lock had been popped off that old file cabinet the human heart, and its dusty folders were getting a second look.

"Nights like this," Glass said quietly, almost gingerly, "they certainly provoke a bit of existential examination."

She smiled. "Oh, Henry, that's *so* romantic."

He shifted his head on the pillow, and ran a hand through his floppy, sweat-dampened hair. "It's funny. For some reason—if I'm being honest, and who knows, maybe I was just in denial this whole time—I never really believed Cairo would be it for us."

"Clearly, it wasn't."

"Why did it take so long?"

"You're asking *me* that?"

"No," he said. "I know it was *my* fault. But tonight kind of makes me ... I don't know ... consider the idea of fate more seriously."

Marissa rolled onto her side to face him. "Like this was *destined*."

"Sounds bloody juvenile, I'm aware. But you and I ... I don't know ... this never felt finished. Whatever *this* is. Whatever we were ... or are, I guess."

"Chap, what we now *are* is in violation of the code barring intimate relations between colleagues of disparate rank."

"Right," he said with a grin.

"You just slept with your boss, you dog, you."

"*Old* dog is more like it."

"Not so new tricks."

"Yes—same tricks."

"Wonder what it would've been like had you not left Cairo so abruptly," Marissa said. Her palms were pressed together, between her pillow and cheek, as if she were sleeping. "Think we'd have lasted?"

It was a question Glass had asked himself a thousand times, a thousand different answers futilely competing for certainty. "I don't know," he said, "what do you think?"

"I think I'm still thirsty," she said, pulling down the comforter suddenly, and rising from the bed. "Back in a jiffy." Stark naked, she scampered off through the doorway, and returned a minute later with two short glasses and bottle.

"Single malt?"

"Suits the occasion, I'd say."

"Marissa White, you *are* a classy bird."

"With unhealthy appetites."

"Just the way I like my women," Glass said. She poured his drink as he sat up. "Now that we're onto the brown stuff, mind if I light a smoke?"

"I'll grant you permission under one condition."

"And what might that be?"

"You share," she said.

And there they were again—leaning against the headboard, splitting a fag, the sound of a cab horn sounding from the street below. Just like the embassy days. And given the vibe, the intimacy, the tangle of work and life and sex—just as it was back then—it seemed only natural for Glass to say, "So—what *do* you make of this Mason business? I'd really love to know."

"Honestly," she said. "It's disconcerting."

"He shouldn't be meeting with them."

"No, he shouldn't."

"What do you think he's up to?"

"Frankly—and pains me to say this—I've no clue."

"I can't believe Tony fucking Mason would have the bullocks to go rogue," Glass said. "So wildly out of character. The man's a pussy—and not too *bright* either."

"There's bound be an explanation."

"There's an explanation alright," Glass said. "But any way you cut it, you've been purposely circumvented. And so have I."

"It's killing you, isn't it?"

"And I have no problem admitting it, Marissa. What they're running down in Zanzibar right now is no small thing. Station liaison retreat or not, I need to be involved in an op like this. We should have all hands on deck. Experienced hands." Glass gestured enthusiastically, drink in one hand, unlit smoke in the other, drops of scotch falling onto the sheets collected at his crotch. "I find it just bonkers such an important operation is being handled like this."

"It was meant to be discreet," she said reaching for the cigarette. "Give me that." She opened the drawer of the night stand next to her and removed a lighter. Sparking it, she inhaled deeply, then exhaled her reply. "I'll discuss it with C in the morning."

"If I were you, I'd call the bugger right now."

Marissa frowned. "Excuse me, Henry, but I know how to do my job."

"I'm not suggesting you don't, but this is going down as we speak. You should request a status check."

"Oh, I get it," she said, only half-sarcastically, "employing sexual tradecraft to extract intelligence from me."

"If only I were so suave," he said with a laugh. "I'm bloody serious, though. This could all being going to shit. At least call Mason."

"You've got to be kidding me."

He took the cigarette from her. "I'm not."

"And I'm not calling Tony *or* C."

"Fine. Then we should look into why he was with the corporate people."

"It probably had nothing to do with the Zanzibar op."

"*Coincidental*," Glass said. "I seriously doubt that." Marissa got up again, walked across the room to the small desk under the window, sat down, and flipped open a laptop. It was an odd sight: Marissa in the nude, pecking at the keyboard, crossing her leg as she typed. Almost erotic. Henry took a long pull of smoke and peered over at the desk. "What are you doing?"

"Against my better judgement, I'm following your advice."

"Checking on the op?"

"No. GLogiX."

"What are you looking for?"

"You know what I'm looking for," she said.

"You think they're paying him."

"No, *you* think they're paying him."

"Where there's smoke."

"One hundred quid, I prove they're not."

"Come on, Marissa, they wouldn't keep something like that on the books, you know that."

"You said he was signing something."

"I said I *thought* they were signing something. And if they were, you can bloody bet it won't be recorded on whatever company ledger you've got access to."

Marissa looked over to Glass and smiled. "I always start in the obvious places—find people are dumber than they let on."

"I'd have to agree."

For a while they were silent, Glass relishing the liberty of a second smoke while Marissa poked around. "Funny," she said after a good five minutes.

"What's funny," Glass said, "is *you* at the computer like a naked little school girl. You *minx*, what did you find?"

"It's what I can't find that troubles me."

Glass perked up. "Yes?"

"Folder containing status reports on the last phase of research. Won't grant me access. Supposed to be open to me."

"What do you take it as?"

"A contract violation, for starters."

"Hiding something, obviously."

"But what—and *why*," she said. "Don't see how that helps their cause. The contract is basically up. Too late to hide the fact they're not getting anywhere." As soon as it came out of her mouth, Marissa cringed.

Glass tilted his head, a bit of intrigue at hand. "Fascinating," he said. "They're up for contract and they haven't produced—not a good place to be."

"That's business."

"How many others bid for this work?"

"Oh, I don't know. Four, five. Frankly, I don't handle any of that. Not really in my purview. This whole thing was a joint project. I have access because of very obvious security implications. We're engaged in fairly stringent monitoring."

"Yet, you've been locked out," he said. "Who else is involved?"

"Usual cast of crusaders."

"Porton Down?"

"Yes, they've got the MOD end of it. On the civilian side it's National Health Service. Centre for Infectious Diseases is the contracting agency."

"Let me guess—they plan on going another direction when the GLogiX contract is up."

"Depends on what the last phase of research has produced."

Glass stared into his drink. "Must make them nervous, the boy."

"GLogiX?" She turned toward him, breasts subtly swinging with the motion of her torso. "And why would that be, Henry?" Her tone said it all: *enough with the conspiracy speculation—this isn't a spy novel*. "Could offer the very breakthrough they need."

He smiled. "That's the plan? To share the boy with them?"

"That hasn't been—" She paused midsentence, brow suddenly pinching. "Oh, what am I doing? This is *insane*, divulging information like this. I'll have you know, I didn't get where I am by allowing men to ply me with liquor and talk me into revealing state secrets."

"You provided the booze."

"That I did," she said, picking up her glass and studying it in the lamplight. "Damn good, too." She finished a sip. "I imagine you're aware that if you were to repeat any of this—to anyone—we'd both be royally fucked."

"Have I ever?"

"You tell me. It's been twenty-five years. And back then, it was *you* doing the divulging. I was a lowly analyst."

"And I regret none of it," Glass said with an ironic grin. "You provided invaluable counsel in uncertain times."

"Ah, so you were using me back then, too!" She got up from the chair and walked over to him, striding confidently. As she moved, Glass's face grew bright, eyes tracing her hips and breasts. She took the empty glass from his hand and placed it on the night stand. Then she leaned into him, drawing his face to her chest, his arms immediately extending to cradle her back." Make love to me again, Henry. This time, like you're not afraid."

"Shouldn't I be," he whispered, kissing her nipples.

***

Before landfall, Amir sunk into a deep, meditative cycle of prayer. The type that renders the mind nearly blank, only the rhythmic mantras of subjugation coursing through it. It was an odd place to pray—footing unsteady, air smelling of salt. But the wind and the bob of the boat only propelled his concentration.

And while the stranger driving twisted round several times to study her praying passenger, she let him be until the harbour lights demanded their undivided attention. "We're five minutes out," she said quietly.

Amir's eyes remained shut for another thirty seconds. Then, just as she was about to rouse him more forcefully from his fugue, he rose. "That's the city?"

"That's it," she confirmed.

Amir nodded and lit a smoke. With the cigarette dangling from his lips, he leaned down and slung the duffle over his shoulder.

"As I said, you'll want to figure out your choice of equipment ahead of time."

"I know what I'm going to use," Amir said.

"Okay. Just want to avoid wasting time once we're on land."

He'd yet to make eye contact with her, concentrating on the shore. "You worry about getting me there. I'll worry about the rest."

"Will do," she said, no sarcasm in it.

The boat soon tacked southward, skirting the harbour's edge, maintaining a safe distance from the reach of its lights. Amir watched the contours of the waterfront keenly, taking in the squat sprawl of Stone Town, noticing the familiar vernacular of colonial architecture peppering the shoreline. He wondered if the whole world was like this—the stamp of European influence fading from its skin. Prominent enough to recognize, diminished enough to feel haunted. Whole sections of Granada felt that way—stuck in between. Conjuring old glory, suggesting new doom.

"Take this," she said and tossed a wound rope to him.

Amir caught the rope with his left hand and eyed it for several seconds, unfamiliar with its intended function. But when they pulled parallel to a small mooring, the purpose became clear. The boat, you fucking idiot—it needs to be tied. As they the edged closer, Amir reached for a dock post and began looping the rope round it.

"Not there … there," she said, pointing at a small cleat on the surface of the landing. "Wrap it in a figure eight and tie it off."

"I'll be more useful on land."

With a smile she said, "For your sake, I hope so." She cut the engine, hopped out, walked down to the stern and secured the rear with another rope. Then she motioned to Amir with outstretched arms. "Here."

"I've got it," he said, cocking his shoulders back to reposition the duffle. In one efficient thrust, Amir hopped up onto the dock, powerful frame making the gun bag appear an easy load. "Now what?"

"Now let's move," she said. "Steady and fast."

"Are we being watched?"

"This is an island. There's always someone watching."

"Try living in a walled city," he said, following her in stride.

"No more talking."

Jesus, thought Amir. *Halfway around the world and you're still taking orders from pushy women.*

The path into town wasn't particularly complicated. Straight up a narrow, quiet road running perpendicular to the waterfront. Then a sharp right, and a quick left onto a dark, equally noiseless side street. After another several hundred metres, Jeff paused at the edge of the road, took Amir by the forearm, and guided him under the shadow of an overhanging tree. She nodded, and he followed her off the street and into the darkness of the foliage. Soon, they were shuffling through underbrush and short bushes beneath a broad canopy of higher growth.

"Stop there," he heard her whisper.

And she meant it literally. His next step brought his torso flush against hers, their faces no more than a centimetre apart. It was virtually pitch black, but he could see her brown eyes staring back with alarm. She placed a palm firmly to his chest, as if to say, you're fine … just be careful. Then she pointed downward and lowered to a squat above the brush.

When he knelt, she held her hands to her eye sockets—forefingers to thumbs—imitating the shape of glasses like a child. He unzipped the bag and removed the mask, studying it in his hands.

"Once on," she whispered, "it should engage automatically—everything preloaded."

Pouting like a toddler, Amir slipped it over his head and gave a half-hearted thumbs-up to indicate it was operational. Again, she lifted both hands, this time extending her thumbs upward, forefingers outward. Through the infrared filter, the look of her wielding pantomime pistols was almost amusing. Like an iridescent little ghost playing cowboys and Indians in the woods.

"The guns," she hissed in response to his distraction.

Amir waved dismissively at the duffle and pointed to the nine on his thigh. Then he reached down, un-holstered it, raised it to within an inch of his visor, and cocked the slide back. With another thumbs-up, he charged forward, too quickly for her to interfere.

Fuck that heavy shit, he told himself.

It took him no more than thirty seconds to navigate the last layer of vegetation and arrive at a clearing. For a good minute he crouched on one knee at the edge of the trees, surveying the property, gripping the gun with both hands. The hotel grounds were dead quiet, and the pair of illuminated windows on the building's third floor showed no movement within.

The mask's guidance system measured the rear entrance a mere fifteen metres away, so Amir risked momentary exposure and darted in a beeline to the door. The mask—in its technological omnipotence—indicated the entrance was unlocked. A metre to its left, Amir stood with his back to the wall, and gingerly twisted the door knob in both directions, probing for resistance. Finding none, he ducked low and pushed the door inward, moving slowly into the interior of the hotel.

Vamos, Duran. One more tally for the fucking match card of life.

Weapon raised, he climbed the carpeted incline of the stairwell, hugging the angles of the outer wall. As he passed the first landing, a surge of adrenaline quickened his pace. Halfway up the second flight, though, the gravity of the situation gave him a strange an untimely pause. And then it happened. A flash of anxiety reared up in his chest. His concealed face went flush. His lungs grew tight. Amir shook his head vigourously, attempting throw off the acidic cloud of panic that had suddenly befallen him.

"Fuck," he whispered under his mask. "Fuck, fuck fuck. Get your fucking shit together." Recognizing the inherent danger of anxiety's unannounced appearance, Amir willed his feet forward, force of momentum the only reliable fix. Take a deep breath and keep moving, he told himself.

And he did—praise Allah—and regained focus long enough to reach the second landing. Flashing his head around the corner, he stole a glimpse of his destination—a room, several doors down on the right side of the corridor.

John Ward

As his foot met the surface of the landing, a searing stream of light flooded the hallway. It was instantly followed by the loud smack of two tangled bodies tumbling into the wall opposite the open doorway of the room. Amir tore the mask from his head, bolted past the man and woman locked in writhing combat and into the room they'd spilt out of.

There was the boy—awestruck—standing in the centre of the room, eyes fixed on the death match outside. Amir paused for a split second and scanned the room. There wasn't much to it but an overturned dish, a mess of rice and some mugs. So, he grabbed Darweshi by the forearm, dragged him into the hallway, yanked him past Kamkin and Suzuki and pushed him down the stairwell, descending so rapidly it was almost a free fall.

As they hurtled past the first floor, Amir shouted, "Wait," and forced the boy down into a sitting position. "Stay here."

Amir darted back upward, recovered the mask from the third floor landing, and paused just long enough to watch Suzuki plunge a blade into the centre of Kamkin's torso. The woman lurched spastically, blood discharging from her mouth with a gasping bellow. Suzuki, face covered in crimson, glanced down the hallway. Before the assassin could disentangle himself from Kamkin's hot corpse, Amir raised his nine and snapped three rounds off. Two struck Suzuki's left side—one in the thigh, one in the shoulder—forcing him to roll laterally. Kamkin's limp body absorbed the third slug, dead weight shuttering on impact.

Amir bounded down the stairwell, heart thumping with each heavy step. When he reached the boy, he paused, threw his mask back on, then took Darweshi by the shirt collar and dragged him out of the building. One hand on the boy, Amir halted halfway across the yard, and, forced his gun back into its holster. Darweshi stared into Amir's bug-eyed mask, body trembling slightly.

"I'm here to protect you," Amir said in wobbly Arabic. "You need to follow me. Got it?"

PART THREE

SIXTEEN

Channel blocked flashed across the panel every time Brit re-entered the code. After six tries she took a swig of cold coffee and dialled for assistance.

"Evening, ma'am."

"Something's wrong with my link," Brit said, "please patch me through to zero-Charlie-zero-Alpha-niner."

"Straight away, ma'am. Stand by." The goofy-looking kid disappeared for moment, the crown, eagle and crossed swords of MOD's crest replacing him on the coms screen. "General Tillman," he said, materializing again. "That channel's locked. Shall I try another?"

"What do you mean it's locked?"

"Not cleared for usage, ma'am."

"I'm running a joint op on that line."

"I don't know what to say, General Tillman—it won't grant me access either."

Brit stood from her chair and lit a cigarette. "It's in use?"

"I've no way of knowing, General."

"You're the bloody operator, what do you mean you've no way of knowing?"

"Sorry, General Tillman. When a channel is locked, it's impossible to tell."

"Oh, give me a fucking break, lad. Get your supervisor."

The operator looked over his shoulder and then back to the screen. "I *am* the ranking desk officer, ma'am."

"Then call upstairs and find me somebody. Christ!"

"Yes, General. Stand by please."

"Yeah, yeah." Brit dialled Mason on her desk line while she waited. There was no response; not even voice mail.

"Um, hi," the kid said upon return, a bit of discomfort in his voice.

"Yes?"

"They told me to tell you there's nothing they can do."

"What?"

"They told me to tell you—"

"I heard you, Sargent," Brit said, tone edgy as a carving knife. "Who's the CO tonight?"

"She's the one whom I just spoke with, General."

"*She*? It's Ferguson?"

"Yes, ma'am."

"Tell Ferguson I want to speak with her directly."

Again, a pained look, as if someone were bending the kid's fingers back. "She told me she's under direct orders to refrain from communicating with you for the next several hours."

"From who?"

"She didn't say, ma'am."

Without another word, Brit killed the feed and called Glass. "Come on…pick the blasted thing up, Henry." Nothing. "Fuck," she said, mashing her half-smoked cigarette into the ashtray and slamming the handheld down.

Five seconds later, the desk-line lit up. Brit jabbed a finger into the speaker button. "Henry, where are you?"

"I'm in London, dear—where the hell else would I be?"

"No, Henry, where are you right now?"

"I'm not at Vauxhall, if that's what you mean."

"They've cut me out of it, Henry … I can't get through on the Coms line."

"Cut you out of what?"

"The operation, Henry! Christ."

"Have you spoken with Mason?"

"No. We're scheduled to be on right now, but they've locked me out of the designated channel."

"You've checked if it's an error?"

"Yes, I've bloody checked," Brit said. "This was intentional. They've even instructed the section chief to refrain from contact with me."

"You're kidding me."

"Wish I were."

"You've tried Duran directly?"

"It's impossible—he's on a single line unit. The one I'm supposed to be on presently."

"Have you tried his phone?"

"His phone is here in Granada," she said. "We collected it before he left."

"Who's he with?"

"Who knows? He's to have met with Mason's contact, by now—probably in the shit of it as we speak."

"Do you have the local's name?"

"It's on a need-to-know," Brit said. "Wasn't given it."

"Jesus. The whole thing bloody wreaks, Tillman."

"Yes, I'm aware."

"Fucking Mason. He's up to something, Brit. I fucking knew it."

"I'm beginning to agree."

"What's that chap's name who works in I.T. for us down there? You know, the gloomy, middle-aged one—bit of a pain in the ass."

"Davis," Brit said.

"Yes, Davis—he's good, he may be able to locate Duran."

"He's not on duty, Henry."

"You had no problem waking me."

"Oh, you weren't sleeping," she said, an allusion to the post-coital dopiness in his voice.

"Have one of the boys get Davis."

"Fine. Henry, can you find Mason for me?"

The line went quiet for a moment, then Glass said, "I can try." And after another pause, "Funny you've been locked out like this … we just experienced a similarly concerning obstruction."

Brit's left eyebrow arched upward. "Who's *we*, Henry?"

"No one to worry about."

After a short pause, Brit said, "What do you think he's doing?"

"Mason? Don't quite know…but I've a strong fucking suspicion it's tied into these corporate arseholes from the Lanesborough today."

"I'm worried about Duran, Henry."

"Don't worry about him, dear. Might not be the ideal candidate for this sort of thing, but what he lacks in experience he sure as hell makes up for in tenacity."

"What if the whole thing's a set-up, Henry?"

"Set up?"

"I don't know," she said. "I don't know what to think of it."

"Our boy's a beast, Brit. Whoever runs up against the bloke, they're the ones you should fear for."

"Right," she said. "Henry, find Mason for me, please. I need to know what the fuck is happening down in Zanzibar."

"You know he won't tell me anything, Tillman."

"Do what you have to … " There was a pause, and Brit rephrased. "Do whatever you can."

"Okay, give me some time."

"We don't *have* time!"

"Brit," he said, a paternal compassion warming his tone. "Just hang in there, dear. Everything is going to be fine."

"Is it, though?"

"You're a damn good leader," he reassured her. "Damn good. Never met a commander who cared so much."

Brit shook her head and lit anther smoke. "Right," she said. "Call me when you've an update."

***

Halfway to the rendezvous point, Amir's adrenaline began to recede.

Which had its trade-offs. He could think straight again—that was a welcome development. No more twitching in the presence of innocuous stimuli. No more jumping at the sound of a snapping twig or the sight of a slinking cat.

But with the edginess gone, some nagging discomforts had crept in. There was that chafing in his crotch; cargo pants still damp from his maiden dip. There was the minor ache in his ankle; a product of his mad dash down the stairwell. And then there was the fucking mask—the least ergonomically-advanced piece of equipment ever designed. Thing weighed a goddamn ton. Poorly ventilated, too. And its lower edges pinched at his neck flesh with the impact of every step.

But there was no way forward without it.

John Ward

So Amir kept it on, face sweating profusely beneath the rubber lining, one stinging eye on Darweshi, the other following the directional prompts telecast across the interior of its visor.

When they finally arrived at the door of the safe house—a ramshackle two-floor grocery—Amir pulled the mask free, gulped in the unfiltered night and took the boy gently by the arm. Leaning over, he tried for eye contact. Darweshi wouldn't engage.

"Are you doing okay?" Amir asked in broken Arabic, the absurdity of the question shrinking his voice to an embarrassed whisper. The boy refused. And who could blame him.

My god, Amir thought. *You've taken a child hostage. A fucking child. Your own son's age. Imagine James in this situation? He'd be terrified, freaking out. Holed up with the Japanese operative, and now this?*

Amir's dark thoughts were displaced by the sudden whoosh of the shop door. Jeff stood across the threshold and motioned for the child to enter first. As they walked in, she eye-balled Amir and the boy—a quick once-over for signs of injury.

"We're fine," was Amir's gruff confirmation.

"Come with me," she said, walking down the centre aisle toward a stairwell at the rear of the cluttered store, and starting up the steps. At the top, she pointed to a dark office opposite the stairs; it's only source of light a laptop, open screen emitting a ghostly, blue flicker.

"Mason is waiting," Jeff said matter-of-factly. Amir looked at the computer and she shook her head. "No. That's mine. Use yours. We'll give you some privacy."

She put her arm around the child's shoulders and led him away. Amir immediately lit a cigarette. After a succession of rapid puffs, he withdrew the device from his pocket. With it held at some distance from his face, Amir squinted, pressed his fingers to the smooth face and waited for London to receive the signal. Almost instantly, Mason's groomed mug appeared on the small screen.

"Agent Duran—glad to hear from you."

"Where's Brit?"

"She's tied up. I presume you're at the safe house?"

"I thought Brit was going to be on, too."

"She's tied up, I said. Now, where are you?"

Amir glanced over his shoulder, then back at the screen. "I'm at the safe house. Shouldn't you know that? You've got a fucking tracer—"

"Everything go as planned?"

"Planned? I don't know, did it?" Amir exhaled from the side of his mouth, lip curling with antipathy. "That was a fucking mess."

"We told you to anticipate resistance," Mason said. "So, you've got the boy?"

"Yes—are you listening? Did you know it was going to be like that? I arrived at a fucking shit show—two operatives in a death match."

For a moment, Mason remained quiet. Then he ran an index finger across his eyebrows and said, "What's his status?"

"The boy?"

"Yes, the boy, Agent Duran. Who else?"

"Oh, I don't know, the fucking guy I shot? Japanese guy? You might be concerned with that."

"The boy."

"The boy's fine … this is quite the fucking operation you're running. We both could've been killed—me and the boy."

"Yet, here you are," Mason said.

"You almost sound disappointed."

"I'm making a point."

"*Making a point.* So this is how you guys do things? Roll the dice, see what happens?"

"Did you kill the Japanese operative?"

"I have no idea. Wasn't about to stick around and inspect my work. Who the hell was he fighting?"

"That's irrelevant."

"Is it? Because she's dead. Small sword lodged in her sternum."

"Good," Mason said.

"Good?"

"Simplifies things dramatically."

"Who was she, Russian?"

"It doesn't matter who she was, Duran. She's dead. End of story."

John Ward

"Matters to me—I still have to get us out of here. What if they're not operating alone?"

"Then you'll deal with it."

"I don't think you're paying attention, Mason. I got lucky back there! Only reason we made it out so fast is because they were too preoccupied with each other to deal with us."

"And it worked out. Now stop all the blabbering and listen. We're wasting valuable time right now—time you'll need if you want to avoid any more of these logistical inconveniences you've such an aversion to."

Mason's tone was sopping with such sarcasm it took every stressed fibre of Amir's being to maintain composure. "I'm all ears, you fucking cocksucker. Just get us out of here."

"Where's the boy?"

"He's here, I said."

"No, right now."

"He's with the handler down the hall."

"Listen carefully." Mason paused. "You've a silencer for your weapon, correct?"

"Of course I do. I didn't use it before, though, if that's what you're asking. I don't use a silencer unless I'm absolutely certain range won't be an issue. I had no idea what to—"

Mason cut him off. "If you haven't closed the door of the room you're currently in, I suggest doing so now."

Amir stood silently for a moment, processing the request, taking in as much smoke as his lungs could handle. After a few seconds, he drew the device closer to his face, and lowered his voice. "You've got to be kidding me. I'm not shooting this woman. There's a fucking kid here."

"I didn't ask you to."

"What are you getting at," Amir whispered, paranoia's icy blade beginning to scrape along his diaphragm.

"I know this is, well, distasteful to say the least," Mason said. And then he drove the dagger in fully. "But the boy needs to be eliminated."

Amir drew back, stammering. "Wha…what did you say?" It was as if the shadows had leapt from the corners of the room and swallowed the meaning of Mason's words before Amir could fully grasp them. "I ... I'm sorry, what?"

"Yes, I'm aware how terribly shocking it must sound. And I apologize for springing it on you in such a way. But you must consider our position. It's a matter of national security, Duran. Can't risk the possibility of the boy being intercepted. Just not something we can allow."

"*Eliminated*," was all Amir could get out.

"And I'll need confirmation. Photos and DNA. Equipment for a blood sample's in the bag. Fairly straightforward. Syringe, test tube. Do it before you kill him, obviously. Once I receive the pictures, I'll forward the extraction details, including where and how to dispose of the body."

Amir lowered the device to his side, walked to the desk, pulled out the seat from beneath it and slumped down. Raising the screen back in view, he stared blankly, incapable of words.

"Agent Duran."

"What?" Amir said, flicking his cigarette butt to the linoleum and lighting another.

"Do you understand?" Silence. "Do you understand," Mason repeated, sharply this time.

"I understand."

"Good. I know this all must feel a bit odd—but you're doing well, Duran." Mason looked to be suppressing a smile. "Field work requires tremendous flexibility. And frankly, a stomach for some rather unpalatable things. So far, you've proven you're up to it, though. Now get to it and send me the photos. We'll have you out of there in no time."

The feed cut out, and with it, Amir's sense of reality.

This is not actually happening. It can't be. Kill the child? It's a joke. A test maybe. Must be a test. Mason—putting you through a test. A trial. See how you perform in the field. Why, though—why would he do that? Where was Brit? Is this whole goddamn thing some sort of protracted simulation? A fucking training mission?

Then he thought of the Japanese operative. Shot—twice. Real. And the woman. Very real and very fucking dead. Was he losing his mind? The sharp pulse in his chest began to amalgamate with an intensifying sensation of nausea.

Breathe, man. Breath. *Eliminate the boy*. Why would they do that?

He leaned back and studied the ceiling above, eyes tracing the water stains snaking across its peeling paint—some faint, some pronounced in the laptop's blue light. Ghastly. Tiny rivers of muck. Mud-brown veins. Repulsive little highlights of human failure. Disorder. Erosion of order. Nature's slow re-conquest. A leaky roof, a burst levy, some spilt blood. False control, flawed judgement—the world was bathed in it.

Amir closed his eyes for a moment and then rose from the chair. He walked slowly into the hallway, drew his Glock—not bothering with the silencer—and raised it up at the open doorway to his right. Jeff staggered backward and looked toward the boy.

"You," Amir said, aiming the nine at Jeff, "out!" When Darweshi got up from his seat, Amir waved his free hand, commanding him to stay put. "No," he said in Arabic and flicked the barrel in Jeff's direction, "Just you." When she moved within reach, Amir slapped an open palm against the back of her neck, closed his grip and pulled her into the corridor.

As she stumbled into the hallway, her eyes bulged with shock. "What are you doing?"

He grabbed her again—this time by the hair—wrenched her head sideways and pressed the Glock's nozzle to her cheekbone. Once through the doorway, he tossed her to the floor. "What is this?"

"What is *what*?" she said with a shriek.

"Don't," he said, dropping to a knee and returning the gun to her face. "I told you … I will fucking unload this magazine into your head, so don't bullshit me!"

"I … I have no … "

"Is this some sort of sick joke?" Amir asked, this time in a lowered, but equally dangerous tone.

"What are you—?"

"What did Mason say? What did he tell you to do once we returned?"

She cowered, tears welling, face turned as far from the gun as her thin, twisting neck would allow. "He told me to have you call!"

"What else?"

"That's it—that's it." She began to shake. "I wasn't … I wasn't even given the exit details. Just told to assist. That's it!"

Amir eased back a bit. "What's your name?"

"What?"

"What's your real name?'

"Jeff!"

"What's your real fucking name?"

"Shiv," she said, the gun three inches from her head. "It's Shiv."

Amir stood. "Get up. Get on the computer," he instructed, nodding at it. "Prove it. I'm sure you've got it in there somewhere. Prove it to me." When she began to weep, he shook his head. "What is your real name?" he repeated, pronouncing every syllable with aggressive, rhythmic clarity. "Last fucking chance."

She wiped at her eyes, utterly discombobulated. "Harkinder," she said with a whimper.

Amir's muscles eased at the deflated sound of it. "*Harkinder* what?"

"Singh."

"Harkinder Singh."

"Yes," she said, a look of defeat replacing the terror in her eyes.

"So, there are limits to your deception."

"Fuck you," Harkinder said, voice rickety. "You don't know anything about me."

"I do now."

"Pleased with yourself?" When he said nothing, she slowly shook her head. "Now tell me. Tell me—what'd I give it up for? *What?*"

Amir was too wired for compassion. "Log on to the computer."

"No," she said. "I'm not doing anything else for you."

Amir cocked his head back. "You want to do this again?"

"I'm not doing shit for you unless you tell me."

Did it even matter at this point? He thought it over. He needed Brit. The laptop was his only option, only way without alerting Mason. Fuck. Couldn't get on it without her.

"Mason told me to kill him."

"Who?"

"The boy."

Watching the confusion sweep over her, Amir instantly knew she had nothing to do with it.

"What," she said. "Why?"

Amir shook his head, no good answer. "I don't know. I assumed you knew."

Harkinder's head was shaking again, long, black hair looking wilder with every turn. "There's … there's got to be a mistake."

As Amir studied her—eyes bloodshot, shoulders slumped—the injustice of their predicament felt more amplified. Ugly, what he'd done; throwing her around, scaring the shit out of her. She was just a pawn. Like him.

"I need to reach my commanding officer," he said calmly, pushing away the guilt. "Will that work?"

"The computer? For what?"

"A coms link."

"I only have email."

"You're kidding me."

"That's how I work," she said.

"Fine. Boot it up." She hesitated, looking wobbly again. "Harkinder," Amir said sharply.

She rubbed her face, walked up to the desk. Hunched, she began typing, face bathed in the light of the laptop screen. As she worked, Amir drifted toward the doorway and poked his head out to check on the boy. But a sudden gasp from Harkinder spun him around. "What is it?" he said, watching her recoil. When she didn't respond, he marched up to the screen, lurched forward for a look.

At the top of her inbox, a single unread message bore Tony Mason's name—no text in the body—the subject line containing a single instruction in all caps:

SEND CONFIRMATION WHEN DURAN IS DONE WITH THE BOY.

SEVENTEEN

It was a feat of strength peeling himself away from the seductive grasp of Marissa's bedroom.

After Glass's phone call with Brit, they'd made love again, ignoring the world for another twenty minutes to reclaim another fraction of years lost. That made three times in four hours—an accomplishment he hadn't known himself capable of at this age. The third time was the most vigourous, totally unencumbered, all inhibitions cast aside. Now, Glass wanted nothing more than to sink into a restful sleep with her warm body draped over his.

But the Mason situation demanded attention. The geezer had something up his sleeve and Glass was certain everything was connected. Zanzibar. The Lanesborough. The locked files. Marissa had expressed her doubts. And before he left, she implored him not to interfere. It wasn't an order per se; more of a plea for restraint. Really haven't changed, have you, she'd said. Still jumping at the opportunity to stick his nose where it didn't formally belong.

Though there wasn't a whole lot she could do to stop him. Commanding his superiors to intervene would certainly expose their little tryst. So here he was, speed walking across town with every intention of confronting Mason.

Despite the hour, Glass had a buoyancy about him. Like a teen-ager invigourated by the novelty of sexual intercourse. More than that, his heart felt lighter, as if all of the hardness—the decades of calcified anguish—had suddenly broken apart and fallen away.

It was bloody remarkable. A resurrection of sorts. An unlikely confirmation that his years hadn't been wasted. That all those times he'd sabotaged his chances for real intimacy with other women, there'd been a greater purpose to it. How wild, the way things work. Flew up to London for a fucking waste-of-time retreat, then—in a turn for the bizarre—growing evidence of a potential conspiracy leads him to the bed of his long-lost love. Just blooming unbelievable; the world anew.

By the time Glass passed the Tate Modern, a low mist had risen, the cool night air coaxing it up from the Thames and over the Millbank. The lights of Vauxhall winked through the fog from across the river. The angular contours of the massive edifice reduced to mere vagaries.

Glass lit a smoke—just for style—his head already flooded with the satiating aftereffects of post-coital bliss. It was all very cloak and dagger, this little mission of his. Might as well play the part. Spy with a cigarette, creeping along the embankment.

On the bridge over, though, he could only think of Marissa, what the future held. He had to remind himself not to get carried away. They'd barely spent an evening together. But hell, what an evening. She'd lost nothing to middle age. Like it should be a surprise. The woman had always been a spark plug, bursting with erotic energy. Only difference now, she kept it hidden under a power suit.

How coy.

Glass had to smile, a bit of self-congratulation in it. Well, nothing stopping you from trying it all on a second time. If she was willing, that is. Oh, she was willing. He'd felt it: her urgent touch; her hungry mouth. Her eyes. He'd heard it in her simmering whispers.

Glass tossed the spent smoke aside, suddenly feeling drunk.

Jesus, man. Get a fucking handle. Sensing he'd lost track of time, Glass reached for the cell in his pocket and discovered he'd missed a call from Brit. Damn it, Henry, get your shit together. Why is the ringer off?

He rang her back and it was barely a second before Brit picked up. "Henry!" she said, all panic.

"Are you okay?"

"No—I mean, I'm fine—Duran though, Mason ordered Duran to kill the boy."

Glass stopped dead in his tracks, only a hundred metres from the entrance of the building. "What? As in *the* boy?"

"Yes, *the* boy."

"Good god … you're fucking kidding me."

"No."

"Did he?"

"Kill him? No, of course not—he's holed up with the handler and the kid right now in some sort of safe house in Zanzibar City."

"Bloody Christ. How did you get in touch with him? I thought you were cut off."

"He emailed me. From the handler's account."

Glass was dumbfounded. "Have you responded yet?"

"Yes. I told him to sit tight. Said I'd talk to you. Henry, what the fuck is going on?"

"You're sure Duran hasn't killed the boy?"

"I'm sure of it. He's freaking out, as you can imagine. As we speak, Mason's awaiting confirmation of the kill—told Duran he'd send extraction details once he's received proof."

"Bastard," Glass whispered. Then he paused, everything becoming clear; the veil, pulled away. "They've got a cure," he said. "They've got a fucking cure."

"What are you talking about?"

"The company, those bastards. That's what this is. GLogiX, Mason—they never intended for the boy to make it back to London. Quite the opposite."

"You think?"

"What the hell else could this be—keeping me out, cutting you out. And if anyone raises questions about the ethics of it—putting a hit out on a child—they'd blame the whole thing on Duran. Rogue agent, unknown quantity. Bastards," he repeated. Then, after a moment: "Kid doesn't get in anyone else's hands, like this. Not the Russians, not the Japanese, and not GLogiX competitors. Bastards'll sit on top of the market from here to kingdom come. The crown will be eating off their hands. Sort of brilliant, actually. Bloody nefarious, but brilliant. Bastards."

The line was quiet for a second, then Brit said, "Glass, listen—I've no bloody idea why this is happening. You may be right. But either way we need to get Duran the fuck out of there. The kid, too."

"Fucking Tony Mason, I still can't believe it."

"Henry! We need to figure this out. Duran can't just sit there.

Mason's expecting him to respond. They've got an RAF pilot on the mainland waiting and Amir's almost certain the Japanese and Russians will come after them too—he's already had a close encounter."

Glass squinted and lit another cigarette, suddenly aware of his proximity to the building, the likelihood someone inside listening. Fuck it, what could he do. "Brit. Can you get one of our planes ready? Or a chopper?"

"Duran's half way around the world, Henry. Even if I could, it'll take ages to—"

"Does Mason know Duran's current location?"

"Yes, I assume so," Brit said. "They're communicating through tracked hardware."

"And where's the RAF plane?"

"Not far."

"And who's the pilot?"

"Only met him once—name's Sparrow. Some sort of specialist."

"Jesus," Glass said. "Duran needs to move. Wet jobs like this, there's always someone standing by, ready to clean up if need be. Sounds like your boy Sparrow might have the skill set." Glass paced anxiously, wondering if anyone from Vauxhall had them tapped. "Tell Duran to unplug his GPS and get the fuck off the system. Needs to get himself and the boy to a new location— somewhere off the SIS grid. And tell him to stay on email."

"They're bound to have her account hacked, Henry."

"Yes, but if she's a pro it'll take them awhile to decrypt the messages."

"Right. Henry … how far up do you think this goes?"

"You mean, are we going to get fucked for interfering? Who knows? Marissa White's not in on it, I can say that much."

"So that's who *we* is," Brit said. "How the fuck did that happen?"

He measured his response: "Something to share over a fag. Nevertheless, she's an ally—might be able to help us get Duran and the boy out safely. Tillman, we should be exploring transport options you've access to."

"What are you thinking?"

"I'm thinking we need to move fast."

***

Kamkin's body still lay in the hallway, eyes wide, head propped against the wall. Her right leg jutted out laterally, knee twisted inward at an unnatural angle. A crimson pool had coagulated on the scuffed hardwood beneath her torso.

There'd be no point in moving the corpse. The safe house was blown. Plus, Suzuki hadn't the strength to do it anyway. He'd lost a considerable amount of blood—mainly from the leg wound—his shoulder only mildly lacerated from the hollow tip that had grazed it.

The past hour had been a torturous study in self-preservation. He'd spent it on the edge of the bed in his blood-soaked underwear, extracting bullet fragments from his thigh with a pair of aluminium travel tweezers. By pure chance, none of the bullet had punctured the artery. It was a complicated procedure, nevertheless—copious amounts of reddish-yellow fluid seeping from his twitching muscles as he dug.

It wasn't until he packed clotting agent into the wound that Suzuki winced and ground his teeth. The excruciating heat sent his frame rigid as if zapped by high voltage current. When the acute searing subsided, he took a gulp of cold tea and went straight for the bandages.

Then it was back to business.

Suzuki retrieved his coms device from the bedspread and scanned the most recent dispatch. His employers were confident they'd locked onto the British operative's location. A store in Stone Town, not far from the harbour. There'd been bit of commotion on the upper level not long ago. They'd even added a bit of editorial commentary.

Convenient, no?

But they were businessmen and missed the point. There was nothing particularly unusual about the British operative's location. Rival spies love to operate in close proximity. The dangerous intimacy, indeed preferable.

As Suzuki rose to put his pants on, he peered through the open door and met Kamkin's wide eyes. They were hollow as an empty shell casing.

John Ward

Suzuki threw his shirt on, gathered his Hissatsu and sheath, attached them to his good leg and grabbed his guns. As he passed into the hallway, he cleared his throat and spit a thick wad of phlegm onto the dead Russian's boots.

She took no offense.

***

"What a totally ludicrous allegation," C said. "And if I were to speculate, nothing more than a red herring—have you traced the IP?"

"Well, no. Not yet. I'm still at my flat and haven't spoken with I.T.," Marissa said, pacing back and forth in her slippers, phone in one hand, a mug of coffee in the other. "But it certainly appears to be the handler."

"And the email was sent to *you*."

"Sent to me," she said quickly, masking the deceit.

"Well trace the goddamn IP. If I were to speculate, I'd say it's the Russians. They do this, Marissa. We've seen it a thousand times, this sort of weak attempt to disrupt our operations. Can't believe you've woken me up for this dribble."

Marissa grimaced. "Have you talked to Tony?"

"I spoke with Mason directly, just before turning in. Everything was going off just fine."

"Sir, with all due respect," Marissa said, "the entire situation feels a bit—I don't know—flimsy. Why would we send an untested agent for such an important op? And put Mason in charge, to boot. I keep running it back."

"*We*, Marissa? You mean, why did *I* tap Tony for this."

"Well …

"If you're going to question my judgement, I suggest you do it in less oblique terms," the old man said. "It's insulting."

"I think you're misinterpreting—"

"I'm not misinterpreting anything. We've been over it countless times. I won't indulge another explanation. Now, if you've finished, I'd like to make the most of what little time I've left to get some bloody rest. I've a meeting with the PM first thing and I'm sure she wouldn't appreciate it if I were to oversleep on account of your misguided meddling."

Marissa put her mug on the counter and cocked her head back in frustration. "Why I am locked out of certain files pertaining to the GLogiX contract?"

"What? What does GLogiX have to do with this?"

"I'd love to know, sir."

"I've no idea what you're referring to. More than that, I fail to see the connection."

"They've been trying to develop a vaccine," she said.

"Yes, thank you for the update. I know what they've been doing for us. Completely irrelevant. And why you've been poking around in there is beyond me. Has literally nothing to do with operational management."

Marissa hesitated for a moment, then came out with it. "I've reason to believe Tony Mason is consorting with GLogiX executives offline."

"Excuse me?"

"I've received intelligence from a reliable source."

"*A reliable source*," C said. "I'm the fucking chief of the SIS, White—not a fucking entry-level analyst. You don't get to withhold sources from me."

Marissa ran a hand through her hair. "I'm sorry, sir. I—"

"Who told you this?"

"I … listen, sir, I know this is … well, irregular and all, but … " She stumbled through an absurdly evasive, circuitous justification for withholding the information.

C let it play for a while then told her, "Marissa, I understand your concerns. There's quite a bit on the line here. But, I think we should table this conversation—pick it up in the morning. In the meantime, I assure you, everything in Zanzibar is going off quite brilliantly. The boy is safe, and this Amir Duran is working out just fine. Should be on their way back to London within the hour."

"Sir—"

"Listen, dear," C said, projecting a sort of paternal benevolence. "This is my suggestion: If it makes you feel better, go see Tony

Mason now. I'm sure he'd be happy to brief you on the operational status. And do check on the IP of that email. I think that'll help ease your doubts."

"Sir, I'm not sure—"

"Marissa," C said, timbre acidic once again. "I'm retiring to bed. Take your concerns up with Agent Mason. You are his boss after all."

"Right, sir ... good night, sir."

***

Tony Mason was fucking around with his putter when the mobile laying on his desk chimed. He took his time answering it, sauntering over with the iron still in his grip, swiping it back and forth with each step. The fun ended when he saw the succession of zeros scrolled across the cell screen.

"Fuck," he whispered, dropping the club to the carpet and lifting the phone to his ear. "Hello?"

"What the fuck is going on in Zanzibar?" C said, growling like an old bear defending his territory.

Mason hesitated. "Sir ... I'm not certain. I should've received word by now."

"Activate Sparrow."

"What?"

"You heard me—activate him."

"What do you mean?"

"You bloody imbecile, contingency protocol is now in effect."

"Yes, but I thought—"

"That's a bloody order," C said. "Ignore it, you'll be sacked."

Mason closed his eyes and shook his head. "Yes, sir."

"And we've had another development. One you'll need to deal with immediately."

EIGHTEEN

A vaporous grey veil clung to London's stone and brick bones. Marissa shivered, the fog unusually cool for the time of year. Her driver was now ten minutes late, clearly unready to be summoned in the wee hours.

Since taking the post, Marissa had foregone driving completely. Just one of the many claustrophobic impositions of her post. Wasn't even supposed to shop for her own groceries. There were ways around it of course. Whenever she felt a touch suffocated, she ordered her security team to go and get themselves a pint somewhere close by. If you don't, I'll reassign you, she'd tell them with a grin. And so, they'd slink off to the nearest pub, always with a bit of apprehension in their eyes.

Tonight had been one of those nights. Told them to bugger off, quite early on. Given how the night had gone, it was damn good thing. Her detail guys had proven a faithful and discreet lot. But with Henry all hopped up on conspiracy theories, she couldn't risk testing her boys' loyalties. Even now, she'd purposely failed to alert her body man she was leaving. He was none the wiser, still sleeping in the downstairs flat of her condo subdivision.

When Glass called, Marissa was on the sidewalk, clicking the toes of her most comfortable pumps against the granite curb, arms crossed at her chest, staring out into the mist.

"Please tell me you're not in a holding cell," she said.

"I'm fairly certain we wouldn't be having this conversation if that were the case."

"Good. I was beginning to—"

"Marissa," he said, cutting her short. "They wouldn't even let me near Mason's office. The wanker's bloody sequestered himself."

"Maybe he's in the middle of something."

Henry chuckled disdainfully. "He's in the middle of something, alright. Have you spoken with C?"

She remained silent for a moment. Then, "I *have*."

"And?"

"He says the email you forwarded was a complete fabrication. A red herring, he called it—presumably sent by the Russians. Also told me Mason says the op is going off smoothly, nothing to be concerned with."

"Oh, that's complete shite, Marissa."

"Is it?"

"Come on," Glass said. "Why has Mason locked himself in his office?"

"Henry, we've zero proof of any—"

"And what about the files? Did you ask C about that?"

"Says he knows nothing about it."

"Spare me," Glass said. "They've developed a fucking cure, and he knows it. Has to. He's the head of the blasted Secret Intelligence Services."

"Listen," she said, watching plumes of fog roll past a street lamp in the distance. "Without evidence your suspicions amount to nothing more than circumstantial speculation."

"*My* suspicions? This isn't a court of law, Marissa. We're not proving something to a jury."

"So very true, Henry. Though I must say, we could very well end up in one if we continue down this course."

Glass grunted plaintively. "We don't have the luxury of methodically gathering the facts right now. We've an agent in jeopardy."

"Henry, don't take this the wrong way," she said, but then stopped herself short. "Listen, Henry, I'm on my way in. Just relax for the time being. Make a cup of coffee or something."

"Relax? The Russians and Japanese are bound to be closing in on Duran. We'll have a dead agent, and the boy will end up in foreign hands. We need an extraction plan. Now! I'm not leaving it to Tony Mason's hired hand."

"He's a topline RAF pilot, Henry—not some mercenary."

"Really? I'd bet my life he's been given orders to finish the job if Duran fails to do so. And trust me, there's no way in hell Duran will kill the kid."

"It's impossible, Henry. I won't risk flying through neutral airspace."

"We did to get them down there."

"In a prop plane, hugging the fucking surface of the earth. Any aircraft capable of getting down there fast enough would light up radar systems from here to Moscow. It'd be an utterly provocative manoeuvre, a blatant contravention of the most recent treaty."

"What about the Navy?"

"Closest carrier we have is in the South Atlantic. Scrambling a jet from there would be just as problematic. Plus, I'm not involving the goddamn Navy, Henry. I've no authority to do so."

"What if they could meet us halfway? Say he could find a way off the island."

"How?"

"I don't know, you tell me. Didn't Duran take a boat to get on island? Why couldn't he take one off? Head south, meet the fleet in the Atlantic."

"For the second time—I'm not involving the Navy," Marissa said, with staccato emphasis, like a mother scolding a stubborn child. "Besides—Agent Duran, charting a course around the Cape of Good Hope? Disastrous. Sure way to guarantee their deaths."

But Glass powered forward. "What about north? He could follow the coast. Much safer—more efficient. Gulf of Aden to the Red Sea, pass through the Suez?"

"*The Suez*. Have you lost your marbles? That's even hairier. The Russian Fifth Fleet are all over Port Said—thanks to the absolutely brilliant arrangement we've struck with them."

"Cairo."

"What?"

"Cairo," he repeated, breathlessly.

"How?"

"Chopper in from the coast. Meet them in Cairo. Avoid Said."

"That'd take weeks—and who's chopper? I'm not having the RAF fly over the Egyptian coast."

"Tillman—she could send one inland. We've got a few transport rigs that could make the trip."

"Henry," she said, exhaustion permeating her voice. "You've just entered the realm of the absurd. Just wait for me to arrive. Please? I'm going to talk to Tony and sort this out."

"Jesus, Marissa."

"Don't *Jesus* me. My driver will be arriving any minute. So hold your bloody horses. Nothing, literally nothing we've discussed holds water. Really, it's rather ridiculous we've gone this far with things. Besides," she said, "There isn't a boat in all of Zanzibar that could make the journey without refuelling."

For a moment, there was silence. Then Glass lowered his voice, a hint of reproach in it. "Marissa. I've high enough clearance to know that Jeddah is an option."

There was silence for a few seconds. "We haven't used the Bedouins for over a year, Henry."

"Precisely—they're damn eager for business. They'd jump at the opportunity to fly Duran and the boy right up to Cairo."

She shook her head. "They are not reliable. And we've made agreements with the ... hold on," she said, the headlights of an approaching vehicle distracting her.

"My ride's here."

"Don't hang up on me, Marissa. We need to work this out."

"I will be there shortly," she said, stepping back from the curb to allow the black Range Rover some space. "I can't discuss this in front the driver." Before she could reach for the door handle, the driver leapt out and rounded the truck's front. "That won't be necessary," she said, "I'll be just fine—"

"No, ma'am. Part of my job, ma'am," the young man said, reaching into his pocket and moving toward her.

"Excuse me, what are you—"

With a flash and a whisper, the shots were in her. One in the chest. One in the neck. And one more in the forehead once she had fallen.

***

"Don't pray for *things*," Jeddo once told Amir. "We're not Catholic. The Catholics pray for *things*. That's why they're so unhappy. 'Why didn't I get a raise? Why doesn't she love me? Why did I lose my football game?' I *prayed* for these things. It's greedy, you see. And it doesn't work. So forget Dua. You don't need Dua. All you need is Salat. Stick with Salat and Allah will take good care of you."

It didn't stop the boy from occasionally casting little wishes toward the heavens. A new bike. A good grade. A better pair of cleats. A chance to see his mother again.

Sometimes he got what he'd asked for. Mostly he didn't. Either way, Jeddo was none the wiser, the boy's requests submitted confidentially. But as Amir grew into adulthood, he embraced Jeddo's philosophy of orison with greater discipline. Sure he'd still utter a passing plea for divine assistance when things got out of hand. Generally, though, Amir's approach had grown more judicious. He'd found—as Jeddo had promised—supplication was indeed the most reliable measure for gaining god's attention.

As the case was now, Amir often imagined the old man right beside him—standing, bowing, kneeling through cycles of prayerful submission. Jeddo's tone an octave lower than his; a harmonious undergirding to Amir's lead.

After a solid ten minutes, Amir opened his eyes. As the old ghost dissolved into the ether, Amir stood and stretched the tension from his limbs. Turning to the open doorway, he discovered Darweshi watching silently. Amir moved toward him, and the boy took a step backward into the hallway.

"It's okay," Amir said, eyes kinder after Salat. "Do you pray?"

"With Babu," the boy said timidly.

Amir smiled, pleased the boy understood his Arabic. "That's good! My Jeddo taught me my prayers. He practiced them with me every morning until I remembered on my own." Darweshi stared back blankly and Amir's enthusiasm faded.

Harkinder emerged from the office at the other end of the hall. "He only knows a little," she said in Arabic. Then, in English, "You should come in here and see this."

"Tillman responded?" She nodded, looking no less burdened. Amir flashed an open palm. "Well what did she say?"

"You're going to want to have a look yourself," Harkinder said.

When Amir arrived at the computer, a graveness returned to his face. Behind him, Harkinder looked on, an arm over the boy's shoulder, the rapidly mutating dangers of the evening seeming to have triggered her motherly instincts.

John Ward

"Jesus," Amir said, reading it for a second time. "We need to get the fuck out of here."

"And go where?"

"To the boat. You read it."

"My boat can't make it to Jeddah—it's thousands of kilometres! And what am I supposed to do? Just leave everything?"

"If you stay, you're dead." They were silent for a little. Then Amir suddenly swiped the back of his hand across the desk, knocking his coms device to the floor.

"What are you doing?" she said.

His boot heel answered her question, smashing down on the device repeatedly, fragments of plastic and glass exploding outward from beneath his foot.

Harkinder looked at the floor and then up at Amir. "They may still be able to trace it."

"All the more reason to get moving. Can you bring the computer, or can they trace that, too?"

"I don't know."

Amir returned to the email, typed out a simple message to Brit, and sent it off without deliberation.

"What did you write?"

"I told them I'd be there," he said.

"Cairo?"

"Yes. The coordinates they sent—pull them up for me. Your computer has a mapping system, right?"

"You'll never get there."

Amir's eyes bore into her, laser hot. "Pull them up."

She shook her head and went to it. "This is crazy. You'll never make it."

"Got a better option? I need a pen."

Harkinder popped open the desk's middle drawer, removed a small yellow legal pad and ball point pen, and handed them to Amir. Amir logged the location—an old luxury hotel, off the Al Ahram, at the edge of town. If the map was accurate, it was a stone's throw from Giza—the mightiest of pyramids. What a fucking trip.

"Grab whatever you need," he said, "we're leaving."

"We have nowhere to go," she said, voice sharp; a bit unhinged.

"It's hard to believe you can't find us a boat. We're on a fucking island."

"Duran, I don't think you understand—the type of boat you need, I can't get something like that! Not this fast."

"Then we'll steal one."

"Are you insane? You know how to hotwire a fishing trawler? You didn't even know how to tie a goddamn skiff to the mooring."

Amir looked away, both hands extended to the surface of the desk, shoulders slumped.

"Uncle has boat."

Amir and Harkinder's eyes locked on the boy.

"What's that buddy?" Amir switched to Arabic and repeated the question, stunned. "Who has a boat?"

"His uncle," she said. "His uncle has one. Christ. His uncle, yes. The Lottos. Christ," she said, eyes darting around the room as if the fishing fleet were right there, somewhere under her nose. "They've got several. Big commercial vessels, I think."

"Perfect. Can you drive it?"

"What?"

"The boat! Focus, Harkinder."

"Right," she said. "I guess. I don't know."

"We don't have much choice. Where are the guns?"

She looked at him, still in a daze. "What?"

"The guns—the black bag—where did you put it?"

"It's in the … the, um, the closet."

Amir whipped the closet door open, lugged the gun duffle over his shoulder and spun around. "How far away is he?"

"Who?" Harkinder asked, still in a daze.

"His uncle—where's his uncle right now?" Harkinder hesitated and Amir lurched forward, grabbing her by the hand. "Listen to me," he said. "You need to get a hold of yourself. I may be the amateur here, but I know this: we stay put, we die. Guarantee it. I admit: this is a shitty fucking scenario. But I'll bet it's not the first you've dealt with. So stop acting like a frightened child and get on your fucking horse."

"I'm sorry," she said, awakened to the immediacy of their predicament. "I can get us there."

"Good."

"It'll be dangerous, though," she said. "What if someone is waiting for us?"

"It's a strong likelihood," Amir said. "But as far as I'm concerned, we don't have a fucking choice. We are in danger. Presently. And we will be until we get off this fucking island. Now let's go."

Three minutes later they were on the street, rushing along its shadowed margins, Amir with his nine out, duffle bouncing off his back, Harkinder and Darweshi less than a pace behind. At the first intersection, Amir raised his hand up, and paused.

"Keep straight," she whispered. Again, he raised his hand, silencing her. "What is it?" Harkinder asked.

"Quiet," he said, turning around and scanning the area from which they'd come. "Okay, keep moving."

At the next intersection, Amir halted and looked back once more. There was no wind, no stray dog lurking in the shadows. No rustling of branches, no apparent movement. Nor any evidence they'd been followed. Yet, his senses told him differently.

"Go ahead," Amir said, letting Harkinder and the boy pass while he held his position. Lowering the bag, he reached into his cargo pocket, withdrew a silencer, and attached it. He picked the duffle up again, and backpedalled several metres, eyes searching every dark doorway on the street.

Still nothing.

Fuck, he said to himself. Just keep moving and quit letting paranoia dictate your pace. Amir pivoted round and accelerated to a steady jog, catching up with the boy and woman in a matter of seconds.

"There's someone following us, isn't there," Harkinder said shakily. Amir flashed an open palm, acknowledging his uncertainty. "Is it Suzuki?" she asked.

Amir stopped in his tracks, the index finger of his free hand shooting up into the space between them. "You need to shut the fuck up. Concentrate on—"

A muted snap sounded from behind. A thin, leafy branch trembled above their heads. There was a second snap, and a spark flew from the asphalt at their feet. The third muffled round slapped the thick nylon of the duffle, jostling the strap on Amir's shoulder. Amir spun round, gun high, searching for the source.

"Go!" he said, spotting a muzzle flash above a short wall fifty metres down the street. He then sent off a hail of suppressive fire, all four shots smacking into the wall's painted concrete. Chips of dust and debris kicked up from its surface. "Get around the corner," he shouted to Harkinder and unloaded two more rounds.

As Harkinder and Darweshi ran toward the intersection ahead, Amir dropped the bag from his shoulder and continued to fire, moving steadily forward in the direction of the shooter. When the trigger clicked without response, he released the spent magazine and reloaded, instincts driving his reflexes at great speed. Receiving a volley of return fire, Amir tacked sideways, ducking into a recessed doorway half the distance from his original position.

Come on, motherfucker, come out from behind that wall. I dare you.

After a period of silence Amir crouched and poked his head out to scope the shooter's position. But there was nothing to see. Be patient, Duran. If they want to hit you, they'll need to expose themselves.

But patience was never his strong suit. After three more seconds of silence, he darted from the doorway, and dove onto the rough fringe of grass directly beneath the wall concealing the shooter.

He counted to five, then sprung up, Glock angled downward over the crest of the wall, trigger finger twitching until every last slug from the cartridge had found a new home.

It was an imprecise manoeuvre. But the odds had broken in Amir's favour. Suzuki now writhed on his side, fingers clawing spastically at the soil, gun just beyond reach. Amir hurtled at the wall. Suzuki coughed loudly, collapsed onto his back and wheezed a red bubble from his lips. Amir approached and the leaky assassin waved a sluggish hand as if to say, *wait—not yet.*

When Amir loaded a fresh clip, Suzuki drew the Hissatsu from his belt. Shakily, the assassin raised the knife, clutching it with both hands, blade inverted. Then, with all the violence he had left, sank the knife into his own gut and wrenched it sideways.

John Ward

Amir staggered backward, nearly tripping on a small rock. He'd seen a lot of shit in his career. But ritual suicide? Not a single motherfucker in Granada had the balls for that. Gut shot, surrounded, skulls fractured, faces half blown off—they all clung to life, the bad men he knew.

A drop of rain shook Amir out of it.

He glanced up at the sky, nodded to Jeddo and hoisted himself back over the wall. Fifty metres up road, his big black bag of guns lay in middle of the pavement like a sleeping bear. Another fifty beyond it, Harkinder and the boy huddled at the shadowed margin of the intersection. Fifty metres further, pure darkness.

Amir broke into a sprint.

NINETEEN

Tony Mason tipped the decanter until his snifter brimmed with brown stuff. He'd just passed along C's orders to Sparrow and the pilot's response had Mason's hands trembling slightly.

Kill the boy? Duran, too? Yeah, no problem. Anyone else while I'm at it?

Mason eyed the rippling surface of the liquor then took two big, burning swigs. "Where do we find these barbarians?" he whispered. "Such little regard."

As he refilled the glass, his desk phone lit up.

"Bloody Christ," he said into the speaker. "How much clearer could I be? Zero interruptions!"

"Sorry, sir. But it's Agent Glass."

"What about him?"

"He's back, sir."

"So, tell him to leave. I don't see why it's so difficult for you to follow instructions."

"He refuses, sir."

"What?" Mason set his drink down and walked over to the broad interior window. With an extended index finger, he inched one slat of the Venetian Blinds sideways. A scrum had developed at the extreme end of the hallway.

Mason returned to his desk and took another big hit from the glass. "What does he want?"

"He's demanding your attention, sir. And he's threatening our staff now."

"What do you mean, *threatening* staff?"

"Says he'll break his way in if he has to."

"Bloody lunatic," Mason said. "Call security, then."

"Security's already up here, sir."

"Then have him escorted out, you idiot!" He paused. "Do you hear me?"

"Yes, sir. Okay, sir."

To the grating pulse of the dial tone, Mason crept back over to the window. A wrestling match had ensued. Glass was promptly forced to the floor by a couple of strapping guards. A great deal of hollering followed—audible even through the thick, supposedly sound-proof office walls.

"God damn," Mason said in quiet growl. "How does he bloody know?"

Mason sped back to his desk, lifted the hand-held and dialled C.

"Oh, bloody Christ!" was the old man's greeting. "What?"

"Glass, sir."

"What in the hell is *glass*?"

"Glass. Henry Glass. Granada station liaison."

"Oh. Yes—what about him?"

"He knows. I don't know how, but he does."

"Jesus," C said, though his tone lacked any trace of dubiousness. "Can you fuck any more of this up? What does he know?"

"I don't know what he knows."

"Then why are we talking right now."

"Because he's here—right now—raising hell."

After some silence, C calmly said, "So you don't actually *know* he knows anything."

"What else would he be here for?"

"Well stop fooling about and talk to the man! Find out what he wants," C said, as if stating the obvious.

"I can't."

"Oh, grow some fucking bollocks, Agent Mason."

"No," Mason said, "I mean I literally can't. Just had him taken in to custody."

"What?"

"He was threatening people."

"You bloody idiot. Get down to holding and speak with him."

"And what do I say?"

"*What do you say.* Say he's acting like a bloody maniac! And if he accuses you of anything, you tell him you've no idea what he's talking about. You tell him he's a paranoid conspiracy theorist and you demand he reveal the source of these absurd accusations." C stopped for a moment. "Tell me we're on a secure line, Mason."

"We are, sir."

"Any word from Sparrow?"

"He should be on Zanzibar shortly."

"Duran and the woman?"

"Still offline," Mason said. "No email from her, and Duran's signal's been dead for some time. Of course, we still have a lock on the transponder. Sparrow's heading to it now."

"The safe house?"

"Yes."

"Good. Now go deal with Agent Glass. We don't want this rabid little pooch cocking everything up for us. And put on a good face for it, Tony. I find a sort of measured disbelief works wonders in these situations. And if he won't back off, then we'll resort to more creative tactics."

"Like what?" Mason asked.

"A bridge I'd prefer to keep at some distance for the time being."

"Right," Mason said, absently.

"Do me a favour, Tony."

"What's that?"

"Now that I'm up, might as well keep me appraised things on a more frequent basis—Glass, Sparrow, etcetera."

"Right. Sure, sir."

"You don't sound sure."

"Yes, well, I can't say the past few hours have been very easy. Seems things have gotten rather, I don't know, chaotic."

"Well, as the Americans used to say, welcome to the big leagues, Agent Mason."

Mason stared at the half-drained snifter on his desk. "I'll go see Glass now, sir."

"Do that. And remind him who's boss, will you."

Mason killed the call and sucked down the remaining booze. "Better pay off, all of this murderous nonsense."

***

The Lottos were back in the parlour. This time, everyone wide awake, a policeman parked on the edge of the sofa, uttering half-

John Ward

hearted reassurances in between bites of stewed chicken. Abasi sat beside the cop, trying to listen; trying to stay calm.

"In any event," the cop said, a mouthful garbling his words, "we've seen situations like this before. As the detective said earlier, I'm sure there will be a ransom call before morning."

"Are you?" Kesi asked. She was stooped on her hands and knees, scrubbing the blood stains clinging to the grout between the floor tiles. "It's almost dawn!"

"Calm down," Abasi said. "Just calm down. You haven't sat down once since ..."

"Since when?" she said, head cocked upward. "Since a man was murdered in my house? Since our nephew was stolen from us?"

"There will be no ransom demand," Babu said. "How many times must I say this?"

"We don't *know* that," Abasi said.

The old man turned to him. "Yes? You think so? Lie to us all you want—lie to the police even. But don't delude *yourself*. He's gone! And there's nothing any of us can do about it. In fact, officer, you might as well go." The cop looked up from his bowl, interested now. "You've got your body, you took your pictures," Babu said. "Your work here is done."

The policeman put his spoon down and said, very casually, "I mean this with no disrespect, sir. But everyone in this room should follow Mr Lotto's advice and simply calm down."

"I *am* Mr Lotto," Babu said. "The only Mr Lotto with enough sense to admit what's happened here."

The officer raised his eyebrows and went back to his stew, adding only, "I've been assigned to protect you for the rest of the evening. Once the next shift comes, I'll be out of your hair."

"I hope you're pleased with yourself," the old man said to Abasi.

"This is my fault?" Abasi shot up from the couch and stomped over to his father.

The cop leapt to his feet, soup bowl upended, splattering the floor. "Everyone relax," he said, struggling to insert himself between the two. "This is helping nothing!"

The commotion halted when Kesi shrieked. "Darweshi!"

She lunged through the open doorway and enveloped the child, kissing and hugging and shaking him about as if to challenge the unreality of his reappearance, testing the physical integrity of this unannounced miracle. Babu hobbled toward them with such speed, the cop gasped. Abasi trailed them more slowly, trembling a bit.

"Darweshi," Abasi said quietly, beginning to weep as he extended his hand to touch the boy. No one—not Abasi, Babu, Kesi or the cop—acknowledged the presence of the two strangers that had arrived at Darweshi's side.

After almost a full minute, the cop nodded at the boy, then looked up at Amir and Harkinder. "Where did you find him?"

"We haven't much time," Harkinder said in Swahili.

Abasi, eyes reddened and bulging, studied Harkinder and Amir as if the pair were creatures from a dimension beyond. "Who are you?"

Amir flicked his head at Harkinder, who began summarizing the surreal circumstances with great efficiency. As she ran through it, Kesi feverishly patted at Darweshi's head, kissing his eyebrows, examining his little body for signs of damage. The three men, however, hung on each word as if receiving revelation from the Archangel Jibril himself. When Harkinder reached the punchline—*we need your best boat*—Abasi had no response, too awestruck by the enormity of it all.

The cop, shaken free from hypnosis by Harkinder's very explicit logistical request, made a feeble attempt to assert control over the situation. "You, you can't take the boy anywhere. He should remain in police custody. This is a matter for the authorities."

Amir raised his nine, switched the safety on and lowered it into his thigh holster. Then he walked up to the stuttering cop and placed a heavy hand on the man's shoulder.

"I don't think you get it," Amir said in Arabic. Harkinder immediately translated the statement to Swahili and continued, verbatim, as Amir went on. "We are getting on a boat and leaving. The boy will be coming. There's nothing you can do to stop us. So don't try."

The cop retreated a step backward.

"I will go," Abasi said; a knife through the tension. "I will pilot the ship."

John Ward

Abasi watched as Amir and Harkinder exchanged a look. After a brief silence, Amir nodded. "Fine."

"Then get your things," Harkinder said. "Whatever you need. We're leaving now."

Kesi shot upright as if suddenly woken from deep sleep. "You can't leave! You can't take him!"

"My dear," Babu said gently. "We don't have a choice."

"We *do* have a choice," she said—a rare act of defiance.

"We don't," Babu said. "What they say—it's as I feared. We must leave here."

"*We?*" Kesi said.

"I, too, will go," Babu said, a resoluteness in it. "Abasi and I must go with Darweshi."

"He can't go," Amir said to Harkinder in English. "No fucking way. We've already wasted too much time here."

Babu turned and addressed Amir in nearly flawless English. "Sir, only death will force me to abandon this child. And trust me—at my age, death is a far less frightening prospect than you might think. So make what choices you must. And if you don't feel like killing an old man today, you'll just have to get used to my company."

"Jesus Christ," Amir said with groan. "Anybody else? Speak now or forever hold your fucking peace." He didn't wait for a response. "Good. Listen," he said, pointing at Abasi and Babu, "get a bag and fill it with as much food you can. Once we leave Zanzibar, that's all we'll have. I assume that truck out there is yours?"

"It is," Abasi said.

"Good. Get me the keys. We're leaving in three minutes."

***

Sparrow arrived to an empty nest and wasted little time scouring the premises for leads. The handler's computer—damaged as it was—confirmed what little intel Vauxhall had sent. Duran was headed off island.

Sparrow snapped the laptop shut and slid it into his rucksack. Down below, the sporadic drizzle had evolved into a soft but steady rain. Sparrow wiped the scooter seat with his glove, then slung the backpack over both shoulders, adjusted the straps, hopped on the moto, fired up the engine, sunk a helmet over his head and flipped down its visor.

In London, Sparrow would've laughed had someone suggested wearing a helmet. But for the mission's sake, it held a great deal of utility. Every inch of his pale flesh and wiry red hair now masked in leather, Kevlar, and polycarbonate plastic. The grey light of dawn no more a threat to his anonymity than the nylon RAF bomber he'd ditched back in the cockpit.

It took less than five minutes to reach a suitable surveillance location. Cutting the engine, he assembled the L118A2 and traded his unwieldy field glasses for the rifle's scope. The rain proved a problem though—forcing the pilot to wipe a finger across the scope's recessed lens every several seconds. Why the extended lip at the scope's rim allowed water to climb inward was something of a mystery. Especially, given that the rain was falling vertically—no angle to it, no wind to propel it sideways.

"Bloody distraction," the pilot whispered.

Distraction was right. The Lotto's truck arrived just as Sparrow began digging into his backpack for something more suitable to wipe the scope with.

"What the fuck?" he said, watching them shuffle out of the vehicle and onto the mooring. "What is this, a bloody family vacation?" Shiv and the boy—each with a bag over their shoulder— helped an elderly man up the ramp and onto the deck. Duran and another man followed, both lugging two sizeable, yellow containers, auxiliary fuel by the look of it.

Crouching behind the scooter, Sparrow picked the rifle back up and steadied it on the surface of the seat. The scope was a mess, providing only distorted forms. Still, it was only 100 metres.

"Fuck it."

The first shot was a ghost—wide—into the water; the snipping whisper of the round unnoticed by the targets. The second and third registered as pings off the trawler's iron hull. Sparrow's targets scurried. In a panic, he sent off three more, trying to adjust, but making no progress.

John Ward

As Sparrow tossed the rifle down and reached for his helmet, a volley of return fire flew overhead, one round blowing a jagged hole into the storage compartment of his scooter. Sparrow dropped to his belly, drew the pistol from his waist, and rolled backward from the scooter. In a frenetic burst, he shot upward and broke into a full sprint toward a waist-high concrete partition at the shoulder of the narrow road leading to the dockyard entrance.

Behind cover, he listened for more shots. When there were none, he stood to take aim, but found the trawler already pulling away from its birth. It was big rig, and moved sluggishly through the crowded inner harbour, a wake of gurgling brown suds rolling outward from the stern. In open water, though, the old boat would find its stride.

"Fuck all," he screamed, lowering his pistol and bolting back toward his scooter.

By the time Sparrow reached the launch and boarded his skiff, the Lotto's trawler had made significant headway. But the skiff's oversized outboard was a monster. He closed on them quickly, rain and froth ricocheting off his visor like someone had a garden hose to it.

Vision half-obscured, the pilot failed to notice Amir at the trawler's stern, raising a black cylinder to his shoulder.

It all happened in a flash: the skiff leaping up from under him; the unnatural roar of fire displacing water, the odd sensation of gravity abruptly inverted. The sky beneath him. The ocean above.

Then, *whoosh*—a wall of liquid crashed over him.

That it wasn't a direct hit became clear once the salt stung his eyes. A blurry second later, Sparrow's limbs regained control. And with a couple scissoring kicks, his head emerged from the water. Forcing the mask free, he swivelled side to side, and caught view of the capsized skiff, rocking up and down in the waves several metres away. On the topsy-turvy horizon, the big trawler appeared no larger than a toy boat.

"Fuck," the pilot shouted, slapping his palms hard against the surf. "You're fuckin' dead, Duran!"

"Where is she?" Glass said, the question a muddled whisper, his jaw swollen from the scuffle.

Mason motioned for the guards to leave. When they hesitated, Mason scowled. "Go—that's an order." Stepping into the cell, he addressed Glass in a delicate, vaguely sympathetic tone. "Now what did you say, Henry?"

"Where is she," Glass repeated, suppressing his rage enough to get the words out more clearly.

"Who?"

Glass shook his head, synapses firing terrible thoughts to the fore. "Did you kill her?"

"Christ, Henry. What in the bloody hell are you talking about?"

"Don't bullshit me," Glass said in a roar, tears beginning to well. "Did you kill her?"

Mason took several paces forward and lowered his voice. "Have you gone mad? I haven't the slightest clue what you're referring to. Now, tell me, what is this about?" When Glass had no reply, Mason's tone ascended a full register. "Look around you, Henry—this isn't a joke! That stunt you pulled upstairs? It could very well end your career. I can't help you unless—"

Glass came violently to his feet, hands grasping for Mason's collar. As they stumbled back toward the open cell door, Mason bellowed. "Security!"

They were back in a rush, restraining Glass by both arms, shoving him inward. With a hiss, the heavy, transparent door slid shut, Glass on the floor, collecting himself, Mason standing in the corridor, trying to look calm.

"Christ, Henry. I didn't want to have to do it like this—like I'm interrogating some sort of criminal," Mason said, an index finger on the intercom button, free hand straightening his jacket lapels.

Again, he turned to the guards. "I'm fine. You can bugger off now." When they did, Mason returned his eyes to the dishevelled spy. "So?"

Glass ran a shaky hand through his bangs and took a seat on the short metal bench fastened to rear wall of the cell. "Marissa."

"What about her?" Mason's face had a pinched look, brow forced downward in feigned confusion.

"What happened to her?"

"What in God's name are you talking about?"

"Don't fuck me about, Mason! What did you fucking do to her?"

"Okay—*this*? What we're doing right now? It's what's referred to as talking in circles. I ask you a question, and rather than receiving an answer, I get another question in return. Given you're the one who's found his way into a holding cell this evening, perhaps it would behoove you to cooperate. So," Mason said, "let's try this again—what is this about? And for the record, I'm not sure where Marissa White is. But if I had to venture a guess, I'd say she's at home, fast asleep, like every other sensible person in this city. More to the point, what's she got—"

"I know about Zanzibar, you bastard."

"What about Zanzibar?"

"Fuck off, Tony."

"Where do you get off?" Mason said, each word sharper than the prior. "You know, I actually came down here to *help* you? Instead, I get *this*. Bloody ridiculous."

"I know you ordered Duran to kill the boy."

Mason drew his head back, the flesh below his chin wrinkling like an accordion. "That's absurd! You've gone so far off the reservation it's almost laughable. *Kill the boy*. I think you need an updated psych eval!"

"You're a fucking liar."

"Careful now, Henry." Mason's voice had reduced to a low sizzle, grease popping from the surface of a skillet. "Don't cross a line you can't come back from."

Glass shook his head again. "You *are* a liar, Tony—and I can prove it."

"*Can* you now?"

"Wait until I fucking get out of here—"

"When you get out of here, you'll be prosecuted in a special tribunal! I can list the charges now if you'd like to begin preparing a defence! Given the cockamamie conspiracy you've dreamt up, I'd say an insanity plea is your best option."

Glass remained silent for a moment, weighing his options. Then he rose to his feet and approached the see-through door. "Put me on the stand. I'd love to tell a magistrate what I know. I'm sure they'd find what I had to say about GLogiX very interesting."

Mason stared, jaw rigid like he'd suddenly contracted Tetanus. Then he shook his head and said, "What the fuck do you—?"

"I was at the Lanesborough, you fucking imbecile."

Mason leaned forward, upper teeth clenched over his bottom lip. "So *fucking* what."

Glass had him now. Not that it was any consolation. "I don't give a shit what you do to me, Tony. It doesn't matter at this point. The game is up, you fucking wanker. Have fun when Duran gets back."

Mason stood straight, glanced down the hall at the guards and then crept forward to the intercom again. "I heard Duran may have run into some trouble down there. Too bad. We almost had a cure on our hands." Upright again, Mason fixed his tie and turned to leave.

"Eh," Glass said, waiting until Mason flashed his head back. "Karma's a fucking bitch, *Tony*."

Watching Mason disappear from view, Glass stood at the door for a while, pressing his palms to its surface, head cocked back. After a minute or so, he returned to the bench behind him. Karma's a bitch. That's the best you could come up with?

Glass's stomach began to turn—remnants of red wine and scotch taking their revenge. He'd gotten Marissa killed, hadn't he? Digging around, pushing her involvement.

Maybe she *wasn't* dead, though. Maybe she was just fine. Went back home. Reconsidered the whole thing. Sent her driver away—decided it could wait until morning. Maybe Mason was right, maybe she was sleeping—nude—her beautiful body, unscathed.

Fuck you.

Don't you dare submit to convenient delusions. If she were okay, she'd have been here by now. This is all your fault. Couldn't help yourself, could you?

Duran better be alive and kicking.

TWENTY

Brit was beginning to confront the loneliness of her position. She hadn't heard from Glass for over an hour. And the last they'd spoken, he was in a frenzy—convinced Marissa White was dead, certain he'd be next.

The plan he'd persuaded Brit to initiate was shaky. She'd told him as much, too. "Henry, this is bordering on ludicrous. All the makings of a monumental catastrophe."

"Desperate fucking times," he'd said in return.

And that much was impossible to argue.

According to plan, Brit's first call went to Corporal Maggie O'Connor, the sole woman in Granada donning RAF credentials. More importantly, Maggie was a seasoned chopper pilot. Earlier in the year, O'Connor had been assigned as Brit's air escort to the satellite facilities. Over the course of several months they'd shuttled back and forth between Granada, Almeria City, Malaga, and the prison at Nijar.

When Brit reached out, Maggie was—despite the hour—up and at it within minutes. Supremely focused, questions limited to logistics. Timeline. Aircraft. Equipment. Permission to select a co-pilot.

"Are we going in hot?"

Brit hadn't an answer to the final bit. Left it open-ended. "Prepare for all contingencies," she said to O'Connor.

The second call was to the coms man, Davis. It was a shot in the dark, but perhaps he could confirm Duran's progress off island.

Davis grumbled at Brit's request. "What in Christ is *Duran* doing down there?"

"Need-to-know basis," Brit said. "Now get up—this is time sensitive."

Another question from the middle-aged malcontent: "I'm assuming he's not stationary?"

"No," she said. "On a boat. Distinctly northbound vector. Point A to point B."

Davis issued a warning. "Needle in a bloody haystack, General."

"I'm aware. Just do your best, please."

The third was a fruitless attempt to re-establish contact with Glass. It went straight to voicemail. Brit hung up, sat back in her seat, and lit a smoke. "There's no way he's dead," she said aloud. "No fucking way."

A few puffs later, she leapt up and gathered her things—jacket off the chair back, laptop from the desk, extra gun from the safe. Glancing down at her wristwatch she snubbed out the half-smoked butt.

Down the hall she poked her head into the ops room and nodded to the night commander. "I'm going."

"Long night, General?" he said, eyes on the backpack slung over Brit's shoulder.

"Yeah…everything good, here?"

"Pretty quiet. Police are dealing with a body in Sec. 3—doesn't look like they'll need help though."

"Okay," Brit said, scanning the room. "Step into the hallway with me for a second?"

As the night commander made for the door, the young soldier manning the dispatch console raised his eyes, a touch of intrigue at hand.

"Close the door behind you," Brit said to the commander.

Out in the corridor, the man's face wore a look of concern. "Something wrong, General Tillman?"

"I'm dealing with a situation that will take me away from the office for an undetermined amount of time. In my absence, I'll need you to run the day-to-day. Check in with me only if absolutely necessary."

"Ma'am, can I ask—"

"No," she said plainly. And they both remained quiet for a moment, only the buzz of the fluorescent ceiling lights filling the silence of the intricately-carved, ancient corridor.

"General Tillman," the commander said softly, "What should I tell command staff?"

"Tell the boys I'll be back soon," she said with a forced smile. "You should try and get some rest right now. You'll need to be up for morning briefing."

"Right, ma'am."

"Good then. Have fun ordering these brutes around—I'll be interested to know how it went when I get back."

***

The Condor required a four-man crew. Tonight, it had two women—one of whom knew nothing about aviation—and a pimply trainee with less than a hundred flight hours under his belt.

"Desperate times," Brit muttered, slipping the helmet over her short, blonde bob, and adjusting the seatbelt.

With a flick of Maggie's wrist, the blades set upon their mighty business. A minute later, the gargantuan bird was airborne, Tarmac shrinking beneath it. Brit breathed heavily, examining the gauges she'd been assigned stewardship of.

"Don't worry," Maggie said. "Once we're up, everything gets far less complicated."

Brit eyed the kid. He looked reassuringly at ease in the cockpit, engrossed in his work like a veteran. "Where you from, private?" Brit asked, diaphragm steadying with some small talk.

"Apologies, General," Maggie said. "Going to ask you to refrain from distracting Private Blake—this is his first real run in the Condor."

"Sorry, Maggie."

"No worries, ma'am. We're all a little anxious."

Brit tipped her head toward the window. Below, the cluttered lights of Granada faded into the sparse twinkle of the labour camps, the ridge-line of the Sierra a dark wrinkle behind it.

"Manchester, ma'am—me blood runs powder blue."

Brit pried her eyes from the vista for a look at Blake. "Football reference, I gather."

"Man City, ma'am—died in the wool."

"So you know a bit about the sport, Private?"

Maggie weighed in before the kid could get carried away. "Just make sure you're doing your job, now, Private."

"Of course, ma'am," he said, straightening up. "Next stop, Favagnana, ma'am."

Brit, eyes back on the bleakness of Sector Five: "Any problem making arrangements?"

"None at all, General Tillman," Maggie said. "I know the boys down there. Stopped over a handful of times during my stint in Monaco."

Brit grinned. "Clearly didn't look close enough at your file, Maggie. Pilgrim in the Holy Land, were we?"

Maggie smirked. "Bloody children's crusade, ma'am."

"*Holy Land*," Blake said. His attempt to join in on the fun drew a chuckle from both women.

"Private," Brit said, "by morning, you, too, shall have something to talk in code about."

"Right," he said, tone betraying bewilderment. "I appreciate the opportunity, General Tillman."

"Thank me when it's over, lad."

The unintended heaviness of the comment shut them all up for a while. As the Condor barrelled forward, rotors casting thunder down on the tin roofs and burlap bunk tents of the African ghetto, the faintest blue glimmer of first light appeared on the eastern horizon.

Brit pinched two fingers over the bridge of her nose, squeezed the thin flesh several times and whispered, "Better get your ass to Cairo, Duran."

***

"Bad news, indeed," C said to Mason. Though, the old man didn't sound too surprised. "Where's the pilot now?"

Mason lowered the phone, shook his head, then returned it to his ear. "On his way back to the mainland."

"And Duran?"

"Duran and party are headed northbound," Mason said, words a bit sluggish. "I've told Sparrow to intercept them when the boat stops to refuel."

Again, C prodded. "How can you be sure?"

"Of what?"

"Where they're going."

John Ward

Mason sighed with exasperation. "Tillman."

"What about her?"

"She and Duran have been in touch," Mason said. He was staring out the office window, passively scanning the opposite bank of the Thames. The mist had only partially cleared, a thin white smattering of it laying over the river like a ruffled bed sheet. "And she's gone after him."

"Hmm. Coming to the *rescue,* is she?"

"Planning to collect them in Cairo."

"Ambitious."

"Quite."

"Well you should get down there too then, shouldn't you?"

"*To Cairo?*"

"Yes."

"That's—"

"That's *what?* Tell me, dear—*what* is it?" There was a pause. "Unnecessary? Overboard? Insane, perhaps? Is *that* what it is?" When Mason remained quiet, C offered a bit of advice. "I don't think so. I think at this juncture you've a salvage operation on your hands, Agent Mason. A clean-up job. And don't mistake it for anything else."

"Sparrow can still intercept them."

"Can he though? You'd guarantee that? Tell me what part of this has gone right so far." C laughed, as if finding some pleasure in Mason's failure.

"So, you're relying on *me* to finish the job?"

"It's your job, damn it! Not mine—not *anyone* else's. You had a real opportunity here, Tony. But so far, you've done nothing but cock it up at every critical juncture."

"*Me?*"

"Who *else* is in charge?"

Silence. Then Mason, addendum. "I can't just fly a jet down to Cairo. What about a drone—wouldn't that be far simpler?"

"If it was about simplicity, we'd have dropped a laser guided bomb on the boy's home a week ago. Jesus, Tony. Maybe you should head home and get some rest." There was a sinister clearing of the throat. "Be careful on your way, though," C said. "Dangerous things seem to be lurking in the fog these days."

"What does that mean?" Mason asked, shock squeezing his pitch.

"Please. That you would think yourself above it is laughable, Tony."

Mason stepped away from the window, looked at the scotch bottle, and took a deep breath. "How am I to get down there?"

"How is Tillman getting down there?"

"Helicopter. One of those big ones."

"I'm sure the same could be arranged."

"A chopper from here to Cairo?"

"My lord. Just go home."

"I'm not going home, sir."

"Then charter a flight to Italy, you nitwit. I'm sure you can find a heli pilot to escort you from there."

"Jesus Christ, this is a royal *fucking* headache."

Mason had only muttered this bit, but C seized it as an opportunity. "No, no," he said. "A royal *fucking* headache would be a parliamentary inquest. Vicious *migraine*, more accurately. Though I've never been the subject of one—knock on wood— I've sat through my fair share. They're no fun. Tend to end badly for the poor soul sitting in front of the microphone. A dose of protracted humiliation typically followed by criminal charges. Not my cup of tea," C said with a snort. "But if you go in for that sort of thing, be my guest—roll the dice with Sparrow. See how it all ends."

"But—"

"And by the way, don't expect *me* to fall on a sword when Duran is summoned to Westminster. I've got no intention of spending my retirement in a cell."

"This whole thing was *your* idea!"

"Was it? Says who? Duran? Glass? Tillman? Our private sector friends? It's your bloody paw prints all over everything! You think I'd be so idiotic?"

"And what if I were recording this right now?" Mason said, a kid kicking at the shins of an adult.

"But you're *not*. Are you, dear?"

Mason slumped down in his leather desk chair and swivelled

John Ward

slowly round to face the window. Day had broken, and his fate lay before him like a foreboding landscape, all swamp and thorns, a fog-strewn mountain on the horizon, its summit invisible.

"Tony."

"What?"

"Get off your ass and stop being such a bloody woman about it. Who knows—things may yet work out in your favour."

"Sir."

"What is it?"

"Go fuck yourself."

C laughed. "That's the fighting spirit, old boy! Now go find yourself a pilot."

Mason hung up with C and put in a call to the RAF, drink in hand as he ran through the itinerary. He'd only a short window before departure. Rather than using it wisely—packing a bag, sobering up with a couple cups of Java—he ventured to the bowels of Vauxhall.

When Mason arrived at the holding cells, he received a warm salutation from Henry Glass: "What the fuck do you want?"

"You're awake, I see."

Indeed, Glass was—though the agent now had the worn-out look of a man who'd seen too much. Less a spy, more of an aging infantry captain perpetually stuck on the front. The wrinkles on Glass's face looked more prominent than usual, eyes bloodshot, harder.

"I said what the fuck do you want, you oily little prick?"

Mason closed his eyes for several seconds, then returned his finger to the intercom button. "I want you to know something."

"Let me guess—"

"Glass," Mason said with a heavy breath. "Just hear me out. It won't take long."

"Take all the time you want," Glass said with a shrug. "You've a captive audience—should be right in your wheelhouse."

"I don't know what you know… " Mason paused, wobbling slightly. "Or what you *think* you know … " His whole body suddenly began to shake, as if he were fighting to maintain balance on the edge of a cliff, violent winds rushing up from the canyon below.

Glass squinted. "What the fuck is wrong with you?"

"I'm fine," Mason said, eyes pinched tight, head dipping. Sweat had accumulated in Mason's quaffed hair, scalp slick under the overhead glare.

"Guard? Better come get him!"

Mason's hand shot upward in protest. "No … no, I'm alright. Just need to … " A heavy stream of brown fluid erupted from his mouth. Keeled over, he let the second wave release itself without resistance. The guards halted several paces away.

"Fucking *kidding* me," the big one said.

"I'm fine," Mason said. He was keeled over, hands still on his knees. "I'll be fine."

Glass grinned. "Bad oyster, Tony?"

Mason stood up straight and stared at Glass. "Fuck you." Then, mumbling, he turned away. "Sick of this."

"*Clearly,*" Glass said. "Come on, now—out with it, Agent Mason. You were about to spill the beans. Cop to it, right old chap? Come on, tell these boys what you've done. It'll make you feel a whole lot better. No shame in owning up to it. Go on—tell them about Agent White!"

"Fuck off," Mason shouted, halfway down the hall now.

Glass looked at the two soldiers standing outside his cell. "What are you waiting for boys—better pick that up."

واحد و عشرون

They'd been huddled in the cabin for at least two hours, watching the rain come down over the bow and listening old man bemoan the drought back in Zanzibar. When the clouds finally parted, the old man grimaced and shook his head.

"See?" he said. "Too good to be true."

Amir ventured outside for some headspace.

Cigarette clamped between his lips, Amir leaned against the starboard rail. As he watched the waves split and ripple off the hull, the deck trembled and swayed beneath his boots.

It was all colliding in Amir's head now. The greedy sun. The vastness of nature. The strange degradation of man's capacity to control it. He tossed his spent smoke into the ocean and lit a second.

Jeddo had once said it all made sense—humanity's sudden and catastrophic defeat at the hands of Mother Nature. He'd said Allah's patience for man's wastefulness had worn thin. Not that the Red Death was an act of vengeance, per se. More of a recalibration. A spiritual rebalancing that returned humankind to its more primitive, trimmer self.

When Amir asked why Allah had purged the earth of so many faithful Muslims, the old man promptly responded that paradise must have had a lot of vacancies waiting to be filled. Amir was too young to appreciate the point—that death could be a form of mercy—that dying could be a reward.

Instead, he'd contemplated the empty hostel down the road, no more tourists to fill its dusty bunks.

He got it now though. And wondered when *his* time would come. Yes, that infamous, unanswerable, recurring question that reared its ugly little head every time he cocked the slide back on his nine or kissed his boy goodbye. Could this finally be it?

Not yet, he thought. Not fucking yet.

Too many of James's football matches left to watch. Too many beers that needed drinking. Too much to laugh about at the dinner table. Too many things he still needed to say to Cristina. And ask. Well, Amir, get out of this jam, you better hop to it, buddy.

Even with the worst weighing on him, Amir felt no anxiety. Maybe it was the water—the bob of the deck beneath him. What a privilege, he suddenly realized. The sea. To experience it up close. This broad, blue, infinite field—a world unto itself—existing only in the imaginations of his landlocked countrymen.

When he got back, he would tell James all about it. How the gulls circled. How the briny air smelt. How shafts of light steamed down through the warm water of the Indian Ocean, schools of fish in purple patches piloting the currents in unison. The world glittered in shades of life-affirming blue. A brilliant contrast to the barren valleys of Southern Spain.

Life, he thought. The good, the bad, and the beautiful.

Unfortunately, *the bad* was one click south and closing in fast. Amir was halfway to the bridge when he heard the buzz of Sparrow's supercharged propellers. The plane came in low, wings tilting slightly as it approached.

"Jesus fucking Christ," Amir whispered, too amazed to panic. The speed with which the pilot had zeroed in on their position was fucking outrageous. Then Amir's instincts kicked in. He rushed into the cabin, grabbed the gun bag, and ordered the boy and the old man below deck.

"What do we do?" Harkinder asked. "Can he fire at us?"

"I don't know," Amir said, trying to recall the plane's design, whether it was weaponized. "Keep driving," Amir said to Abasi. Abasi nodded, eyes forward. "Take this," he said, switching the safety off one of the automatic rifles and handing it to Harkinder.

As she took it from him, Sparrow roared past.

"He would've fired at us if he could," Amir said, stepping out of the door to gain a view of the plane circling round for another pass.

"What am I supposed to do with this," Harkinder said, joining him on the deck. She held the machine gun out from her body as if it were something poisonous.

"Shoot it."

John Ward

"I don't know how to use it!"

"Just aim and pull the trigger—not complicated." Amir nodded at the gun. "Just make sure to brace yourself. And wait for my mark."

"I don't get it—what is he doing?"

"If we're lucky, he's just taking a look, checking our course. I expect he'll to try an intercept when we've stopped to refuel. We shouldn't wait for that, though."

"We're going to shoot him down?" she said, looking terrified.

"We're going to try," he confirmed, leading her toward a suitable place on the bow. "Get down like this." With the grenade launcher on his shoulder, Amir stooped to one knee, loaded a round and steadied his aim.

"Can't he see us?"

"Yes," he said, tracking the plane's approach. "When he gets within range—"

"What's within range?"

"Stop panicking. When he gets within two hundred metres, start firing—and don't stop until the magazine is empty."

But as the plane came within distance, she failed to follow through on his instructions.

"Now!" he screamed. With a spastic lurch her gun clacked out a flurry of poorly placed rounds, the recoil knocking her thin torso backward. It wasn't enough. Amir's plan to provoke Sparrow into a lateral manoeuvre had failed. As the plane ripped past, Amir spun around and fired toward the twin prop's tail.

"Fuck," Amir barked, watching the grenade coast past its target by a significant margin. Like a frustrated parent, he tore the rifle away from Harkinder. "Goddamn it," he said, raising the gun to his shoulder and taking aim. But the plane was out of range now, rising in altitude and tacking east. Twenty seconds later it was out of view.

"Sorry," Harkinder said. "I've never shot one of these."

"How the fuck have you survived in this business?"

"I'm sorry," she repeated.

He looked at her gangly limbs, loose clothes, her oddly innocent big, brown eyes—and saw a girl instead of a woman.

"It's fine," Amir said, lighting up a cigarette. "He'll be back before you know it."

***

"Muhammed was illiterate," Babu said in Arabic. "Did you know that?"

It wasn't clear to Amir whom he was addressing, but the boy responded. "I knew that, Babu."

"Good." Babu smiled, eyes shifting to Darweshi. "And did you know he never proclaimed himself to be Devine?"

"Oh, how do *you* know that," Abasi said with a snort.

"Have some faith, son." The old man returned his attention to Amir. "Do you pray?"

Amir looked around. "Who me?"

"Yes, you."

"He does," the boy said. "I saw him."

"How did you know I was Muslim?" Amir asked the old man.

"I didn't—that's why I asked. I used to think I could tell who the faithful ones were. But you know, life is ... you never know."

"Please spare the man," Abasi said in English.

The cabin was cramped, but they were all packed into it. Abasi at the helm, Amir beside him, the boy, his Babu and Harkinder in a cluster toward its rear. Outside, the clouds had cleared completely, the calm open ocean and blue sky rolling out in every direction, an almost indiscernible divide between air and water.

Amir, cognizant of the father-son tension turned fully toward Abasi and said, "It's fine, it's not a problem." Then he faced the old man. "I'm half Arab. But my mother's father, he raised me in The Faith."

"Your *Jeddo*."

"Yes."

"He taught you to pray?"

Amir thought about it. "He taught me everything."

With a subtle, wrinkly smile, the old man said, "Where are you from, young man?"

Abasi shook his head. "Babu, leave him be."

"Spain," Amir said after a few seconds.

"*Spain*. I thought that might be the case. Whereabouts?"

"Granada."

"Granada! One of the world's great cities."

"I wouldn't know," Amir said. Harkinder looked on with interest. "It's a bit of a disaster now … Have you ever been?"

The old man nodded, smiling broadly. "Many, many years ago. Truly gorgeous place. And so much history. The Alhambra? Magnificent—a jewel of Islamic culture."

"It's changed."

"Yes?" the old man said, a graveness creeping into his tone. "Do you still visit?"

"You could say that." Amir paused. "When I was young, we'd pray there every morning, my grandfather and I."

"How blessed you are."

Or haunted, Amir thought. As he studied the old man and the boy at his side, a pang of longing tightened Amir's chest.

"Would it help to pray?" the old man asked, staring into Amir's pained eyes.

"Now?"

"Yes," the old man said. "I think all of us could use a nice talk with Allah."

"Okay."

Babu looked at the boy and returned to Arabic. "Darweshi—why don't you join us?"

Darweshi nodded and gave his Babu a sweet look—familiarity and uncertainty tied together. One that made Amir immediately think of James.

Harkinder and Abasi remained inside as the three of them walked out under the sun and onto the deck of the stern. The old man rested his cane near the wheelhouse encasing the spool of cable from which the nets were cast.

"My knees aren't what they used to be," he said to Amir, who provided a hand as the old man steadied himself for prayer. The boy flanked Babu's other side, holding him by the forearm. "Thank you," the old man said. "Now—shall we begin?"

They did so in unison, Darweshi and Amir each buttressing

the old man with a supportive hand as he strained to meet the physical requirements of the ritual. And so it went—the bowing, the kneeling, the prostration—three good Muslims embracing under the brassy glare of Allah's midday sun.

What the boy and his grandfather experienced it as, Amir could only guess. But Amir felt strengthened by the communal spirit of the moment—a rare and novel return to faith as a shared experience. It had been years since he'd prayed with anyone else—anyone living, that is.

When it was over, the old man said, "Good! Don't you feel better now?"

He was looking at Amir, but Darweshi answered. "Yes, Babu. I do."

"Good," the old man said. "Now go keep your uncle Abasi company—he's probably getting bored in there. Be careful on your way in though, okay?"

"Yes, Babu," the boy said, then sprung toward the old man, hugged him, and quickly set off for the cabin.

When the boy was out of ear shot, the old man addressed Amir in English. "I realize I don't even know your name, sir. Now, I understand if you don't want to tell me, but I figured I'd ask out of politeness—what do you prefer to be called?"

"Amir … and that's my given name. Amir Omar Duran."

The old man leaned heavily on his cane, eyebrows raised. "Well then—you're telling me the truth, aren't you?"

"I've got no reason to lie."

"Don't all spies lie?"

"Not a spy," Amir said after a moment. "Not really."

"So why are you here then, Mr Duran?"

"Long story. But if it's worth anything to you, it wasn't my choice."

"The will of Allah, then."

"Maybe."

"Definitely. Definitely the will of Allah. Have you ever made the pilgrimage, Mr Duran?"

"Please, call me Amir. And no, never. What is your name?"

"These days everyone calls me Babu. You might as well, too."

Then with a flicker of a smile, "Besides, I get easily confused at this age—so let's keep it simple."

"Could have fooled me," Amir said, taking out a cigarette.

"Those will kill you, Amir."

Amir shrugged. "We'll see."

"Ah—I *do* see. You're one of those fatalistic types. Makes sense in your profession. Whatever profession that is, I'm not quite certain of. But I suppose you'd have to be."

"Allah's will."

"Touché," Babu said with a chuckle. "*Allah's will.*" Then Babu straightened up as far as his sloping spine would allow. "Be honest with me, Amir. Do you believe we can make it—all the way to Cairo—with that maniac after us?"

Amir exhaled deeply, smoke fluttering swiftly from his mouth into the rippling currents of wind.

"Be honest with me now," the old man repeated.

"I think we can."

Babu shifted on his cane and shook his head. "So you *do* lie. You don't think we'll make it—I can tell by your eyes."

Amir gave him a hard look—a look the old man didn't really deserve. "It doesn't really matter what I think. What matters is how we handle the situation. And for the record, I just don't know. How the *fuck* could I?" Amir took a deep draw of smoke, steadied his tone. "I'm sorry. What I can tell you is this: I've been in a lot of difficult situations before. A lot. Ones that have required me to go head to head with some incredibly dangerous men." Babu tilted his head as Amir went on. "Most of those men are either dead or sitting in a cell right now. I admit—this situation—this scenario we're in right now? I've never been through something like this. I'm not a spy. I'm not some sort of experienced operative that specializes in this sort of thing. I'm a fucking cop. But, I can also say—" He took another drag and let it out. "I can say, I will do everything in my power to keep you, your son, and that little boy in there safe. That's a promise."

Babu nodded and gave Amir a placid smile. A swift gale swept across the deck. Amir flicked his cigarette into the water and cast his eyes outward, scanning for signs of the winged mercenary.

TWENTY-TWO

The Z-7 Zeus's frigid cargo hold was a Spartan contrast to the heated mahogany and leather cabins Tony Mason had grown accustomed to. No attendant in heels. No magazines. No dry bar stocked with booze.

Mason's off-manifest jaunt was proving anything but smooth. Indeed, the sheer mass of the rig provided nothing in the way of stability. With every patch of turbulence, the nylon safety belt pinched at Mason's ruffled sport coat and wedged him deeper into the rigid contours of the steel and rubber torture device that passed for a seat.

And then there was the deafening roar of the jet's turbines. A thousand nails down a thousand chalkboards, amplified over a thousand loudspeakers.

The only other person subjected to this distinct little slice of hell was the pilot C assigned to the second leg of the mission. Mason had arranged to connect with a chopper crew on arrival to the Italian coast. But when he showed up at Northolt, there was the pilot, standing on the Tarmac, duffle bag at his boots, smoking a cigarette and jibber-jabbering with all three members of the Z7's flight crew.

The way he'd introduced himself was distastefully informal. "You must be Tony. I'm an Anthony, too. Call me Ant. I'll be handling the second stretch."

When Mason requested his credentials, the man smirked and without a single *sir* or *sorry, sir*, said, "No can do. Need-to-know basis."

"On whose orders?" Mason had said.

The pilot had shaken his head in refusal. "Need-to-know."

Now, the man sat across from him, eyes closed, appearing to be—through some miraculous feat of training, or complete lethargy—sleeping. "Jesus, where did they find these men," Mason whispered. "Bunch of bloody pirates."

Eying the pistol holstered on the pilot's thigh, Mason wriggled his seat, and then checked his watch. "Christ."

"You alright, there, Tony?"

Mason looked up to find Ant's staring back at him. "When do we touch down?" Mason asked.

"Just relax."

"*Relax*," Mason said, eyes back on Ant's sidepiece.

"Don't get your panties in a bunch—all goes right, you won't even need your weapon."

"That's not what I asked," Mason said. "I'm concerned with logistics. Are you sure you've a good sense of timing?"

"Listen," the guy said, "I'm not a fucking rookie. Don't overcomplicate this."

"Do you even know what we're doing down there?"

The man smiled. "You don't spend much time in the field, do you?" Mason hadn't a retort. "Just sit tight," Ant said. "It'll be over before you know it."

Mason leaned back against the vibrating headrest and ground his teeth. Just as the pilot closed his eyes again, Mason said, "You like that nickname—*Ant*? Or is it something you got stuck with as a child?"

Ant grinned. "You like *Tony*?"

"Why don't you call me Agent Mason from here on out." Ant laughed. Mason grimaced. "What's so funny?"

Ant raised an index finger and pointed round the hold. "Pay attention, Tony. You're a long way from home."

"What's that supposed to bloody mean?"

"Means you don't get to give orders anymore. You, my friend, are simply along for the ride. So pipe the fuck down and get some rest. As I said, it'll all be over before you know it."

***

"You're in better spirits."

"A bit of food and coffee tend to do that for me, ma'am."

"Good," Brit said, adjusting her headset. Then, with a smile, "Davis, you better not leave tortilla crumbs all over that consul. Damn expensive piece of equipment."

"Course not, ma'am."

"So," she said into the mouthpiece, "find him?"

"In a manner of speaking, General. Bit of a process."

"Where is he?"

"Um, I expect he's roughly 100 kilometres north-northeast of Mombasa—making fairly good progress, too."

"You *expect*?"

"I don't have a direct lock."

"You lost him?"

"I didn't, ma'am. Never had a lock, actually."

"You've lost me."

"Well," Davis said. "Bit of a workaround, ma'am. Struggled to locate him myself, so I started poking around the network. Found someone at Vauxhall was tracking movement in that region. Less we've other active ops down there, I'd say they've eyes on your boy. Though I must say, whoever's watching him doesn't have very consistent data. Course is entered as plot points—not an unbroken signal."

"Fine," Brit said. "Stay on it."

"Ma'am," Davis said, some tension in his tone. "I've got to warn you. I can't access that system for more than a few seconds at a time without alerting Vauxhall. And even then … if someone's paying attention closely enough, we're at risk of—"

She cut him off. "Just stay on it, Davis."

There was a fuzzy pause over the radio.

"General Tillman," Davis said, tone oddly diminutive, "would you mind telling me what Duran's up to?"

"Yes, I would mind. Now please, keep me updated more frequently. We've been in the air for far too long to just be receiving word now."

"Well, it was rather complicated for me to—"

"Davis!"

"General Tillman?"

"The proper response would be *yes, ma'am. Right away, ma'am.* Save the rest."

"Yes, ma'am."

"Thank you, Davis." Brit paused for a moment. "Listen, can you figure out who's tracking him at Vauxhall?"

"It's someone with higher sec clearance. Don't have access to that portion of the index."

"I need you to make a call for me then."

Hesitation. "To whom, ma'am?"

"Agent Tony Mason."

"Um, okay. What do I say?"

"Ask him if he's heard from Duran."

"Okay, I'll be back to you shortly."

"Good. Over."

"Over and out."

Brit tilted her heavy, helmet-crowned head toward the window and took in the burnt, rippled earth below. She was on the right side of the Condor's cabin. Her view faced southward toward the vacant, dusty reaches of the northern Sahara. The desert stretched out in a thousand shades of brown, the occasional, black up-cropping of an abandon oil field breaking up the monotony. It was a skeletal world, reduced to its natural rudiments, only the faintest trace of bygone civilization clinging to its harsh crust.

Brit shuddered and returned her attention to the cockpit. "You've your masks, correct? Should've asked before departure."

"Aye," Maggie said.

The kid nodded. "Got mine too, ma'am."

"Good," Brit said, eyes back on the otherworldly waste.

"Ma'am," Blake said. "Can I ask you something?"

"Speak freely, private."

"Nobody seems to agree on it. It's gone, it's not gone. Which is it?"

"The Death?"

"Yes, ma'am."

"Bit of both, I suppose ... I don't say that to be evasive, either. From what I know ... well, without going into detail, it's thought to be active some places."

"How could it be active if everyone else is dead? Besides Russia and Japan, I mean." There was silence for a moment. Then, the young pilot's eyes came alive, revelation afoot. "Christ," he whispered.

"Life finds a way," Brit said.

Maggie's brow rose. "You can say that again."

Brit ran a finger along her jawline. "You remember when the news came down?"

"Like yesterday."

"Where were you?"

"The academy, ma'am. Flight school. Commander walked right into the mess hall and delivered the announcement. Never seen anything like it—could hear a pin drop when he finished. Then everyone rushed off to make phone calls to family."

"I was in the recruiting office, if you can believe it," Brit said.

"You enlisted after me? Ascended the ranks pretty quick, ma'am."

"I'm not sure I'd call twenty plus years quick, Maggie."

"People put in forty and never get to lieutenant."

"Right place, right time," Brit said.

"What ever happened to General Thatcher?" Maggie asked.

"Thatcher? He's okay, I think. Recovering from something like that takes time."

"He was in pretty bad shape, wasn't he?"

"Yes," Brit said. "Very. Tough man, though."

"That's what I hear. Rank and file really liked him, though."

"What do they say about me?"

Maggie held back for a moment, then flicked her eyes toward Brit. "Can I be honest, ma'am?"

"Please."

"I'm sure you know this—but there's still a lot of grumbling about having a woman in charge."

"Sure," Brit said.

"I wouldn't take it personally, though, ma'am. Same would be true if I were in charge."

"I know that, Maggie."

"Boys will be boys."

"You've got that right," Brit said with a laugh. "Private Blake, what are the young bucks over at—?"

"Heads up," Maggie said, interrupting.

"What?"

"Something just popped."

John Ward

"Bogie," Blake said, explaining. "Triggered the warning receiver."

"I thought we were NOE," Brit said.

"We are—and have been entire flight," Maggie said. "Well below what's even considered a safe altitude."

Brit craned her neck for a look at the centre console. "So what is it?"

"Judging by its velocity, a chopper."

"Russian?" Brit asked.

"No way of telling without a visual. Seems unlikely, this far west."

Brit scanned the illuminated radar panel. "Maybe it's one of ours."

Blake squinted at the radio controls. "Why wouldn't they make contact?"

"I need you to mind your business, pilot," Maggie said. "Ready defence systems."

"We're going hot?"

"Stop talking and arm us. Full suite. Flairs and everything."

"Jesus," he said. "I've never operated hot."

"Only one way to learn," Brit said. Which obviously wasn't true.

Blake entered the codes and glanced at Maggie. "Systems up, ready to operate."

"Good," Maggie said. "Tacking south to avert contact."

"No," Brit said. "Don't divert from the course."

Maggie turned to her. "Ma'am, with all due respect—"

"That's an order O'Connor."

"What if they engage?"

"They won't."

Maggie grimaced. "Should I attempt contact?"

"No. Sit tight. Let it play."

For two minutes, only the hum of the Condor's blades and the steady, high-pitched pulse of its radar system could be heard in the cockpit, everyone bracing for a host of unknown dangers.

When the console lit up red, Maggie broke the silence. "They're hot," she said, no trace of panic in it.

"Do we have a visual?" Brit asked.

Maggie waited. "Visual confirmed. Blake—if the flairs dispense, hit them immediately with the M2's."

"Roger," he said, hands trembling as he calibrated the targeting system.

"Just so everyone's clear," Brit said, "we are not on offense here. Do not—I repeat—do not engage unless fired upon first."

"Roger," Maggie said, leaning left toward the window, and pointing at the brown Kamov-54 hurtling toward them. "It's the Russians alright. Coming in fast, too. Hold tight." With a jolt, the Condor leapt upward so suddenly, so violently, its cabin rattled like a wooden shack on a quaking fault line.

As Brit's blood plummeted toward her toes, she dug her fingernails into the hard rubber armrests and closed her eyes. "Tell me what's *happening*, O'Connor!"

"Executing evasive manoeuvres, General. Hang on."

Within seconds they were stabilizing, centripetal force loosening its grip.

"Passing beneath us ... now," Maggie said.

Then Blake took over the play-by-play narration: "Here they go, ma'am—circling back. Still have a lock. Still locked."

"Hold," Maggie said as the desert-hued, second-gen Erdogan attack chopper rounded in a wide loop less than a kilometre south of their position.

"What do you want to do ma'am, what do you want to do?" Blake asked frantically. "He's circling back, ma'am. Permission to engage!"

Brit raised a rigid palm toward the kid. "Do not engage, private! Do not fucking engage!"

Blake's eyes were darting up and down between the blinking consul and the windshield. "They have a lock on us, their systems are hot!"

Maggie whipped her head around toward the rattled gunner. "Blake—calm the fuck down! Do not engage unless fired upon first. Got that?" He didn't respond, wide eyes still glued to the window. "Private! Do you understand me?"

"Copy," he finally said.

With one had on the throttle, the other tapping away at the touch screen to her left, Maggie said, "They're coming in beneath

John Ward

us again."

Blake lifted his visor and wiped the perspiration from his eyelids. "What are they doing? I don't get it."

"They're taking a look," Brit said, watching the chopper zag past. "If they wanted to hit us they would've already."

"A look?" Blake said, voice jittery. "Why the fuck are their weapons systems red?"

"Same reason ours are," Maggie said.

ثلاثة وعشرون

The Gulf of Aden shimmered like polished platinum beneath the big, white moon. They'd passed the Horn ages ago. And were it not for the chirping blink of the boat's navigational system, Amir's sense of progress might have abandoned him completely.

With no land in sight, his days had been reduced to a disorienting succession of recurring transitions. Dream world to waking. Blinding sun to star strewn sky. Rationed breakfast to communal dinner. Meandering conversation to imposing silence. Anxiety to boredom. Fishing to card games. Constant prayer.

So much prayer.

Five, seven, ten times a day or more—as if the trawler were a desert caravan of map-less pilgrims, devotion both a means and an end.

The adults had taken to a steady rotation at the wheel. Amir had just finished another turn, quietly passing his duties on to the boat's owner, another unceremonious recognition of time's passage.

Amir wanted to sleep but wasn't quite tired. Fuck it, he thought, lighting up a smoke. Might as well ask. "Don't have any booze stashed somewhere, do you?"

Abasi raised his eyes from the radar screen. It was the first time Amir had spoken to him in English. "Thought you were a man of God."

"When it suits me."

Abasi gave him a tired smile. "Take the wheel."

When he returned to the cabin, he held a dark glass bottle, a third of it spent.

"Brilliant," Amir said. "What is it?"

"You don't want to know," Abasi said, twisting off its plastic cap and taking a swig. "Does the job though."

Amir took the bottle and studied it. Then, after a long pull, exhaled loudly, eyes squinting, mouth contorted. "Jesus that's strong."

"Do you have a spare?"

Amir passed Abasi a cigarette and lighter. "Didn't take you for a smoker."

"Didn't take you for a drinker," Abasi said with a grin.

"Where I'm from, everyone's a drinker."

Abasi reached for the bottle and reassumed his position behind the wheel. "What does your son think?"

They'd discussed James twice now, but only in the context of football.

"Of what?" Amir said, finding the question off-putting.

"Of your drinking and smoking."

"He's got no idea. I mean, I drink at home—a few beers or whatever. But never smoke."

"You really think he doesn't know?"

"Does your son?"

Abasi's brow creased. "My son?"

"Darweshi."

"Darweshi's not my son."

Amir took a drag and thought it over. "What is he?"

"My nephew."

"Guess I just assumed."

"He's my sister's."

Then Amir remembered—the bar with Brit. *Let me guess, your lot had something to do with it.* He wanted to ask Abasi about it, but said, "Like a son though, isn't he?"

"Yes, he is. Always has been."

"Seems well-raised."

Abasi looked up at the moon. "It's not easy for him. My kids, they're all ... they have it easier."

The statement left a heavy silence between them for a minute or so, until Amir reassured him. "He'll be fine. We'll make it."

"Will we?"

"Yeah. We will."

"Then what?"

Without an answer, Amir took a hit from the bottle and thought about James. What time was it in Granada? Was he sleeping yet? Was Paco curled in a lump at the foot of his comforter? What about Cristina—had she turned in, an open book resting face down on the night stand, an empty wine glass teetering at its edge?

"Then we figure out how to get you back home," Amir finally said, an aspirational fortitude in his tone. Abasi expelled a humourless chuckle. "Can I ask you something," Amir said.

"Please."

"Your father and the boy—they pray. Why don't you?"

"Well," Abasi said, "can I be honest?"

Amir raised two open palms. "No judgement here."

"I think it's a bunch of—how do you say it—hocus pocus." It sounded funny, Abasi's accent shaping the English expression, an over-annunciation of consonant sounds.

Amir lit another smoke. "I hear you."

"Then again," Abasi said. "What do I know?"

"There was a while when I thought it was bullshit too."

"What changed?"

"I became a cop," Amir said. Abasi turned back from the wheel to glance at him. Amir understood the look. "I know it sounds strange. But once I started to see a bunch of shit in the field— violence, death—the faith, it sort of inexplicably returned to me."

"You'd think it would be the opposite."

"Yeah, I know. Hard to explain."

"Sometimes I wish I *did* believe," Abasi said, wearily. "It would make things simpler."

Amir grinned. "Don't be so sure."

"You're married?"

"What?"

"Are you married?"

"No. I mean—"

Abasi smiled. "Ah, but you're thinking about it."

"I am."

"So your son, you're not with his mother?"

Amir grinned. "Fuck no."

Abasi let out a hearty, full-throated laugh. "Women are hard, my friend. Very hard. Sounds like you may have a good one, now?"

"I do."

John Ward

"Must worry about you."

"You can say that again. More so when I was a cop."

"Granada must be one hell of a dangerous place," Abasi said, tone raised. Then, watching Amir's face, "She doesn't know you're here, does she?"

Amir shook his head, smoke trailing from his mouth. "No, sir."

"What did you tell her?"

"Told her I'm in London."

"What if something happens—?" Abasi stopped himself. "Does she even know what you do?"

"Sort of."

"Must be kind of nice, not having her nose around your business all the time."

"I tell her some things."

"But not everything," Abasi said with a quick tilt of the head.

"Of course not."

"Well, at least you have a *reason* to lie to her. I lie to my wife all the time, just so the woman will leave me alone."

"About what?"

"Oh, I don't know," Abasi said. "Little things. *Did I call the repairman? Did I pay the electric bill?* You know, the stupid things women get crazy over. Where is James's mother?"

Amir shrugged. "To be frank, I've no idea. Nor do I give a fuck."

"She's in Granada, though."

"Yeah," Amir said. "Nowhere else to be."

"She sees him?"

"No. Hasn't seen him for years."

"That must be difficult for the boy."

"He was so young when she left—he doesn't know the difference."

"Trust me," Abasi said, motioning for Amir to hand over the booze, "he knows the difference."

***

The lobby of the Mena House hotel was a perfect little analogue of the apocalypse, replete with well-preserved artefacts future archaeologists might interpret as evidence of a once-thriving, but doomed civilization.

Its marble floor was littered with discarded paper and random articles of clothing. Broken light fixtures dangled by wires from recessed gaps between intricate sections of mirrored ceiling. Where artwork had been torn from the walls by looters, small metal hooks projected upward at severe angles, freed from their opulent burden.

Most haunting was the intricate, gold-embossed, arabesque pillar-flanked reception desk, behind which an array of office equipment and miscellany lay in a heap. Ink jet printers. Computer keyboards. Fragments of sheetrock. An upended leather chair. Some Egyptian currency littered about, now no more valuable than a scatter of fallen leaves. And then there was the dust—fine and blonde, clinging to it all.

Brit and her team had their masks off, inspecting the ruins of luxury for the fuck of it. The prior evening, they'd claimed the Presidential Suite as a staging area and camping quarters. They'd taken night watch in turns, the spotter stationed on the balcony behind a massive set of field glasses. All had been quiet.

At first light, they gathered some gear and set out to explore the palatial grounds.

Blake kicked aside some cushions near the lobby entrance and turned to the women in charge. "You think it's odd there are no bodies anywhere?"

"What, here?" Brit said. "In the hotel?"

"That'd be a classy death," Maggie said, no smile to be found on her freckled face.

"Seriously," the kid said, "where did they all go?"

"Hospitals," Brit said. "Airports. The ocean." She paused and looked around. "Half of them tried to make it to Europe. Some took to the streets and rioted. A lot died at home, too."

Blake shook his head. "Must've been a bloody nightmare."

Maggie laughed. "Understatement of the century."

"Hey," Blake said, more spiritedly. "Can we check out the pyramids?"

Brit turned to him. "What, sifting through trash hasn't caught your fancy?"

"I was just thinking—you know—it's all right here. Pyramids of Giza, the Sphinx? I mean, wow."

"A little *sightseeing* at the necropolis," Maggie said with a chuckle. "I can see the headline of The Sun now: Giza reopens to tourists after twenty-five-year moratorium."

"What's a necropolis," Blake said. He got no answer.

"What's Duran's timeline again, General?"

"To be honest, Maggie, I'm not quite sure. Could be today, could be tomorrow. No more tracking data to go by."

"And he's coming in by air from Jeddah?"

"That's the plan."

"What if they don't make it," Blake said.

"Private."

"Yes, General?"

"Let's try and stay positive here. Okay?"

"Yes, ma'am. Sure thing, ma'am."

"Good. Thank you … Blake?"

"General?"

"You really want to see the pyramids?"

"Yeah! Why not?"

"I can think of a few reasons," Maggie said, a bit haughtily.

Brit stood at the centre of the lobby bouncing her mask against her thigh, head tilted, studying her reflection on the grimy mirrored panels above. "To be frank, I haven't a clear idea whether it's safe out in the open. The Russians obviously know we're here— Condor's parked in the middle of the bloody golf course."

Blake laughed a little. "Can't believe they built a golf course here."

"Oh," Maggie said, "how charming. The Private hasn't yet discovered that nothing is sacred."

Blake shrugged his shoulders and smiled. "I'd say let's get a quick nine in, but I forgot my clubs. Besides, whole thing's a bloody sand trap now, anyway. Am I right?"

Maggie shook her head and grinned. "And he's a brilliant sense of humour, too. I knew I picked the right airman for this job." Then she looked at Brit. "Seriously though, I'd be shocked if they weren't watching."

"No doubt," Brit said. "Russians and SIS. The Satellites aren't my concern, though. It's the possibility of flesh and blood recon that worries me." She paused. "Blake, I know it'd be thrilling and all to take a look up close, but it'd be irresponsible of me to compromise us like that."

"What about the roof, ma'am? I bet we'd get a good view from there."

"Blake, let it be," Maggie said, an older sister scolding.

Brit motioned at the ceiling. "Actually, Maggie, getting up there might provide us some advantage—survey the layout of infrastructure, perimeter and whatnot."

"Higher ground," Blake said with a smile.

"Precisely."

"You don't think they'd ever hit us with a drone, do you?"

Maggie nudged a chunk of drywall with her boot toe and looked out through the dust-coated windows. "That'd be in direct contravention of the treaty."

"They wouldn't," Brit said, tone lacking certainty. "They would send in a team, though. So if we go up there, we need to exercise caution."

"Right, ma'am," Maggie said. Blake made his way to the reception desk, placed his pistol down on its counter, and pressed a finger down on the button of the silt-covered call bell. Its high-pitched ring echoed through the lobby. Brit and Maggie both flinched.

"Sorry," Blake said, clenching his teeth with embarrassment. "Ma'am, I know I asked you this already … and I do get that it's above my pay grade and all—"

"So why are you asking again?" Maggie said.

"I don't know, I … I'm just confused, you know? It's not lost on me I'm not really qualified for this. Not in the least, if we're being honest. I mean, why are we down here? Why are we doing an extraction like this?"

"Blake," Maggie said, trying to interrupt.

But the kid went on. "Like, what's so special about this Duran guy, that a General leaves post to personally retrieve him from deep in neutral territory—and who's he with?"

Maggie tossed aside a crumpled hotel bill she'd been perusing and marched up to Blake. "Are you fucking kidding me, Blake?"

"Maggie," Brit said. "It's fine."

Maggie shook her head. "It's not *fine*, ma'am. I've been over this with him."

"O'Connor," Brit said firmly. "I've put you both in a difficult position. You're right, Private Blake—this is a highly unorthodox arrangement. But everything we're doing here is on me. No one else. And the less you know, the better off you'll be. That may seem like a cop out, but it's true. And you need to trust me on that. Okay?"

The look in his wide eyes betrayed a youthful vulnerability.

"Okay?" Brit again asked.

"Okay, ma'am."

"Good. And thank you. Let's go to the roof."

When they arrived at the upper landing of the emergency stairwell, the exit was jammed shut.

"Put some back into it, Private," Maggie said as the kid leaned on the door and twisted its handle. After several more attempts, he backed up several inches and thrust his right shoulder forward against the steel surface. When it budged outward slightly, he repeated the motion several more times and succeeded in creating roughly half a metre of open space for them to squeeze through. "You should start hitting the weights more," Maggie said, needling him.

"Ha-*ha*," Blake said, stepping back and drawing his sidearm.

As he raised it, Brit interrupted. "No. I'm through first. Maggie, you bring up the rear."

Brit's first step through was a doozy, a plank wedged between the bottom of the door and the overturned sofa behind it almost catching her feet. "Careful," she said, striding broadly to avoid it. Several metres out from the door, they halted in unison, arrested by the grizzly scene.

"Good fucking god," Maggie whispered, lowering her weapon.

There were bones everywhere. Skulls. Tibias. Rib cages. Human skeletons picked clean, clothing shredded to rags. It was an open tomb, the whole thing, maybe a hundred unburied skeletons.

"There's your answer, Private," Maggie said.

Blake just stood, looking on with disbelief. Maggie and Brit fanned out across the cadaverous clutter, moving at quarter-speed, cautious not to disturb the bones where they lay. There was an unreality to it, as if they'd stumbled onto the soundstage of macabre thriller, the celluloid undead, waiting to be roused to by the nudge of a misplaced boot.

The kid remained paralyzed, stammering. "I … I don't, I don't understand. They all—why did they all come up here? Why would they want to die up here?"

Brit squatted beside a skull, leaning to inspect it more closely. "They were trying to get away."

"What do you mean," he said, vocal chords giving over to the trembling that had overtaken the rest of his thin frame.

"This skull has a hole in it," Brit said. "Bullet right through the base."

"What does that mean," Blake said, motioning with his pistol.

"Careful with that piece, Private," Maggie said. When he lowered the gun she explained. "It means they were gunned down. Probably came up here to wait for help."

The kid raised his pistol again. "Gunned down by who?"

Brit rose to her feet. "Egyptian Army."

"Why?"

"Trying to contain things, likely. Who knows," Brit said, pointing at the area around her. "This lot—they'd probably been infected."

"Jesus," Blake whispered.

Maggie and Brit shared a look, then Maggie said, "Happened everywhere."

Beyond the roof, blurry waves of boiling air climbed upward from the sand-shrouded grounds of the Mena House. Past its rows of raggedy palms rose the defiant, limestone titans of the Giza Necropolis, impervious to the elements, inured to the self-destructive tendencies of the species that birthed them.

With a hand cupped over his brow, Blake took in the view.

Without a sound, Maggie O'Connor pitched forward.

Brit squinted. "Maggie?"

John Ward

Maggie's legs buckled. Brit raced toward her, bones cracking beneath her feet. "Blake," screamed Brit. "Get down!" Blake froze in place, watching Brit force Maggie to the deck. "Blake," Brit again shouted, "get inside!"

Instead, Blake rushed toward them, dust and debris kicking up where the sniper's rounds met the roof. He grabbed Maggie by the waist and heaved her body upward. Brit grabbed hold as well, and in a flurry, they lugged Maggie's limp body across the rooftop, bullets pinging off the steel door as it snapped shut behind them.

TWENTY-FOUR

The block was dark. Glass hadn't slept more than a few hours over the past several days, but he was achingly, acutely, manically awake. His brain raced, fires of rage bathing his psyche in noxious fumes.

"Guard," he said, completing the last of his push-ups and rising from the cold concrete. He must have done a thousand since he'd been detained. He felt like a mad man. "Guard!"

The soldier lumbered up to Glass's cell and punched his end of the intercom on. "What in the bloody hell do you want now?"

"What time is it?"

"I don't know."

"Bullshit. That's bullshit," Glass said. "I demand to know what time it is—and that's a fucking order!"

The guard laughed, big, booze-reddened nose honking like a swine's snout. "You're fucking hilarious, you know."

"What, are you Scottish? You're Scottish, right?"

"Fuck do you care," the guard said, accent rolling from the roof of his mouth.

"What," Glass said, "ashamed to admit it?"

"Why would I be ashamed?"

"My father was a Scotsman. A *real* one. Not like you, you bloody slob."

"What's that supposed to mean," the guard said with a growl.

"He could handle his liquor, for starters. You? You fucking reek. I can smell you from here. Just off a bender, are we?"

The guard began walking away, shaking his big head.

"Hey, I'm fucking talking to you."

The guard spun round and pressed the talk button again. "Put a sock in it!"

As the guard marched off, Glass slammed his palms to the door. "Pussy!"

The big lug could've throttled him with one hand. But Glass couldn't hold it back—his venom burnt for a flesh and blood target. Plus, if he could provoke the man into doing something stupid, he might have the opportunity to speak with a higher-up. Glass pounded the door again. "Forgot your fucking bollocks, you pussy!"

No response.

Glass knocked the aluminium tray of uneaten slop from the cell's bench and slumped down. What fucking time is it, god damn it. Time. Ha. What a fucking sick illusion. Runs out when you need it. There in abundance when you don't. What a bloody twisted, weird universe.

Embracing the anger had kept him afloat. Teetering on madness, but afloat. It was the guilt he was avoiding. The fact he'd gotten Marissa killed. And the excruciating self-loathing and sorrow that came with this admission.

For a good half hour, he sat, stewing in his juices, contemplating all the ways he'd take his revenge. He'd skin Mason alive. Rip him limb from limb. Snip his balls off and serve them up on a paper plate. Burn the man's designer wardrobe in front of him first.

No need for public shaming. This was personal.

When the fluorescent lights came to life, buzzing like a hundred dying horse flies, Glass leapt from the bench and called for the Guard again.

Instead, C emerged in the pallid glow, rickety-looking in loose tweed. "Agent Glass."

"Sir," Glass said, straightening, concerned his bloodshot eyes were playing tricks on him.

"Heard you've been giving the guards quite a time of it down here." Glass hadn't a response and C went on. "Pardon my language, Agent Glass, but you've stirred up quite a shit storm upstairs—colleagues wondering whether you've completely lost your marbles."

"Sir," Glass said, "I—why am I down here?"

"Hmm. Might it to do with the myriad offenses you've perpetrated? Violence, threats of violence, intimidation. And let us not forget the unfounded accusations."

Glass gritted his teeth, restraining a reply.

"I'd been warned many times that you were a loose cannon,

Agent Glass. And as many times I'd come to your defence—*personally*—reminding people of your undeniable talent, trustworthiness and dedication. You've done great work for us over the years. Of course, our business provides few accolades for jobs well done. Nature of the beast." C ran a bony index finger over the cleft bulb of his chin. "You've left me wondering, though—has Agent Glass lost his nerve? Have the years of thankless labour worn away at his good judgement? Have the endless rigors of the job become too much for this tired soul?" C tilted his head slightly, removed his wireframe glasses and began wiping a small handkerchief across the lenses. "Now, to be frank, I'm bloody confused about this situation. I'm hoping you can clarify a few things. Starting with all of this Zanzibar talk."

"Where's Marissa White?"

"*Marissa White*—what's she got to do with this?"

"She's dead, isn't she?"

"My dear boy, you really *have* come unhinged, haven't you?"

"Sir," Glass said, dropping his head in dejection, "something's happened to her."

"Henry—you don't mind if I call you Henry, right?"

"I don't care what you call me."

"Henry, Marissa's got nothing to do with any of this."

"Where is she then, sir?"

"Oh," C said, pity in his voice, "I understand what this is about, now. You and Marissa. *Right*. You'd thought you'd rekindled your flame—spent a romantic evening together. Hashing out the past, making up for lost time. Then, suddenly, she goes radio silent. Out of touch, as it were." C shook his head and sighed loudly. "My dear, my dear. *Love*. What a painful endeavour. I thought you had more self-control than that, though, Henry. I mean, all of this?" He subtly motioned toward the intercom and the chrome titanium at the upper portion of the cell door. "On account of a broken heart? *My god*."

Glass shook his head violently, feeling the concrete walls shrinking in on him. Was C really part of this? "So where is she, then, sir?"

"Christ, Agent Glass—how should I know? She'd scheduled

time off this week. The woman works ungodly hours. Leaving her be, while she's on holiday is the only decent thing to do."

"Holiday? Are you fucking kidding me?"

"Watch yourself," the old man growled, "you're in a bloody compromised position already, need I remind you." Then C eased back, the vitriol vanishing from his tone. "Now, Agent Glass, shall we discuss the Zanzibar operation for a moment?"

"What time is it?" Glass asked, walking toward the bench and sitting.

"What?"

"Do you know what time it is, sir?"

C looked down his nose at Glass and ran thin hand over his wrinkled jawline. "Forgive me, I don't. Never remember to put my bloody watch on before leaving the house." Then, "Glass, Agent Mason tells me you're quite upset about being left out of the Zanzibar operation. And, apparently, you've been poking your nose in places it doesn't belong."

"Like the Lanesborough?"

"The Lanesborough? I don't follow."

"Tony Mason—GLogiX."

"I'm sorry," C said. "I haven't the faintest notion of what you're referring to."

Glass peered through the bars at him. C wore a well-contrived look of confusion. "They've a cure."

"Excuse me?"

"Where is Tony Mason, now?"

"Not your concern, Henry. Now tell me exactly what you're talking about—what do you mean they've a cure?"

"They have a cure—*a cure*," Glass repeated. "GLogiX, Tony fucking Mason—they've a cure. And Mason has rigged this whole Zanzibar op to be a catastrophic failure."

C's head jerked back as if a hornet had dive-bombed his nose. "That's ludicrous."

"Is it? Where's Duran, then?"

The old man hesitated for a moment. "You know I can't disclose that information, Agent Glass. My god."

"Well, I suggest you check in with Mason, see what's happening right now."

C slipped a card from his sleeve. "Are you suggesting the operation is compromised?"

"Compromised is a bloody understatement. Marissa—"

"Marissa, *what*?"

"If you're so convinced she's alive and well, go and ask her about it. She was on to him."

The old man removed his glasses again, and let a potent silence settle in for several seconds. Then he slipped the spectacles back on and said, "These are serious accusations."

Glass rose from his seat. "I don't give a rat's ass what happens to me at this juncture. But I won't sit here pretending all this bad business isn't actually happening."

Their eyes met, and C ceased the moment. "I respect your fortitude, Henry. I do. But, let's pray you're not right about this." C turned his attention to the soldiers at the end the cell block. "Guard! Get this man some breakfast. And not that shite you've been serving him the past few days."

***

A waxing day-moon hung above the harbour. The Lotto's trawler crept through the wide central channel. Massive container ships lay dormant on both sides, decks stacked to the brim with undisturbed cargo; ten stories of rainbow-painted steal deprived of a destination.

Their plan was to disembark below the port's loading cranes. Amir was nervous, though, and had Abasi dock several hundred metres away, between the cover of two small tankers. He wanted to go before them, scout the situation.

The Glock and couple extra clips would've ordinarily suited a simple recon job just fine. But with Sparrow still in play, Amir chose not to skimp on the hardware. From the portside of the boat, Abasi handed Amir the grenade launcher and an L92A2—a mid-sized, suppressed machine pistol. Its prototype was a German make, but the SAS had grown so fond of its utility in close-quarters combat, a British contractor began manufacturing their own model after The Death wiped Deutschland off the map. No patent litigation necessary.

With the bazooka strap slung over his shoulder, Amir unlocked the safety on the machine gun, and slid an auxiliary magazine into a slot on his Kevlar.

Amir nodded to Abasi and instructed him to arm himself while he waited. "If this takes longer than a half-hour," he said, "leave."

Abasi frowned. "What do you mean?"

"Take the boat and go."

"Where?"

"Home," Amir said, scanning the docks. "Go home. Got it?"

"Yes," Abasi said, still looking concerned. "Got it."

Amir set into a jog, eyes tracing the columns of containers that flanked his path toward the loading bays. Reaching the edge of the loading docks he lit a cigarette and dipped behind a lone fork-lift parked at a diagonal angle from several anonymous pallets of cellophane-wrapped who-knows-what.

For several minutes he crouched there, searching for movement. It must've been a hundred degrees. Every time he spit in between puffs, he considered how odd the process of evaporation truly was—that his saliva would sizzle up and join the atmosphere from which he drew breath.

Growing impatient, Amir rose and ventured to the assigned meeting place. Almost instantly, he heard the roar of an engine. Within seconds, a monster black pickup truck was bearing down on him, its jacked up carriage bouncing violently over the suspension springs and over-sized tires, windshield tinted so dark it was impossible to make out the driver. As Amir raised his gun, it skidded to a screeching halt several metres from where he stood.

The driver's side door swung open. A white-draped Arab donning a traditional Bedouin turban and fluorescent green sunglasses with chrome lenses leaned out from the truck's running board at a forty-five-degree angle.

"You Amir?" the driver asked in choppy English. Amir, startled by the haphazard approach, stepped backward, saying nothing. The Arab withdrew a Kalashnikov from the cab. "You Amir or no?"

"Yeah," Amir said. "Who the fuck are you?"

"Rashid. Friend of Glass. Where the rest?"

"Who?" Amir said; a meagre test of the man's credentials.

"The boy," the Arab said. "I don't know. Maybe a lady too?" He then tossed the rifle back on his seat. "I'm on tight timeline. Get in truck."

Well, here's to the beggars everywhere, thought Amir, weapon raised, walking to the passenger's side.

"No—in back."

"Are you out of your fucking mind? I'm not riding in the payload!"

"Hey. In back or no ride."

"Where are we going?"

"Mecca."

"Mecca?"

"Plane is in Mecca. You want ride or no?"

Fuck it, thought Amir. "I need to go get them."

"No, we pick them up. We drive over to the boat."

"How do you know where the boat is?"

"I see you come in," the Arab said, pointing his gun toward the docks.

"Well why'd you let me go out in the open like that?"

"Want to see how stupid you are." Rashid said with a laugh. "Now I know."

"Stupid isn't the word for it," Amir muttered.

"What?"

"Let's go."

The back of the truck was a sandbox, myriad construction tools and a blue tarp crumpled in the front left corner just behind the cab. As soon as Amir settled into a stable position, the cab's back window slid open.

Rashid's turbaned head twisted sideways toward the mirror as he spoke. "Cover up with that."

"The tarp?"

"Yes. That."

"I won't be able to see anything."

Rashid twisted back further in his seat so he could make eye contact. "Whatever you want."

Then the truck lurched forward, Amir bracing against the

raised edges of the payload. He figured Rashid was indeed as young as he looked, given the almost-adolescent aggressiveness with which he handled the vehicle—barely braking as he ripped through ninety degree turns, accelerating on every straightaway.

In less than a minute the truck skidded to a stop at the trawler's side. Amir motioned for Abasi to send the party forward. So they came, the two able-bodied adults gathering far more from the cabin than Amir would've suggested had he been aboard. Babu and Darweshi emerged, hand in hand. When Abasi extended the steal gangplank from the trawler's side, Harkinder descended first and handed Amir the weapons bag, arms trembling under its weight. Next was the old man and child, single file, Babu limping forward without his cane.

"Come on," Amir said, motioning for them to hurry.

Abasi stood at the centre of the bow, breathing heavily through his nose, scanning the iron contours of his trusty vessel. "She is my best one," he said solemnly.

"And she served us well," Amir said. "Now let's fucking go."

Abasi nodded, patted the deck railing and stepped out onto the gangplank. Halfway down, a jolting pop sounded from above and a bouquet of sparks erupted from the ridged metal at Abasi's feet. He spun round to re-board the trawler, but a second burst of rounds ricocheted off the spool of chain suspending the ramp and Abasi lost his footing.

As he tumbled into the pale water with a thumping splash, Amir sprung from the truck. "Down! Everyone down!" Machine gun raised, Amir scanned the stacked containers surrounding them. A third series of shots snapped through the air, several striking the roof of Rashid's truck's. The Arab's door swung wide and a deafening rattle of shells flew from his AK.

Amir unleashed a torrent too, though had no target in sight. "Where is he?"

Abasi pulled himself up to the concrete surface of the dock and when he gained his feet, thrust a finger toward a set of containers a hundred metres to their left. "There," Abasi said. "He's right there!"

First, Amir caught sight of the muzzle flash. Then he felt the bullets—two at the centre of his chest, one in his lower right abdomen. He collapsed backwards onto the concrete.

"Duran!"

Harkinder yanked a weapon from the gun bag. As Amir peeled himself from the ground, she unleashed a chaotic volley in the direction of the shooter. Hot shell casings spiraled down on the boy and the old man as they lay flat on the payload beneath her, hands pressed to their ears. Staggering, Amir ran both hands over his chest. He found no discernible damage. A cracked rib, perhaps. Though adrenaline tends to reduce one's sense of trauma, and he knew it.

"Everyone in the truck," Amir said, lifting the grenade launcher from the truck. "And stay down!"

As Amir took aim, Rashid popped another clip into the Kalashnikov, and resumed his assault. The A-K rattled with such intensity and volume, Amir struggled to focus. Then, steadying himself, he pressed his index finger to the red trigger button. A ball of fire leapt from the containers beneath the shooter. As the smoke rose, it was impossible to determine the effect of the explosion. Rashid kept up the onslaught.

"Stop," Amir said. Then, "Darweshi, get inside the truck. Babu, you too!"

Rashid glowered. "No one in truck."

Amir tossed the empty grenade launcher back into the payload and drew his Glock. Safety on, he pointed it toward the Arab. "They're riding inside."

"You kidding me?"

"Do I fucking sound like it?"

After helping the boy and Babu get in, Amir returned to the payload. Left foot on the fender, he stretched his right leg over the tailgate. A stabbing pain bolted from his side and up his back. As Harkinder reached to provide support, Amir winced. "I'm fine," he said, inserting his fingers between the Kevlar and his ribs. "Keep your eyes on those containers. Can't assume he's dead."

As the truck picked up speed, Amir relaxed into a sitting position, and slowly removed his hand from behind the vest. In the rusty light of the descending sun, his fingers glistened deep crimson.

God fucking damn it.

PART FOUR

خمسة وعشرون

There were two roads to Mecca, one old, one new. The former, meandering. The latter built for speed. The encroaching wilderness had reduced the latter's width to one narrow lane. But nature was no match for the gigantic treads of Rashid's steel beast.

They must've been travelling one hundred forty kilometres per hour, and every time the truck hit a turbulent patch of highway, Amir's abdomen seared as if someone had pressed a hot poker to it.

The pain he could bear. It was the waves of wooziness he found unsettling—a clear indication of the wound's severity. He'd never been shot before. A small miracle given his line of work. Now, with the wind rippling loudly, and his body leaking strength, everything seemed fragmented, yet strangely familiar.

The falling crimson sun. The intensifying desert moon. The craggily, low mountains—hard, raw and brown. The slap of hot air against his face. It was Andalusia in a dry spell. But for the battered Arabic road signs reminding him that it wasn't.

He looked over to Harkinder. She was studying the machine gun in her hand. Then to Abasi, whose eyes were peeled wider than an amphetamine freak's. Who the hell were these fucking people? Where were James and Cristina?

Amir's eyes drew closed. His little family's beautiful faces loomed behind his lids. Their voices echoed in a windy whisper through the warm, dark chambers of his memory, beckoning for his return.

Jeddo's voice joined in the chorus. "Amir—you need to stay awake."

Amir leaned forward and opened his eyes. The truck's velocity had diminished. Around them, the outskirts of Mecca grew up in tangled clusters, appearing exactly as one might imagine. Sand-worn. White and tan. Dense. Referential to the desert. Every edifice clinging to the next, like, don't leave me all alone out here.

Amir rapped the back of his fist against the window of the cab. It slid open. "Are we here," asked Amir, straining to raise his voice.

"Mecca," was Rashid's response.

Mecca. It didn't sound right. That Mecca might be a real place. A wave of nausea rolled over Amir and he breathed deeply to contain it. "Do you have masks?"

"Have what?" Rashid asked.

"We need masks."

"Why?" Rashid said, head flashing back toward Amir.

"The Death."

Rashid laughed. "No death here."

Nothing here, thought Amir, the world blurring a little, the abandoned cityscape whizzing by, no trace of the chaos that had ensued in urban centres the world over. No overturned or burnt-out cars. No roadblocks or abandoned tanks. No bullet-riddled building facades or refuse-blanketed sidewalks.

Had there been no rioting? No bloody skirmishes? No looting?

With the sun disappearing behind them, early evening shadows began to soften and bleed into the all-encompassing, watery blue of twilight. Rashid turned on the headlights, bathing what lay before them in a stark, concentrated glow.

They soon turned off the expressway and onto the Umm al Qura, approaching—according to signs overhead—the Al-Masjid al-Haram.

"Where is he taking us," Abasi asked, still bug-eyed with the gun bag at his feet.

"I don't know," Amir said, groggily. He was beginning to shiver now, and the intense searing below his ribs had produced a steady side-effect of queasiness.

Harkinder eyed Amir's gut. "Is it bad?"

Amir closed his eyes. "I'm fine."

"You need help," Abasi said.

"I'm fine," Amir repeated, fending off reality. "Honestly, it's … it's not that bad."

Then, the most delirious white lie of his life. "I've been … I've been shot before … trust me," he said, willing the words forward, "this isn't that bad."

But truth wouldn't be denied, and suddenly—as if someone had drawn a heavy curtain over his eyes—everything went fuzzy and dark.

"There's nothing fortuitous about it, Amir. It's all part of the plan."

Amir had no idea what Jeddo was talking about. "Whose plan?"

"Very funny," Jeddo said. He was dressed like that Bedouin maniac driving the pickup truck. Even had those ridiculous sunglasses on.

"You look weird in that outfit," Amir said. "The turban—it's too much."

"I like it. Plus, it was all they had available."

"Who?"

Jeddo pointed to the men circling the Kaaba. There were hundreds, maybe thousands of them. All dressed like Jeddo—draped in white, eyes concealed behind cheap fluorescent shades. The steady swirl of their bodies around the cubical structure made Amir dizzy.

"Who are those men?"

"Pilgrims, Amir—who else?"

Amir tried to move but he couldn't, prone body glued to the sandy steel payload of Rashid's truck. "How'd they get this in here? Get me off this thing!"

Jeddo chuckled at the suggestion. "Amir, you're far too heavy. You were eight years old the last time I picked you up. And I threw out my back. You don't remember that?"

"Please," Amir said. "Don't let me die in this fucking truck!"

"Die? Why would you say that? You're not going to die."

"I'm bleeding, Jeddo—I'm bleeding badly. Look. Look at my side!"

"I don't know what you're talking about. Have you been drinking? I told you to stop drinking so much. It's terrible—makes a man weak."

"I haven't been drinking—Jeddo, please. Please get me out of here." Amir felt like crying, but held it in.

"You know, Amir, I never wanted to tell you this—but your father—*he* was a drinker. Wrecked him. Utterly pitiful at the end. When I met him for the first time, he was such an impressive young man. But the drinking just destroyed him. Couldn't control it. Couldn't control himself. It ruined your parents' marriage. You were too young to remember any of it, praise Allah. I was hoping I'd never have to share this with you, but now—to see you here like this—here, of all places, the most sacred space on earth— and you can't even stand up! I thought you'd have shown more respect. My goodness. This is how you end your Hajj?" Then Jeddo paused, folded back one of his sleeves, looked down at the gold watch on his wrist, and rather casually, as if a bartender just notified them of last call, said, "You better sober up. You'll miss the plane."

"Jeddo. Jeddo, I can't move. I'm stuck!"

"You're not stuck. You're drunk."

"I'm not drunk—I'm shot! Look!"

"Let me see," Jeddo said, frowning as he opened tailgate. He climbed in gingerly, then knelt to inspect Amir's wound. Silent, he removed the sunglasses, and leaned forward for a closer look. "Well, well. You're right! Looks like you have been shot. Sorry— forget what I said about your father. You're nothing like him, really."

In one, powerful motion, he scooped Amir into his arms, stood fully, walked to the edge of the tailgate and hopped down, Amir's dangling limbs bouncing as Jeddo's feet met the earth.

"Let's get you fixed up," the old man said. Then he kissed Amir on the forehead.

***

A tugging sensation brought Amir to.

He was shirtless, back flat against the pale stone floor, a large cloth bandage wrapped around his torso. A pleasant, warming sensation radiated from beneath the dressing. An ancient man with olive skin and a bristly, chalk-white moustache hovered above him, muttering in a dialect Amir found difficult to identify.

As the man adjusted the bandage, Amir remained silent, fixated on the teal twinkle in the man's eyes.

The nausea had subsided. As had the acute burning in his side, obviously the work of whatever balm had been applied. Had the bullet been removed? That'd be some fucking handiwork. How long had he been out?

When the man stepped away, Amir gained a clear view of an elegant beige stone arch directly above him. And in rolling his head from right to left, the hundreds of blue-lit pillars and archways constituting the Masjid al-Haram's interior facade.

It was breathtakingly simple, a sprawling achievement of sacred architecture—its openness overtly, magnanimously inviting passage.

Amir breathed deeply, anticipating what stood before him and then hoisted himself onto his elbows.

And there it was, just a stone's throw away: the sight to end all sights; the object to reduce all objects, the imposing, solitary, pristine geometric work of genius, the Kaaba—an onyx and gold gift box from God. Amir forced his frame upward, relying on every fibre of muscle to gain his feet. Upright, he staggered slightly, then regained balance after a wobbly moment.

"Seven times," a whisper told him. Then a thin hand took him by the arm. "Come," Babu said, gently drawing Amir forward toward the Kaaba. "I've done it twice already—and trust me, it doesn't get old."

And so they went—slowly—both limping but determined.

"What sort of prayer," Amir asked.

"Any one you want," Babu said, letting Amir's elbow go as they processed around it. "Though one of gratitude seems fitting."

Overhead—beyond the illumination of the Mosque, beyond the silent intricacies of the holy city, far beyond the mortal remains of those buried beneath it—the desert stars vibrated wildly, the moon glittered like a platinum broach pinned to the breast of heaven, and the untouchable, unknowable, percolating edge of time-space roared outward at immeasurable speed.

Amir could feel it spin above him, moving as he moved, no trace of inertia. No barriers. No boundaries. No impediments to Allah's cosmic ambitions.

Rashid was right—*no death here.*

Not in the seeping wound above his belt. Not in the disintegrating bones of the entombed. Not in the spinning fires of the firmament. It was all life—cycling and swift—stretching from creation to eternity.

***

A half hour up the coast from Jedda, on the King Abdulaziz International Airport's sandstorm-battered runway, Sparrow barked orders at the old Arab carrying a hose. Sparrow was in a pain-induced tizzy, beard singed, brow raw, leg dripping from his latest encounter with Amir Omar Duran.

"This better not be the wrong type," the pilot said. "I'll blow your bloody head off if this thing shits the bed."

The man said nothing and attached the nozzle to the tank. When the job was done, Sparrow staggered toward the man, and jutted a finger into his chest.

"I want you to stay exactly where you are until I'm in the air, got it?"

The Arab nodded. But when Sparrow started up the steps to board the plane, the man shuffled quickly toward the gas truck, wrenched the driver's side door open, and flung himself up and into its cab.

"Hey! What the fuck are you doing," Sparrow screamed, bounding down the steps at the reversing tanker. "I said wait!"

Sparrow limped toward the truck, drew his Beretta level, and squeezed off every round in the magazine. The tanker glided backwards into the overgrown brush at the Tarmac's edge, its driver in a bloody pile behind the wheel.

"Fucking bastard," Sparrow said in a growl. Then he turned around and re-boarded the plane. "Fucking sand-nigger prick. Where does C get these fucking amateurs?"

In the cockpit, Sparrow held his breath and turned the engine over. The ignition failed to respond. He grabbed his headset from the passenger's seat and spiked it off the windshield. "Fuck all!"

Sparrow closed his eyes and muttered Amir's name, over and over in a boiling whisper.

One laboured minute later, he dragged himself across the

runway, climbed into the tanker, tossed the body from the cab, and kicked the truck's windshield out. His GPS insisted Mecca was over 100 kilometres away.

"Christ," he said, then yanked the shift back and drove the gas pedal to the floor.

***

Sparrow was a disaster on wheels. Steel splinters lodged in his left quad. Sweat pouring down his seared face. Torn tee shirt reeking of gun powder and petroleum.

Despite the growing list of maladies, he'd made good time. Headlights killed, he barrelled off Ring Road, around a looping interchange and onto Route 15—a stretch of industrial highway the Bedouins had converted into a makeshift runway.

Sparrow hadn't brought his field glasses. Only his rifle and pistol. But the night was clear and the southern portion of the 15 was lit well enough to expose the sand-worn turbo prop he'd come to intercept.

Roughly four hundred metres from the plane, Sparrow brought the tanker down to second gear. He'd plenty of cover to choose from—vacant factories, defunct refineries, anonymous storage containers abutting the road's edges. Two hundred metres further, he parked the truck behind some rusty rigging equipment and hopped from the cab.

Machine gun raised, Sparrow limped along the road's shadowed margin—moonlight only jumping over him as he passed between buildings. A hundred metres from the turboprop, Sparrow dipped behind a row of blue outhouses at the edge of an empty lot and took a knee in the dust.

Ten minutes of observation produced nothing of value, Duran and his ragtag crew of Zanzibaris nowhere to be seen. Sparrow shook his head and stretched his wounded leg out. "Where the fuck are these assholes?"

"Who you calling an asshole?"

Sparrow flashed his head round and received a hard smack from the steal barrel of Amir's Glock. The pilot tumbled onto his back.

"Shit hiding place," Amir said, collecting the pilot's rifle from the dirt. "You *are* fucking dogged, though, I'll give you that." Sparrow's hand inched toward the holster at his waist. "Don't do that," Amir said. "Seriously. *Don't.*"

"How in the bloody *hell*," Sparrow said, a touch of resignation in each word.

Amir bent forward to disarm him and winced. "I know it must be painful for you to hear this, *mi amigo*—but you're a fucking mess. Now get up. We need to go."

Sparrow rested on one elbow and studied Amir. "Think you're fucking better than me, don't you?"

Amir looked at him, thoughtfully. "Tell you what I think. I think you and Mason underestimated me. I also think whoever's pulling the strings back in London never figured it would come down to this. So they choose the only imbeciles stupid enough to get mixed up in this car wreck of an op. Either way...makes me wonder about the SIS."

"Calling me stupid?"

"I'm calling you *and* Mason stupid. Now get the fuck off the ground. And Sparrow, just because I didn't have the heart to shoot without fair warning, doesn't mean I won't pump two rounds in your fucking head if you try anything."

Sparrow rose, smiling a little. "See I got one in you at least," he said, pointing at the white bandage poking out from behind Amir's vest.

Amir returned the smile. "Simple suggestion, Sparrow. Go for a headshot next time."

TWENTY-SIX

At the ripe age of twenty-one, Tony Mason signed up for six months abroad in Florence. A sure means of gaining a leg up on every aspiring auctioneer at Cambridge.

Three days prior to his scheduled departure, the exchange program was suddenly cancelled.

Terrorism, he'd said to his roommate. *In Italy? Bloody crock of shit. What, the jihadists are suddenly obsessed with purging the West of homoerotic perversions? Was Michelangelo now Koranic enemy number one? Doubtful.*

Mason transferred out of the art history program the following semester to pursue a degree in economics. Ironically, failure to follow through with his original major became the one thing his father ever praised him for. *Good*, the bastard had said. *At least now you have a fighting chance to do something productive with your life.*

"Yet to be determined," Mason whispered. He now stood at the edge of a sprawling heliport built atop the southern ramparts of the Castello Maniace. Mason had never been to Sicily before. Indeed, he'd never set foot in Italy up until this point. And the Sicilian RAF base was a far cry from Florence's Piazza del Duomo.

As Mason waited for Ant to load his last bit of gear, a swift wind rolled in from the eastern Mediterranean and flapped at the lapels of his blazer. Mason buttoned his coat and flipped the bird to the winking heavens.

"Ready to roll, Tony?"

He turned to the pilot. "Roll?"

"Yes. *Roll*. Run. Ship out. Get *ghost*, as the RAF boys like to say."

"I *know* what you bloody mean."

Ant smiled. "Then why'd you ask, Tony?"

"Just making sure you knew the difference between a helicopter and dump truck."

"*Ha*," Ant said with a chuckle. "They told me you were a prick. But a *pithy* prick? I lucked out with this op."

"Tell me," Mason said, fixing his eyes on the sea below. "What *is* this op?"

"Oh, you know exactly what it is." With that, the pilot strode off toward the mat black fifth-gen Chinook. "Come on, Tony—don't be late to your own party!"

"Wouldn't dream of it," Mason said under his breath.

Once in the chopper, though, he had more questions for the pilot. All of them eliciting unsatisfactory answers.

"You can fly this on your own?"

"Thank the blokes in R&D for that."

"What about range—won't we have to refuel?"

Dismissed again: "Beauty of a nearly bottomless defence budget."

That shut Mason up for a minute. But, Mason wasn't really the silent type. "Okay, well what happens when we get there—won't they know?"

"Fuck yah, they'll know."

"What does that mean?"

"Just what it sounds like. Now stop distracting me—I've got a 200 million quid bird to fly."

"Wait," Mason said, "don't I need a gun?"

The pilot didn't even turn his head. "You mean you didn't bring yours?"

***

The big moon had fallen some. Brit stood on the balcony eying it, machine gun hugged to her breast as if someone threatened to disarm her. A large set of field goggles dangled from her neck and cigarette hung from her lower lip.

Inside, Blake lay prone on the carpet next to Maggie's cot. He'd been asleep for a good two hours.

When Maggie gasped, though, the private sprung to his knees within seconds. "O'Connor," he whispered, immediately reaching to feel her neck. After sixty seconds, Blake removed his fingers from Maggie's pulseless jugular. Then he closed his eyes, lowered his head, and rested it on her lap. After another full minute, he rose to his feet and made his way to the open doorway of the balcony.

"Stay inside," Brit said, voice low and flat against the hum of the locusts down in the overgrown rough of the golf course below.

"Ma'am," Blake said. "She's gone." Brit shifted only slightly from where she stood, eyes still out on the night, still searching the shadows. Blake's head slumped downward. "What do we do?"

"About what?"

With trembling vocal chords, he reminded her. "O'Connor, ma'am. She's—she died, ma'am."

"Blake."

"Yes, ma'am."

"Call me Brit, okay?" When he didn't answer, she persisted. "Will you do that?"

"Okay."

"Thank you," she said, still unable to face him.

"May I have a cigarette, ma'am?" Without looking, she removed the dwindling supply from her pocket and extended it back in his direction. "Thank you, ma'am," he said. "I mean, Brit, ma'am. I mean—"

"Blake."

"Yes?"

"It's fine. Can't change who I am anyway."

"Okay, ma'am."

"Blake," she said, sliding past the private and making her way to Maggie's side. "Do not go out there."

For several minutes, Brit lingered above Maggie, studying the pilot's face in the moon's pale, watery glow. There was a simple beauty in Maggie's features—her small, freckled nose; her thin, angular jawline; the gentle rise of her upper lip. Brit ran a hand over Maggie's forehead, and then turned around to face Blake.

"Blake."

"Yes, ma'am?"

"Let's go kill this fucking bastard."

***

"Repeat it back to me," Brit said. They were flat on their bellies, faces coated with soot and bone dust from the crawl.

"When you get to the corner, I shoot the flair," he said in a whisper.

"Blake."

"Yes, ma'am."

"*Listen* to me. When I get into position, I will light *my* landing flair. If he opens up, I return fire. Only then, do you shoot your flair. Aim high and in the direction I'm firing."

"What if you don't see him?"

"I will, if he's there. Maggie—" she paused. "Based on Maggie's wound, he must've been close."

"What if he moved?"

"Blake."

"Yes, ma'am."

"He's in one of those buildings," Brit said, pointing. "We've only got an hour or so before it's light. We need to take our shot. Copy?"

"Copy, ma'am."

As she crawled away, big gun slung over her back, Blake breathed heavily, chin raised, the flair pistol in one hand, his service weapon in the other.

A minute later, the far corner of the roof was ablaze in flaming pink, phosphorescent sparks splashing over Brit and the remnants of death surrounding her.

When the sniper's silent shots arrived, Brit tossed the flair sideways from her body, sand and bone splinters splashing up from the roof's surface. Then her gun muzzle joined the wild dance, rattling the dry night air, bottled thunder uncorked.

Blake trained the flair pistol and pulled the trigger. It ripped upward with a shrill whistle, then crested in a tremendous green burst. But the explosion was too high to help Brit's cause.

"Blake! Another one," Brit said in between rifle bursts. "Right at the building—top level!"

Blake reloaded and squeezed off another shot, this time under a volley of rounds from the sniper. As it collided with the building, a crouching silhouette appeared between a cluster of deck furniture on the opposite roof.

"The roof!" Brit screamed, unloading every bullet in the magazine. "Send one at the shit on the roof!"

When Blake did, the sniper leapt from his position and darted toward a small storage structure behind him. With her eyes locked on the fleeing target, Brit fumbled for a new clip, swearing as her opportunity receded.

Suddenly Blake's service weapon snapped off from the flank. Repeatedly. And by some miracle of latent marksmanship the moving shadow collapsed in a heap onto the deck.

Brit shrieked, scampering toward the private. "Brilliant! Bloody fucking brilliant! Let's fucking go!"

Blake sprung from his knees, staring with disbelief at the dying light of the flare on the opposite roof. "Where?"

"Come on," she said, ripping the exterior door wide, and bolting down the steps.

Blake bounded down, several stairs at time. "Ma'am! Ma'am, wait for me!"

They burst through the front lobby and out its entrance, rounding the hotel's facade, and charged toward the enemy's edifice like kids set loose in a game of tag.

"Weapon up," Brit said, yanking at the handle of the building's side entrance. Locked, she raised her gun and discharged several rounds from point blank range. Sparks jumped as the handle flew to pieces. "Stay close and cover the flank."

Brit went first, rifle extended from her shoulder at ninety degrees, moving with the steadiness and speed years of tactical training had instilled. Blake, though, had never learnt to ride that bike, and as he brought up the rear, his head swivelled wildly from side to side, hands trembling over the service weapon.

They arrived at the foot of a stairwell and Brit signalled upward with two fingers and launched forward. Eyes peeled, chests heaving, they raced to the top. On the landing above, they huddled silently behind the roof door.

Brit raised a fist and counted off. One finger. Two fingers. Three. Her free hand returned to the gun, and her foot drove the door wide, the thud of her boot toe followed by the vicious clap of her gun.

And then another clap. And another. And then a jarring rhythm of thunder as the shots rang out in succession. Blake froze in the open doorway as Brit pitilessly unloaded the remainder of her clip—forty plus rounds battering the dry air like a snare drum.

The brimstone perfume of spent powder filled the silence that followed. After several seconds, Brit tossed her rifle down, drew her pistol and approached the lead-riddled corpse.

"Ma'am," Blake said. "Ma'am … I think you've got him."

But Brit's vengeance was incomplete. With an icy remove and ease of motion, she knelt at the sniper's side and placed the gun barrel to his forehead. Blake winced as blood and brain matter exploded onto the deck beneath the gunman's skull.

"Bastard," Brit said, rising to her feet. "You know what that is?" Blake stared blankly. She pointed to the man's weapon. "That's an L131A1. You know who uses that?" Blake shook his head. "The SAS," she said. "Exclusively."

***

"The important thing," C said, "is to avoid rushing to judgement."

The old man was leaning over his office dry bar pouring a sizable serving of his finest scotch, talking to Henry Glass as if Glass were an agent in training. Glass was seated on one of the burgundy leather chairs at the centre of the room, barely listening. He took the scotch from C and drained it in a single, burning slug.

"I'll have another," Glass said.

"Careful, now."

"Pour it."

C gave Glass a serpentine grin. "I suppose you've earned it." He turned to fetch another round and continued the lecture. "Let's focus on what we know. Obviously, Tony is in cahoots with those bastards at GLogiX—we've confirmed that much." He paused, handing Glass the drink. "I've had them taken into custody, by the way."

The statement didn't elicit a congratulatory response.

Instead, Glass silently drained the second scotch, and handed the empty cup back. "Another."

"Christ, Henry. I suggest you slow down. Don't want you vomiting all over the oriental."

"*Another.*"

C sighed. "Anyway, the man is in way over his head."

"Where is he?"

"I can't disclose that, Henry."

Glass rose slowly from the chair, body loose with liquor, and swaggered toward the old man. C shuffled back a step.

"He's gone to Cairo—yes?" Glass was inches from C's face now, hot, boozy breath infusing the air between them. "Send a team."

"You know I can't do that, Agent Glass."

Glass gave him a mad smile. "Because it would expose this little mess."

"Oh, spare me," C said with a snarl. "I could give a shit about the bloody optics of it. This isn't about politics."

"Then do it."

C leaned forward, reclaiming some ground. "I'm not going to violate a fucking international treaty. Get your fucking head straight."

Glass wouldn't move though. "And the boy?"

"Well," C said, relaxing again. "We'll have to hope for the best. Duran and Tillman know what they're doing—they've made it this far."

Glass raised his chin and peered down his nose at C's forehead, weighing his next move. Violence was an option. A satisfying one, at least. It'd complicate things, though.

Having spent God knows how long in a bloody cell, Glass chose otherwise. "Put me in touch with Mason."

C smirked. "And how do you propose I do that?"

"Who's flying him?"

"If we knew that, we wouldn't have such a conundrum on our hands, now would we? You need to go home, Henry. Get a hold of yourself. Eat some food, get some sleep. They tell me you've been up for days."

"I'll be here," Glass said, pushing past the old man, and snatching the bottle from the bar. Decanter in hand, Glass sauntered toward the door.

John Ward

"Agent Glass—where do you think you're going?"

"Wherever I bloody please."

By that, Glass meant the coms centre. When he arrived—rapping at its broad glass window like a dishevelled vagrant harassing restaurant goers—the graveyard shift boys exchanged glances, like, *are you going to handle this?*

The door hissed open and a young redhead emerged in the corridor. "Can I help you?"

"I doubt it," Glass said, pushing past the man.

"Sir, you can't just—"

"*Can't* I?" Glass said, scanning the room. "Who's got a cigarette?" Again, the coms team sat in silence. Glass shook his head. "I'm Agent Henry Glass, the Granada station liaison. Now who's going to give me a cigarette? I know at least one of you smokes ... come on lads, give it up."

"I know who you are, sir," the ginger said. "I was there for the trade security presentation earlier this week."

"Lovely," Glass said. "Now be a good boy and get me a smoke."

The overweight, frumpy one at the console stood up and dug a pack out from his cheap sport coat.

"Ah," Glass said, lifting the cigarette to his lips, "there's a real man among you. Light, please."

The redhead looked horrified. "Sir, you can't smoke in here."

"Says who—*you?*" Glass motioned at the fat boy with an upturned palm. "Lighter."

"The equipment," the redhead said in protest.

"The equipment, *what?* Will cease to function? You little minions need to get out more. Now, come on, man, hand the bloody lighter over." The chubby kid shrugged and handed it to him. Glass sparked the flint, took a deep tug from the smoke, and exhaled slowly. "Don't get your panties in a bunch—the fire alarm won't trigger. Excuse me," he said, making his way to the empty seat the fat one had previously occupied.

"Sir, what are you doing?" the redhead said.

"Calling home."

"Sir, there's a process in place for this sort of thing."

"If you've a bloody problem with what I'm doing, put a call into C's office—I'm sure he'd be happy to straighten you out."

"Pardon?"

"You heard me—call the old man. I just came from meeting with him."

"I'm not calling C's office, sir—that's totally inappropriate!"

"Then bugger off."

When Granada came online, the operator wore a look of shock. "Sir!"

"Hi Jenkins—where's Davis?"

"Um, he's right here, sir. Hold on, sir."

It took a few seconds for Davis's big, bald head to appear on the monitor. In that time, the surly redhead disappeared from the coms room—ostensibly, to search for someone who might heed his complaints. Best of fucking luck.

The other coms operators, though, were rapt with curiosity, shirking their assigned duties for a front seat to the action.

"Agent Glass, where in the hell have they been keeping you? A fucking *dungeon*?" Glass and Davis weren't equals, exactly. But the endless litres of Spanish beer they'd shared over the years had shaped a degree of informality between the men.

"Best not get me fucking started," Glass said.

"That bad, eh?"

"Bad doesn't begin to describe it. What's the word on Tillman?"

Davis squinted, and then looked over his own shoulder. "You sure you want to do this right now, Henry?"

"No better time."

Davis shrugged. "Your call. Anyway—I haven't a clue where the General is. Wouldn't disclose her destination. Though she was somewhere over the Libyan desert last we spoke."

"How long ago was that?"

"Days, Henry."

"Haven't you been tracking her?"

"She's radio silent—said she had to be. Couldn't be running commo in a DMZ or whatever. Russians would be all over it." Davis cleared his throat. "So would SIS—though I take it that's no longer a concern."

"What about Duran?"

"Ask your friends at Vauxhall. Only data we had down here

John Ward

was coming from London. But it's been ages since we've heard anything. Whoever was tracking him stopped—or went off-system with it. Either way, I haven't the foggiest."

"God damn it."

"Last coordinates we have for Duran is a hundred clicks east of Mogadishu, if that helps. Again, that was days ago."

Glass rubbed his eyebrows. Then he ran a hand back through his greasy hair and twisted round to take in the baffled faces behind him. *Wankers.* He took a quick drag from his dying butt, tossed it to the floor, gave the room a hard stare and returned to Davis. "I gather you haven't been in touch with the Bedouins."

"The Bedouins?"

"Jeddah."

"You've lost me. Hank—Tillman's kept me entirely in the dark."

Glass was silent for a moment. Then, "Davis, what's your schedule today?"

"Just started."

"Good. Expect to hear from me again shortly."

"Sounds like a plan," Davis said with a smirk. "Henry."

"Aye."

"You look like shite."

"Aye," Glass repeated. Then came his first smile since everything went to hell. "Looks can be deceiving."

سبع وعشرين

Their arrival was something out of a movie: Beat-up plane barrels down narrow fairway; debris flies up at its nose; landing gear bounces violently along the sand-blanketed turf; plane skids to a halt just metres from a row of sun-beaten palms.

Bedouin pilot smiles proudly.

"Hole in one," Rashid said in English.

"And on a par five," Amir said with a chuckle. "Nicely done."

"Shukraan," the pilot said, still beaming with satisfaction.

Amir turned to Sparrow, unable to resist. "Bet they didn't teach you that shit in flight school."

"Fuck off," Sparrow said, rolling his shoulders, and lifting his zip-tied wrists. "Can you loosen these bloody things—cutting my goddamn circulation off."

Amir shook his head and said, "*Lo siento, mi amigo.*" Then he stood from his seat, unstrapped the Glock from his thigh holster and addressed his crew. "Okay—here's the drill. Me and our friend here go first. Then Harkinder, Darweshi, Babu, and Abasi—in that order. Rashid, you cover the back. Stay close and move quickly. We're making a beeline to the hotel. Looks like a bit of a hike, so stay alert." Amir leaned down and unzipped the duffle that lay in the isle. "Take this," he said to Rashid, handing the pilot a machine pistol.

"What you want me to do with this tiny thing?"

"It's fully automatic."

Rashid raised the gun to his eyes and shrugged. "How many bullets?"

"Plenty."

When Amir popped the hatch, the low dawn sun splashed into the cabin. Squinting, he gained his first glimpse of Giza's surreal beauty, the indomitable pyramids rising up from the desert beyond. "Let's go," he said, pulling Sparrow by the arm and shoving him onto the top of the foldout steps.

Sparrow grimaced and shook free. "Get your fucking hands off me."

"Listen—I'm going to say this for the last time: follow my directions." Then he leaned into Sparrow's ear and lowered his voice. "Or I'll beat you fucking senseless."

"Fuck off," Sparrow said, wincing as he staggered down the steps.

"How's the leg?" Amir asked, as they waited for the others to join them outside.

"How's the bullet hole in your side?"

"Healing nicely—thanks for asking."

Sparrow's eyes narrowed, and again he shook his head. "Really think you're some sort of hero, don't you?"

"Just an ordinary man living an extraordinary life."

"Read that somewhere?"

"*En una pared del bano.*"

"What?"

"*No hablas espanol?* Funny—I was fluent in English by sixth grade."

"Sucks being colonized, doesn't it?"

"That was *before* the invasion, you ignorant shit." Amir was having a good time of it, fucking with the man who'd shot him. But as Rashid emerged from the plane and descended the steps, he refocused on the business at hand. Amir pointed with his gun across the course. "Here we go everybody—quick and steady."

They marched ahead in unison, Sparrow limping in front of Amir at a respectable pace. Ordinarily, Amir would have kept his gun trained on a prisoner's back. But he was satisfied with the extent of Sparrow's disadvantage. Instead, Amir held the nine low, palming its grip with both hands, eyes scouring the shortening shadows along the course's perimeter, every so often glancing up at the majestic monuments of Giza.

Heartbreaking, thought Amir, suddenly feeling the urge to see them up close; to give them the proper attention they deserved. Attuned to the eerie silence of his surroundings, he wondered whether the boy behind him might indeed hold the key to restoring the world's magic.

Fucking hope so.

Amir hopped a heap of sand and the throbbing in his side

jumped to the fore. The pain prompted more practical considerations. Where the hell was Brit? She must've seen them land. Maybe not—maybe she's just holed up inside, avoiding the eyes in the sky. Had the Russians simply backed off? No way. Not with young Darweshi Lotto in the world.

After rounding a large, concave section of earth—a former sand-trap by the look of it—they passed through a dense line of dried-out palms and low scrub. It was challenging terrain for the hobbled Sparrow.

"Keep it moving," Amir said, poking Sparrow's back with the muzzle of the nine.

"Why the fuck aren't we going round this shit?"

"Great idea," Amir said. "While we're at it, we can shoot off a bunch of flairs—start screaming—make sure everyone knows we've arrived."

Sparrow returned his attention to the craggy terrain. When they were through to other side, though, he stopped in his tracks, eyes locked on the massive transport chopper one hundred metres away at the crook of a dogleg fairway.

"It's Tillman, isn't it?" Sparrow said.

"What makes you say that?"

"That's O'Connor's rig."

Amir motioned for the group to keep moving and drew shoulder to shoulder with Sparrow. "How do you know O'Connor?"

"Who doesn't? Only bird in the PAF who knows what the fuck she's doing."

"We're in good hands then."

"Speak for yourself." They were closing in on the hotel now, and the weight of the pilot's predicament was clearly wearing on him. "I wish you'd put a bullet in my head and been done with it."

"You know," Amir said, "you've got a good case on your hands—just following orders, and all."

"Spare me the fucking pity," the pilot said.

"Didn't take you for a martyr, Sparrow."

In another hundred metres, they passed from the edge of the course onto the resort's back lawn. A massive, muck-filled swimming pool lay at its centre. From the pasty, shit-hued surface of the pool, rose an almost unbearable stench. Another raw statement of nature's reclamation.

They charged past it, pinching their nostrils, even the hobbled among them moving with great efficiency. Just beyond the range of the stagnant water's awful scent, they arrived at the hotel. Amir waved for the group to join him under the cover of the building's rear portico.

"Stop here," he said as everyone shuffled under the simple arches of the portico ceiling. "Rashid, you'll be on watch." There was still no sign of Tillman. And weary of a potential ambush, Amir had no intention of leading the ragtag platoon inside. Cocking the slide of his Glock back, he looked off toward the corner of the building. "Under no circumstances do you come after me."

Harkinder—who'd remained remarkably silent until now—stepped forward as if she'd been designated group spokesman. "And what if you don't return?"

"Just sit tight," Amir said. Abasi and Darweshi took the instructions literally, helping Babu take a seat against the wall, and quickly plopping down next to him. Harkinder did the same. When Sparrow attempted to join them, Amir flicked his gun barrel in the pilot's direction. "Not you," he said. "You're with me."

"What do you need me for?"

"Sometimes I get lonesome," Amir said, his best Eastwood impression drawing a smile from the old man. Then, Amir shrugged. "I don't know, Sparrow, maybe I'm just feeling nostalgic. Me and you—we used to be thick as thieves." Sparrow straightened up. "Come on," Amir said, allowing the pilot to proceed first.

They made their way along the back of the building, then around its side. As they turned the front corner, Amir placed his left hand to the pilot's left shoulder and raised his weapon up over Sparrow's right.

"Using me as bloody shield?"

"Bingo," Amir said, slowing their pace as they approached the front door. "Now open it and move inside. Try anything and I'll be sure to do you that favour you asked for."

With the steal of Amir's nine two centimetres from his jaw, Sparrow drew a massive breath.

"Easy," Amir said, tapping Sparrow's ear with the gun. "Go ahead."

Gradually, the pilot drew the door open and shuffled in, Amir shadowing in lockstep, eyes adjusting to the darkness of the lobby as they entered.

"Whoops," Sparrow said, halting less than a metre in.

Amir craned to see over his captive's strapping shoulders.

"Took you bloody long enough," Ant said, baritone cockney booming through the room.

Amir leaned left for a better view. Not fucking good. Mason, Brit, and some kid in nylon flight gear stood shoulder to shoulder, each blindfolded, hands bound. The men looked terrified, though Tillman was the one with the pistol angled at her temple. The guy holding it was half hidden behind the human wall.

Amir dipped back behind Sparrow, wrenched left his arm round the pilot's neck, and jammed the Glock to his head. When the pilot tensed up, Amir only pressed harder.

"Brit," Amir said, "Who the fuck is this guy?"

"The cavalry," Ant said. "Now here's how this goes. First, you'll let go of the pilot's neck. Once you've released him, you'll step to the left and place your weapon on the ground. Stand back up, raise your hands out in front of you, interlock your tan little fingers, and rest them on the crown of your head. Then—and pay close attention to this bit—take six very slow paces toward the centre of the room and kneel down."

"After that?" Amir asked, a simple interruption the only toe hold he could find.

"Glad you asked," Ant said. "After that, our pal Sparrow's going to fetch me the lad. When he gets back, we'll sort out who lives and who dies."

Without a clear play at hand, Amir began to drag Sparrow backward. Ant raised his gun up and cracked a shot off into the gilded moulding above Amir and Sparrow. A brown blizzard of dust rained down on their heads.

Amir froze. "Brit?"

John Ward

"Amir," she said, voice oddly steady. "Get the boy and go."

Her punishment for speaking out of turn was a swift strike from the butt of Ant's pistol.

"Listen, *Amir*—I don't have all day," Ant said, returning the gun to Brit's slumping head. "Let go of the pilot."

"Fuck off."

"Bloody Christ," Ant said, suddenly shifting his pistol to Blake's skull. There was a jolting clap. The kid flopped sideways, body collapsing face first to the floor. Brit shuddered, and Mason released a pitiful howl. Ant poked his head forward to inspect the damage and pointed with his gun. "Now that's on you, Duran."

"I'll put a bullet in Sparrow's head," was all Amir could come up with.

"For all I care, we can play this out until you and I are the last ones standing—have a little duel if you're up for it."

"Are fucking kidding me," Sparrow said, windpipe struggling to project under the pressure of Amir's forearm.

"Sorry, Sparrow, nothing personal," Ant said. "Why don't you tell Agent Duran who I am? Might help his decision-making process." When the pilot didn't answer, Ant said, "No? Well, Duran, I'm what the SIS warmly refer to as a Garbo. You know—as in *garbage man*. Not the most glamourous of titles. But I assure you, it's an apt pseudonym. I'm the one who cleans up all the crap everyone else has trouble with. Seems there's been bucket loads recently. Now, I don't know much about you. But you should ask yourself—why are you here? From what I gather, it's because you've bumbled your way into this mess. Me? I'm here to sort you out."

Amir flicked his head. "That's supposed to scare me?"

"No, that's supposed to set the record straight. I kill for a fucking living. And if I weren't good at it, there wouldn't be a gun to this bitch's head right now. So, what's it going to be—more blood on your hands?"

"I can send Sparrow for the boy," Amir said, "but he won't make it back." Which wasn't simply posturing, given what he'd observed of Rashid.

"No? Let's make this simple then."

Amir—more so than most men—was well-accustomed to the disorienting nature of gun violence. But when Sparrow pitched back from the shot to his chest, Amir experienced the sound of the aggressor's weapon only as an aftereffect. Like a delayed clap of thunder in the wake of distant lightning.

More startling was the blurring rush of action that followed. A hand on Amir's shoulder, yanking him sideways. The rapid bark of an automatic weapon. Brit and Mason scattering in opposite directions as splinters of wood and metal exploded from ceiling. Ant crouching to return fire, gun muzzle flashing as he did.

Rashid's unannounced arrival had whipped the lobby into a tornado of chaos. After a split second of resisting the whirling momentum of violence, Amir's instincts launched him headfirst into its winds. He slid flat onto his belly, eyes tracking Ant's torso, arms extended forward in a V, both hands gripping his Glock at its apex. One, two, three shots—fast and even—sprung from his pistol, tagging Ant squarely in the chest, colliding him with the reception counter.

Amir sprung athletically to his feet, charged Ant, and raised his Glock level to the assassin's head. Their eyes met briefly, Ant's wide with an unflinching, fatalistic calm. The pistol was still in Ant's hand. When he raised it—quickly, but with an almost perfunctory casualness—Amir had already won the draw.

Clack.

Shot to the head.

Clack.

Shot to the neck, just above the collar of Ant's flack jacket.

The assassin's upper body bounced awkwardly off the reception desk and then slumped to the floor. Amir turned to find Abasi kneeling over Rashid. Brit was several paces away, bound hands aiming the Bedouin's pistol at Sparrow. The pilot writhed, clutching at the blackened impact point on the left side of his Kevlar vest. Mason was curled into a foetal position at the base of an overturned couch, shielding his face from the action.

"There's a helicopter," Abasi said to Amir.

"What?"

"There's a helicopter flying at us."

"Out," Brit said, "now."

Amir nodded at Rashid. Abasi's head shook regretfully.

Amir ran toward Mason and pulled him up by the arm. Mason legs wobbled like a newborn colt, and the strength it required to hoist the shaken agent upward sent a bolt of pain through Amir's ribs. He pointed his Glock at Mason. "Get a fucking hold of yourself," he said, tightening his grip on Mason's arm and pushing him toward the door.

Abasi, who hadn't moved from Rashid's side, looked at Amir, crestfallen. "What do we do with him?"

"Nothing," Amir said, "he's dead." Amir then paused, free hand locked over Mason's elbow, and rapidly shook his gun at Rashid's body. "We can say a prayer for him once we're up. Now let's go."

As they passed through the glittering, refracted sunlight of the foyer, Amir could hear the chopper closing in but failed to locate it, pupils adjusting to the full power of the glaring sun.

When they arrived at the back of the building, Harkinder was staring out toward the western sky above the pyramids. And there it was—a Russian twin turbine gunship—ripping toward them.

"Anyone else?" Brit said, looking at Amir, like, where did all these fucking people come from?

"No," he said. "Abasi—help your father."

And they were off—the wounded, the young, the infirm, the adversarial captives—sprinting, united by a common threat.

Halfway across the fairway Amir reared up. "Harkinder, where the fuck is the bag?"

"I—I left it," she said, pointing.

Amir looked back toward the hotel, and Tillman screamed. "Duran—leave it! They won't open up on us." When he hesitated, she stopped and made her command more exact. "That's a fucking order, Duran!"

As they piled in, the Russians made a short loop and came to a hover above the building.

"Sparrow, you're driving," Brit said.

"Me?"

"Yes, *you*."

He stared at her, a faint grin emerging on his lips. "You trust me?"

"You're the only one who can operate this thing. Now get in the cockpit."

"Why the fuck should I help you?"

"Amir," Brit said, "cut me loose."

Amir drew a knife from the sheath at the back of his belt and clipped the plastic ties from Brit's wrists. In a flash, she had the gun to Sparrow's head. "Get this thing in the air."

When he held his stare and didn't move, she backhanded his face with the machine pistol. He drew his tied hands to his face, blood flowing heavily from his nostrils.

"You broke my fucking nose!"

"It'll be a bullet next time. Get the fucking show on the road."

"What if they fire on us," he said, getting oriented at the controls.

"It's an extraction team," said Brit. "They're not here to make a mess. Amir, get up here—we need you."

Amir looked at Mason, then Abasi. "Make sure this prick behaves," he said to Abasi and handed him the Glock. Then Amir turned to the old man. "Babu."

"Yes, son."

"Say a little prayer for us."

"Bismillah," he said with a slow nod.

Amir nodded. "*In the name of God.*"

TWENTY-EIGHT

"Never thought I'd say this, but Duran—he's fucking remarkable, you know. You are too, for that matter." Glass was in the coms room with an earpiece in, not really giving a shit if C had the line tapped.

It *was* remarkable, what they'd pulled off. Even the fat kid who'd been feeding him cigarettes for the past few hours was brimming with a sort of second-hand exhilaration. And he made no attempt to disguise it—eyes as big as saucers, mouth nervously chomping on a candy bar as he listened to Glass's half of the conversation.

"Well," Brit said, "save your praises until we're back in one piece, Henry—we're running on fumes here."

"You'll be fine," he said. "Carrier passed Crete an hour ago."

"Still unsure of what to do with our friends here, Henry."

Glass gave the coms room a quick look over. "Don't give them over to the MPs—we'll never see them again."

"What do you suggest?"

"Have Duran babysit them until you're back."

"Back *where*, Henry? They'll have us all in debriefing as soon as we step foot on the carrier. Guarantee it."

He thought about it. "You're a general, Brit. Throw your weight around a little."

"Right," she said shakily. "Last few days, Henry. I don't know up from down, anymore."

He sighed deeply. "Almost home, Tillman."

There was silence on the line for a good ten seconds. Then Brit cut through it, tone heavy with emotion. "I want them to receive full honours, Henry. No bloody secret ceremony. Full colours, O'Connor and the kid."

"Okay," he said. "Just remind yourself, lass—they died in service of something important."

"Cold comfort."

"Aye," he said. "How is Duran?"

"Pretty banged up. You know that stubborn bastard, though—

wouldn't admit it if you paid him." Again, she went quiet for a stretch. Then, "Can't believe I allowed this all to happen."

"Had no choice, dear."

"I should've called you straight away."

"You couldn't have known," Glass said, voice tremulous.

"Henry."

"Yes, love?"

"Are you okay?"

"Just tired is all."

"Tell me about it."

"Trust me," he said, "I will."

"I should go."

"Call me as soon as you touch down, dear."

"Roger," she said, and cut the line.

***

The big rig was cruising now. Amir had moved to the cabin, sitting silently among the rest of them. By now, the adrenaline should have subsided. But every time he forced his lids shut in an attempt to rest, they sprung open defiantly.

Jesus fucking Christ, he was dying for a drink. And a cigarette. Whatever the Bedouins had given him for the pain had worn off completely. Fuck a beer, he thought. Need some morphine for this job.

"Can't sleep?" Harkinder said. She was opposite him, the boy draped across her lap, snoring softly. Every few seconds, she ran a hand over his tight-cropped hair, looking natural in her surrogate duties.

Amir rubbed his fingers against the scruff on his jaw. "Dying for a smoke."

"You must be excited to see your family."

Amir looked up, and then stretched his neck, head pivoting side to side. "How are you feeling?"

"Exhausted," she said, eyes on the boy. Then with a faint smile, "Happy to be alive, I guess."

"Praise Allah," he whispered.

John Ward

"Sorry—didn't hear you."

"Nothing." As Amir watched her caress the boy's head he felt a pang of compassion for her. "I can't promise you anything," he said, "but we'll try to get you back home when this is all over with."

Harkinder took a deep breath and brushed some hair strands away from her face. "You know, I've been in this business for more than half my life. And I'm not even forty years old."

Babu, who had appeared to be sleeping in the seat suddenly cracked his eyes open. "Time to leave this business behind, I'd say."

She nodded and gave a hollow smile. Amir considered it, too.

"What about you, Amir?" the old man asked. "Are you going to keep all of this up?"

"What else would I do?"

"Take care of your family," the old man said.

Amir twisted in his seat slightly, collecting memories of boyhood; of being James's age. Of coming home after football to a warm kitchen, his mother moving between the sink and the stove, asking whether he'd completed his homework before practice.

Si? Perfecto—off to the shower.

Then, Jeddo calling from the other room: *How many assists today?*

After washing up, Amir would settle in on the couch next to Jeddo and review every highlight.

Don't be over confident now, Amir. You'll find your match one of these games.

Never really happened though, did it? Even when he'd gone off to high school. In high school—motherless, under the cold, compassionless supervision of the British—the anger propelled his game to a new level of aggressiveness and tenacity. He'd grown unstoppable, frankly. His adolescent body, a pliant weapon wielded mercilessly against the competition. His broad shoulders, his long legs, his sharp elbows, his nuclear grade right foot. All added up to the most formidable arsenal in the league.

Amir wondered if James's relatively struggle-free childhood

would handicap the boy later in his athletic career. Would the lack of adversity soften James's instincts?

Amir hoped so.

"Excited to see them?" Babu asked, interrupting Amir's reflection.

"Yes."

"You will propose?"

Amir smiled. "Soon enough."

"Don't wait," Babu said. "As they say—timing is everything."

***

They barely made it, fuel gauge sounding its shrill warning for the final few kilometres of the journey, Babu muttering prayers until the chopper's big tires bounced down on the carrier deck.

"You owe me," Sparrow said, tossing his head set to the cockpit floor.

Brit leaned within a few centimetres of Sparrow's face. "Thanks for the ride," she said in a whisper. When he went to pull away, she grabbed him by the collar. "Know that I seriously considered killing you back in Egypt."

The pilot's grin faded. "Fuck off."

Near the top of her lungs, Brit made an announcement. "Duran, cut Sparrow and Mason loose before you open the door. Once we're out, they stay with us. Under no circumstances do they leave our sides. Let's go everyone."

But when the hatch opened, their greeting party had other ideas. "Send the prisoners out first," the masked soldier in the front ordered.

Brit pushed her way past Amir and Sparrow and leaned forward in the scalding sun. "We don't have prisoners."

The masked soldier in all black fatigues turned to the MP next to him, then back to Brit and waved his gun. "General, not only do you lack jurisdiction on this vessel, I'm operating under direct orders from the Secretary of the Navy. Unless you want to spend a night in the brig, I suggest you comply."

"Is this a bloody joke? Get the admiral."

"Admiral's not coming down, ma'am. Turn 'em over or we're boarding the chopper and placing everyone in custody."

Sparrow smiled again. "Pardon me, ma'am—seems I'm needed elsewhere."

Mason wasn't so willing. "To bloody hell with that," he said to Brit. "I'm not going with them."

Brit receded back inside and looked Mason in the eye. "Now's your chance to come clean. Can't help you otherwise."

Head tilting, Mason opened his mouth, preparing to respond. But the masked soldier in black was suddenly aboard. Arm on Mason, he nodded toward the boy.

"Him too."

Babu hobbled forward, inserting his body in between the door and Darweshi. "Where he goes, I go!"

"And me," Abasi said.

"I don't think so," the soldier replied, angling his rifle in Abasi's direction. "Step aside."

Amir stepped forward and Brit extended her arm across his chest. "Stand down," she said quietly.

He met her eyes and stayed put. "This is—"

"This is fucked," she said, completing his complaint. "But interfering won't help. Not right now."

The masked soldier stared at Amir. "Listen to the general, Agent Duran. I don't want to have to put you in custody. But I will if necessary. Now move," he said, pulling Tony Mason by the arm and then shoving him out of the chopper. Mason stumbled on his way out, falling to the cement deck and rolling awkwardly. From the door, Amir watched the MPs place shackles on Sparrow's wrists, then Mason's, and led them off toward the nearest helicopter.

"I won't let you take him," Babu said, now holding the boy to his side.

The soldier reached for Babu, and Amir thrust a hand forward. But the intervention was swiftly defended with a downward chop. Then, in one fluid motion, the masked man snatched the sidearm from his holster and drew to within a hair of Amir's face. He now had two of them in his aim—Babu, at the end of the rifle, Amir at the nose of the Beretta. Even by Amir's standards it was an impressive manoeuvre, a staggering feat of coordination and speed.

"You really want this?" the masked man said calmly. "In front of the kid?"

Amir worked the calculation through—the angle of approach, the distance between he and his adversary.

Watching him, Brit raised her voice. "No, we do not. Duran. Stand down."

As soon as Amir stepped back, the soldier returned the sidearm to his waist.

"I can't believe this," Babu said in a hiss, old eyes bulging with disbelief. "You're going to let them take Darweshi?"

"We don't have a better option," Brit said sharply. Softening her tone, she elaborated. "Resisting won't help. I'll do my best to get him back to you—you need to trust me on that."

"Trust you?"

"You can trust her," Amir said, acknowledging the limitations of their situation.

Babu grimaced and shook a crooked finger at Amir. "I've misjudged you."

"Babu," Abasi said. "Please—they're *right*. Do you want to get us killed?"

"Go ahead—shoot me—do it! Shoot me," Babu said, waving his hand at the soldier. "See what I care! You're all a bunch of cowards!"

The two MPs had returned to the open door of the chopper, both armed now.

"Stay there," the masked soldier said, flicking his free hand back in their direction. Briefly, then, he studied Babu. "Sir, last chance. Give me the boy."

"Over my dead body!"

To Amir's relief, Babu's suicidal invitation elicited a restrained response—an inverted application of the masked man's weapon, no gun shot sounding through the cabin, just the muted crunch of a rifle butt colliding with Babu's jaw. As Abasi leapt forward to break his father's fall, the soldier scooped Darweshi up by the waist, and hustled him out. The MPs weapons remained trained on Brit and Duran until the squirming boy had been safely transferred into the second chopper.

Once Darweshi was in, the masked man made his way around its nose and boarded the other helicopter. Just before the chopper's massive door slid shut, Sparrow waved his bound hands in Amir's direction, an open-mouthed smile signifying his satisfaction.

Within seconds, the whirring of the turbines amplified and both choppers leapt upward in practiced synchronization—one peeling left, the other right—and set off on opposite trajectories.

Fucking Sparrow, thought Amir. *Laughing all the way to his grave.*

***

A few clicks west, Sparrow nudged Mason with his elbow and lifted his hands.

"Oy" he said, turning his attention to the masked man. "You can take these off now." When it drew no response, he raised his voice. "Hey. I'm talking to you, friend. Wouldn't you say it's well and safe to remove these bloody things?"

"Lower your hands."

"What?"

"I said put your fucking mitts down."

Sparrow scooted up in his seat. "What's the fucking story here, mate? Get these fucking cuffs off me. Wrists are bloody killing me!"

The man said nothing. Sparrow, in near slow motion leaned back, singed face a perfect picture of confusion. He turned to Mason. "What's his fucking meaning, Mason?"

Mason closed his eyes, leaving the pilot all alone with his thoughts.

Sparrow adjusted his wrists in the restraints, winced a little, then twisted his head toward the small, oval window at his shoulder. Nothing but ocean and sky. A day so blue and clear, true believers the world over might offer it up as irrefutable evidence of the Devine. The pilot took a deep breath and rolled his tongue around the inside of his cheek.

When the masked man got to his feet and wrenched the door open, Sparrow drew the hard wind in through his nostrils. "Now that's more like it," he whispered. The masked man's side arm went up to his head and Sparrow said, "No—no, bullets. Just let me jump. No mess that way."

The masked man shrugged and pointed toward the open hatch with his pistol. Fast air wrapping at his tee shirt, Sparrow stood up, approached the door, steadied himself, took another long breath, and closed his eyes. Then the gun went off behind him, and his body spiralled down toward the waves.

Mason had to be violently removed—kicking, screaming, a large tear opening along the back of his sport coat. A blow to the neck folded him over in the raging wind.

Stooped, heaving, he looked up at his killer, and issued a final word. Rhetorical question, really. "Think you've got it all figured out, don't you?"

29

It would remain a mystery.

Perhaps he wanted them debriefed at Vauxhall. Perhaps it was all for show. Perhaps it was a result of parliamentary pressure. Or maybe more nefarious intentions were at play. But C had Abasi, Babu, and Harkinder immediately flown to London once the chopper touched down in Granada.

As with most rushed departures, the goodbyes were awkward, emotions withheld. No hugs, kisses, or well wishes. Just a quick succession of stiff handshakes, the foreigners' impassive faces belying a collective trepidation.

Not that Amir or Brit were ever good at offering comfort to the vulnerable anyway. Their strong suit was in providing protection, maybe the vague promise of order. So they lent a few generic words of encouragement to Babu, Harkinder and Abasi. *Don't worry. Things'll turn out fine. It's been … it's been good to know you.* What else could be said? Amir detested insincerity, and feeling it leak into his farewell was enough to send him marching off the Tarmac, without looking back. Brit followed, just one step behind.

Officially speaking, the mission had been accomplished. Child saviour transferred to custody of The Crown. But the cost in blood and the erosion of trust had taken a toll. With the rotor wash spilling over them, they made their way toward the idling Land Rover, Amir feeling like an exhausted rodent scurrying toward the exit of a laboratory maze. Brit, silent and solemn, shoulders sloped under the invisible weight of leadership.

On the ride to the Alhambra, neither spoke; too damn tired. It was late afternoon, and the sun hung low over the pine slopes above. *At least there was that,* Amir thought. The familiar contours of the land. The soft cascade of brown and green. The beige and tan buildings rolling up from the valley. The long wall separating sector five from the city—age from industry, preservation from squalor, power from the marginalized.

It wasn't pretty. But it was home.

Back at base, they split off from one another. Amir headed toward his truck, Brit to her office—not a word between them—only a nod toward tomorrow. When Amir arrived home, the house was quiet. No Cristina, no James, no Paco chirping for a treat. What fucking day is it, he thought, heading straight for the shower. Halfway down the hall, he peeked in James's room. A small pile of clothing sat atop the tightly made bed. Then he noticed the uniform—the away jersey thrown aside.

Home game.

Shower aborted, he threw on a clean shirt. Not bothering to change out of his fatigues or take his holster off, he rambled out of the apartment, down the steps, and to his truck. It was rush hour, but the labyrinthine back streets did the job.

He arrived at the pitch just as the whistle heralded the start of the second half. And there he was. *Número siete de FC Albaicín*, streaking toward the eighteen, ball on foot, defence failing at every turn to dispossess him. James's shot went slightly high and wide, catching the outside corner of the top left ninety, ricocheting back into the field of play, the goalie snatching it on its way down. James sulked a little as he scampered back to position.

"Seven—pick your head up and get moving!" When James pivoted round toward Amir, his face lit up and his posture straightened. He paused for a moment, letting the player he was marking cut loose, and gave his dad a huge smile and tiny wave. "Get moving," Amir repeated, though the adoration in his eyes delivered the real message. "Go," he mouthed to the child, arm scooping diagonally upward.

Then the boy burst forward, hurtling downfield like a rock from a sling. Heat-seeking missile was more like it—rapidly closing distance on its target. Amir took a deep breath, feeling truly safe for the first time in days. Or was it weeks? As he watched James run circles around the older boys, Amir's thoughts wandered toward Darweshi. But a tap on the shoulder drew him back.

"Agent Duran, I see you've returned home in one piece."

It was like seeing her for the first time. Glowing and perfect under the pink radiance of the late day sun. Wide brown eyes so generous, he suddenly wondered if he was worthy of their attention.

"*Besos*," she said.

When they kissed, he had to dig deep to remain in control. Every inch of his battered body yearning for her flesh.

"What's this," she asked, running a hand over his side where the bandage bulged beneath his shirt.

"A souvenir from London."

"They kept you very busy, I see."

Amir smiled and pointed over at the pitch. "*Veo que el esta jugando con quince y bajo ahora.*"

"*Si*," she said, snuggling up to his ribs. "And he's *still* kicking their asses."

"Good boy," Amir said as he kissed her forehead. "*Como estas, mi amor?*"

"Happy to kiss your little face."

"No one's ever called my nose little before."

"Not your nose," she said with a chuckle. "That's still big."

"Like my dick."

"Don't flatter yourself," she said, lightly jabbing at his side with her hand.

"Owe!"

"*Lo siento! Olvide!*"

"*Tranquilo*," he said, wincing but smiling. "I love hearing you speak Spanish to me."

"You really missed me, huh?"

"Baby, you don't know the half of it."

"Digame."

"It can wait," he said. "I've got more important things to tell you."

THIRTY

C requested they fly to London the following month for the medal ceremony—a rather unusual public honour, given the surreptitious catalyst for said valour. Amir surmised it had something to do with deflecting scrutiny in the wake of the GLogiX scandal. It was all put on Tony Mason, of course. But that didn't prevent Parliament from berating the old man for letting it all play out under his nose.

"I insist," C told Amir—personally—over the phone. "Such bravery deserves recognition. It'll be a bit of overblown pomp and circumstance, sure. But what you did for that lad—Tillman too—it's the stuff that makes this nation worthy of empire."

But Amir had a conflict. Coincidentally, so did General Brit Tillman and Agent Henry Glass. Two, actually.

When the old man persisted, Amir made his case clearer. "Listen, just won't work," he told C—no thank you or sorry sirs attached. "Oh, and might as well get this out of the way, too—I hereby tender my resignation from Special Unit. Tillman has the hard copy."

The old bastard was flabbergasted. "How dare you!"

"How dare I *what*?" Amir said. "Live a normal fucking life?"

The first ceremony was of the sombre variety. Sunrise. Glass, Brit, and Amir standing silently on the Alhambra's Patio de Machuca, each holding a folded Union Jack, the sweep of Granada below, dawn's pink light splashing across the red roofs of the city, the sturdy, comforting buttress of the Sierra to the north, its deep green pines whistling in the stirring wind. There'd be no bugle, no rifle salute—just the sun and the wind, the spirit of fallen comrades echoing through the hearts of a lover and a friend.

For Brit, the ritual resonated with loss and finality.

For Glass, it was one more wrenching chapter in the tale of unattainable romance, Marissa's disappearance officially determined a casualty of conspiracy, Tony Mason most definitely to blame.

For Amir—who barely knew Brit and Henry's fallen friends—it was one more reminder of the Crown's inherent corruption. And further affirmation he'd made the right choice to return to policing. After they were done, Amir stayed behind, lit up a smoke, and offered some funerary prayers in remembrance of Rashid. A martyr in the truest sense of the word. And a real fucking man, if he'd ever met one. *Rest in peace my friend. You died like a warrior.*

The second ceremony—less than one week later—was something for the ages. Sunset—a *brilliant* sunset—on the back terrace of the Gran Mezquita. Hot reds streaked across the cloudless heavens. The unpigmented exterior of the Mosque reflected every subtle hue the sky possessed. Amir stood hand in hand with Cristina. She, in a simple white dress which flowed loosely to the knee, a crown of Spanish Bluebells wrapped round her drawn-back hair. He, in a traditional, regal thwab—just to make Jeddo happy. His best little man, James, to his left, looking spiffy in a tiny suit and tie, face beaming with satisfaction.

Brit performed the ritual. Her part in English. The secular vows in Spanish. Glass serving as official witness. Cristina's mom looked on with moist eyes. Her dad's expression vacillated between pride and scepticism. *A Muslim cop?* A few of Cristina's girlfriends had also gathered with them. And in typical fashion, spent the ceremony dabbing at their running eyeliner, and pining after the handsome groom.

When Cristina and Amir sealed it with a kiss, an eruption of tearful cheers followed. Dinner was served right there on the back terrace of the Mosque. The new, young Imam, Julian Rahim had granted permission to keep the wine flowing all night. A toast was offered by Brit, simple and to the point: *Amir, you're a bloody lucky bloke; Cristina, may God grant you a bottomless well of patience; the two of you deserve nothing less than a life of love and happiness.* Then, under the moon and stars and twinkling fairy lights strung along the trimmed juniper trees, they danced until their feet hurt—even Amir.

James's sweaty little head eventually came to rest on Brit's lap. Glass sucked down his scotch, lighting one cigarette after the next, thoughts never far from Cairo's Marissa White. Cristina's parents retired slightly past midnight and took James with them overnight. Glass and Brit said their goodbyes around two. At three, the last of their friends departed, leaving the couple to relish the short hours in quiet embrace. Around four, they made it home. Around five, they fell asleep, after an hour of making love. Around six, the day cracked open, its subtle beginnings peeking through their open window. Around seven, he woke her up and suggested an early breakfast. Down del Darro, on the open expanse of Plaza Mayor, they dined on *juevos y pan y jugo y café* and decided to make a baby, pending Amir's rehire to the force.

A month later, she was pregnant, and Amir was back in his shitty police-issued Mitsubishi, sipping Turkish coffee, digging a smoke from his jacket pocket, weighing whether he should load his Glock with hollow tips or standard rounds.

Decisions, decisions.

ACKNOWLEDGEMENTS

Many thanks to Jessica Bell and her Vine Leaves team, without whom, you would not be reading this.

And to my family, endless gratitude.

VINE LEAVES PRESS

Enjoyed this book?
Go to *vineleavespress.com* to find more.

CPSIA information can be obtained
at www.ICGtesting.com
Printed in the USA
FFHW02n1456241018
48910096-53159FF